The Eyes of Bach

A NOVEL

MARC MOSKOVITZ

One Printers Way
Altona, MB R0G 0B0
Canada

www.friesenpress.com

Copyright © 2024 by Marc Moskovitz
First Edition — 2024

All rights reserved.

Front cover illustration by Teri-Ashley McCallum
Author photograph by Michael Forhez
Rear cover background: Bach Cello Suite No. 6, Prelude, as copied by Anna Magdalena Bach

No part of this publication may be reproduced in any form, or by any means, electronic or mechanical, including photocopying, recording, or any information browsing, storage, or retrieval system, without permission in writing from FriesenPress.

ISBN
978-1-03-832089-6 (Hardcover)
978-1-03-832088-9 (Paperback)
978-1-03-832090-2 (eBook)

1. FICTION, HISTORICAL

Distributed to the trade by The Ingram Book Company

Also by Marc Moskovitz

Alexander Zemlinsky: A Lyric Symphony

MEASURE: In Pursuit of Musical Time

Beethoven's Cello (co-author)

For my musical colleagues everywhere

How are we never at an end with Bach? How he seems to grow more profound the oftener he is heard.

—Robert Schumann

AUTHOR'S NOTE:

In the spring of 1750, the traveling English oculist John Taylor passed through Leipzig, where he operated on the eyes of Johann Sebastian Bach, intending to restore the 65-year-old composer's failing vision. Nothing is known about the procedure itself, save that shortly thereafter, Bach's health began to fail and within a few months, the composer was dead. While Taylor probably understood the human eye as well as anyone of his day, he presumably blinded as many as he helped. He was also widely regarded as a charlatan.

Prologue

IN THE SUMMER OF 1750, I became a man.

Admittedly, my rite of passage was neither kindled by a passionate romance nor born of an intellectual or spiritual awakening. Instead, the season that marked the beginning of my adulthood was occasioned by the death of my master, Johann Sebastian Bach.

As I pen these words, the year is 1810. It has been sixty years since Sebastian Bach passed from this earth. Nevertheless, the events surrounding his demise and the role I played remain deeply etched in my memory. I know I am not to blame for what happened. I am also as powerless to change the outcome writing about it now as I would have been had I spoken up at the time. Nevertheless, the tragedy significantly shaped the narrative of my life. Having reached my seventy-fifth year, I feel an urgency to share my story before time runs out.

Should fortune be gracious enough to allow these pages to survive fire, flood, war, or simply time itself, then perhaps my story will find its way into the hands of those who harbor curiosity about Sebastian Bach or his surgeon, John Taylor—for I knew them both.

Our intimate, walled city of Leipzig is noted for two institutions of learning: the St. Thomas School and the University of Leipzig. St. Thomas, located on the western side of town, was Bach's final home and workplace; I was a student there when my story begins. The imposing school building adjoins the stately St. Thomas Church, where Bach often led performances and which, like the school, traces its provenance to the early thirteenth century. In fact, the present St. Thomas, where boys learn to sing the liturgy, dates back to 1254, when evangelical monks sang the service. Some 300 years later, Martin Luther would preach at this church. Given his omnipresent spirit, one might surmise that the antagonistic Augustinian never left.

Today, the church and the neighboring school remain connected by a lovely courtyard that the Bach family and all the students crisscrossed daily. The massive medieval fortification that encircles the city runs directly behind the school; beyond that, further south, flows the picturesque Pleisse River. To the north stands the market at the center of town. Further north lies the Brühl, home to shops, cafés, and stately boulevards lined with linden trees, from which Leipzig—or *Lipsk*—gets its name. On the eastern side of town, directly opposite St. Thomas, sits the imposing St. Nicholas Church, in whose loft Bach also performed and conducted. Still farther east, backing up to the *Grimmaische Tor,* or Grimma Gate, is the University and its church, St. Paul, another of Bach's frequented venues. Here, in March of 1750, placards announced the arrival of the famed oculist, John Taylor, known as "Chevalier."

Although he was entirely unknown in Leipzig, I later learned that Taylor's reputation, as expert or charlatan, depended on the nature of one's acquaintance with him. He claimed to have traveled "day and night" throughout England and the Continent, "giving sight to the blind"—whether pauper or pope—and he had amassed a supposed string of honors to prove it. Nobody thought to question his titles: *John Taylor Esq., Chevalier, Ophthalmiater Pontifical, Imperial and Royal, Oculist to the King, Knight of the Order of Portugal, Doctor of Physick*, etc. etc.

Taylor arrived in the week preceding Easter and presented a lecture that Saturday, one day after Good Friday. A second followed on the Tuesday of the Octave of Easter, at which point he began soliciting business. I did not attend the first of these lectures, but news traveled swiftly; Bach had soon heard enough about the famous visitor to request that I attend his second talk. I returned with a glowing report, for Taylor undoubtedly possessed uncommon knowledge of the eye.

As for his ability to restore sight, that ultimately proved an entirely different matter.

Though English by birth, Taylor's lightly accented German was exceptional, the product of a keen mind well-traveled, though how many other languages he spoke I cannot say. I can also report that our visitor cut an impressive figure and made no apology for his elegant, even extravagant appearance. His dress, cut of modern, colorful cloth, stood out within our parochial community, and the glimmer of his bejeweled rings and necklaces, his diamond studs, and the gold cross he wore on a fine chain about his neck, caught every eye. Taylor veritably sparkled from the stage. Given my subsequent experiences with the man, I suspect these abundant jewels were gifted by those wishing to honor him or given up as payment for services rendered.

At the conclusion of his second lecture, I made my way to the stage, only to find the doctor surrounded by those desiring his services. Rather than wait and speak with him directly, I slid a note into a pocket of his frock coat, indicating that Sebastian Bach, Cantor of St. Thomas, requested an evaluation with the possibility of surgery. Given my master's prominence among Leipzig's notable citizens, I suspected we would hear from the doctor before too long.

The Chevalier called on Bach at his St. Thomas apartment that evening and performed what seemed a rather superficial examination. The eyes of my master were all but useless by this point and the source of constant irritation. He received the doctor ill-naturedly.

Standing in the doorway, I could hardly bear to witness Bach's vulnerability. This giant of a man and peerless artist commanded an entire cathedral when he performed, possessed an almost superhuman ability to create at will, and constructed music of unsurpassed complexity and beauty. As *Thomaskantor*, as he was officially known, Bach harnessed the energy to run a school, teach its students, and provide music on the grandest scale for every significant day of the church year. At home, he was a devoted husband who had sired twenty children. Yet now, as I quietly observed, he sat defenseless before this itinerant stranger.

Still, what was he to do? To compose was all but impossible without the use of his eyes, and Bach was nothing if not forever pushing the limits of his musicality. He could conceivably give up his routine and dictate to an assistant but is not the true act of composition as much about the scribbles of sudden inspiration and the crossing out of rejected ideas as it is the finished work? In any case, Bach would refuse to allow anyone else to commit his ideas to ink until no other options remained. And now, seemingly out of nowhere, John Taylor had appeared, trumpeting the bloated claim of *Giving sight to the blind*. Admittedly, it would have been well-nigh impossible to turn away from such a promise.

PART I
FAMILY

Chapter 1

MY NAME IS CARL FRIEDRICH Barth. I grew up in the village of Glauchau, a half-day coach ride to the south of Leipzig. My father, Georg Samuel, a businessman, and my mother, Christiana Sophia, passed from this life of fever shortly after my first birthday. Thus, I have no memories of either. My brothers and I were sent to live with an uncle who did his best with boys not his own. In time, he enrolled us at nearby St. Thomas, believing that our parents, lovers of music, would have chosen this school had they lived long enough to do so.

I was 12 when my brothers and I first crossed over the St. Thomas courtyard and through the school doors. What remained of our family estate had been applied to our tuition, room, and board. After those funds were exhausted, the school would pursue other options, as was often the case with students of limited income. And this was how I came to find myself living with the Bachs.

My initial impressions of Johann Sebastian Bach were hardly encouraging. Not long after I arrived at St. Thomas, he took over for our ailing Latin teacher, a fellow easily half Bach's age. Until that morning, I had observed Bach only from a distance, but it was a well-known fact throughout the school that he was a severe taskmaster. Indeed, moments before he joined us, my mates began whispering that he routinely and ruthlessly dismissed students from both the classroom and the choir loft. One maintained that the cantor had once become so angry that he tore off his wig and hurled it at a helpless organ student, thundering that the boy would make a better cobbler. We all laughed heartily, imagining the red-faced old man arming himself with a wig. Admittedly, however, we were more than a little apprehensive about what might be in store.

When Bach strode breathlessly into the room, we rose as one. He stood dressed in a stark black coat and white wig. As Bach was never seen without either, some students jokingly maintained or perhaps truly believed that he must have worn both to bed. His foreboding gaze rested on each student in turn, signaling we had better have learned our lessons well. It was not that Bach failed to appreciate the importance of Latin. On the contrary, he regarded Latin as a holy language in which he addressed God and concluded most of his music, proclaiming His glory always. And, to be sure, the cantor had taught his share of Latin throughout his time at St. Thomas. But it was obvious that he harbored little desire to be here now, standing in front of a roomful of young boys who, he well knew, would have preferred to be most anywhere else.

For the record, I welcomed the change and looked forward to what was to follow. My peers would soon mark me as studious and introspective, which is to say, I likely harbored greater sympathy for the bewigged disciplinarian than anyone else in the room. In the short time he remained with us, I was to find him demanding and uncompromising, yet fair.

Only gradually would I come to appreciate the full extent of Bach's responsibilities and accomplishments. His daily activities at St. Thomas included courses in musical instruction as well as private vocal and instrumental lessons. Moreover, he oversaw the musical activities of no fewer than four city churches. Each demanded he compose for Sundays, feast days, and special events, and rehearse its choirs and instrumentalists. Bach had even been part of a student inspection rotation for which he was obliged to conduct morning and evening prayers, account for all the boys involved, and ensure that none boozed at meals or before bed.

Given such myriad commitments, it's no wonder Bach didn't want to be burdened with additional teaching. His expectations were high, although certainly not unreasonable, and he rarely lost his composure. Furthermore, despite his age, he maintained a sturdy constitution, and one could easily imagine him defending himself. Indeed, a story circulated about a much younger Bach fighting off a fellow student who had threatened him with a knife. My classmates also gossiped that not only must he have worn out his first wife, who had died young, but also that he was well on the way to using up his second, having sired some twenty children between them. But let it stand that his second wife, Frau Magdalena, was anything but used up. Such vulgarities were as misguided as my initial impression of the man himself.

When I first encountered Bach tête-à-tête, several years after entering St. Thomas, the experience did little to allay my fears of his uncompromising standards. It came about as musicians were being selected for the upcoming Advent performance, and I had come to play my cello for him. In truth, I harbored little hope that I would be accepted into Bach's orchestra as a cellist so soon. Back home in Glauchau, I had begun my musical studies as a violinist, with instruction from a local musician. However, before long, the cello had been all but forced into my large hands. And while I quickly took to the instrument—indeed, it was a far more natural fit than the violin had ever been—I remained uncertain of my abilities.

As I now came to be seated before Maestro Sebastian Bach, I regarded myself as wholly inadequate, yet I did my best with some well-worn music that must have previously passed through the hands of a dozen or more cellists. With a sigh, the cantor shoved the pages aside and placed something before me that I suspected he had composed. Although I believe I acquitted myself respectably, given the circumstances, he cut me off and grumbled, "No, that won't do, though perhaps with time ..." He then instructed me to lay the instrument aside and sing for him.

Everyone at St. Thomas who could reasonably carry a tune performed in one of the choirs; when I told him I was a baritone, Bach raised an eyebrow. I remarked that my voice had begun to change when I was 11. He turned, went to the keyboard, and asked that I repeat the phrases he played. As this was no problem for me, he next tested my range with a sheet of music from the nearby cabinet. This time he accompanied me, expanding the harmony as I did my best to sing from sight.

"Good enough," he responded brusquely after a few phrases. And then, motioning toward the door, which I understood to mean our time was up, he said I was to join the first chorus rehearsal, two days hence, ". . . at which point we shall see if you possess the makings of a sensitive musician. That will be all for today, Herr Barth." As I stepped into the hallway and his footsteps receded behind the closed door, I could not help but wonder what impression I had just made.

The answer came in November 1749, about a month past my sixteenth birthday, when Johann August Ernesti, rector of St. Thomas, summoned me to his office. I had no idea why he wanted to see me. I could not recollect having missed more than a single church service in months, a transgression that frequently caught up with other students and one for which several were repeatedly disciplined. By contrast, I was a responsible student and had begun making a solid showing as both a cellist and a singer. Thus, I was more than curious about why I had attracted the rector's attention.

It was well after vespers when Ernesti greeted me at his door. The study behind him was lit only by a large candle at the edge of his desk. A familiar portrait of Martin Luther hung on the far wall, slightly luminous in the flicker of candlelight. The rebellious monk's image created the illusion of a living, breathing soul, a perception many of us conjured regularly during our years at St. Thomas. Books lay scattered across the rector's desk, some thrown open. Others rested in small piles about the floor. I noted the names Cicero and Ovid on several covers and assumed there were many volumes by other ancients in which Ernesti was thoroughly versed.

Pipe in hand, the rector gestured toward a seat in front of the desk. He dropped into his chair and exhaled a cloud of smoke, which I found not at all unpleasant, reminding me as it did of home and my uncle's predilection for tobacco. Ernesti's demeanor was severe but calm, and after acknowledging my accomplishments at the school, he put me fully at ease by telling me nothing was amiss. Instead, an opportunity had arisen.

In short, Sebastian Bach needed an assistant for various musical tasks. I begged the rector's pardon, indicating I was under the impression that Herr Bammler, a theology student at the university who had been increasingly filling in for the cantor, especially at concerts, was serving as his amanuensis. True enough, Ernesti confirmed, but Johann Bammler's duties, which included directing the St. Thomas choirs, had become so onerous that his university studies had begun to suffer. He could no longer dedicate sufficient time to Herr Bach.

"Herr Barth, it is no secret that the cantor and I have had our differences over the years. He is a proud man with a history of butting heads with his employers." Taking a deep breath, Ernesti looked away before again meeting my eyes. "I say this with the greatest respect, for besides the fact that my apartment sits directly across from his own, and therefore one must strive to be neighborly *and* collegial, I am honored to serve as godfather to two of his children. Nevertheless, we haven't always maintained a peaceful coexistence and on occasion have nearly come to blows."

After a long drag on his pipe, the rector continued more reflectively. "I also concede that much of what flows from his pen goes right over my head. It all seems so complex. Admittedly, I like my music like my Sekt: light and effervescent. Besides, I have more than enough intellectual challenges with all this," gesturing towards the volumes splayed upon his desk. "I simply haven't the capacity to be challenged by the music of our St. Thomas cantor or that of anyone else!"

After a moment's pause, the rector continued. "And yet, how many of us have entertained the King?"

I had naturally heard about Bach's travels to Potsdam and his audience with Frederick the Great, a fateful meeting had occurred a few years earlier. Cutting himself off again, Ernesti waved a hand in the air. I was unsure whether he was attempting to clear the tobacco smoke from before his face or redirect his thoughts.

"But never mind all that, Herr Barth," he said. "What concerns us now is *you*. Herr Bach came to me a day ago, requesting a replacement for Bammler. Because of your impressive musical progress and what he deemed your earnest disposition, the cantor believes you might do him a valued service, so he asked me to approach you about the matter."

A haze of tobacco smoke now floated before Luther's portrait, mercifully freeing me from the severity of the monk's disdainful gaze. "Coincidentally," the rector added, "it also appears that the money from your estate has been nearly exhausted. Unless you have any other family who might help support you and your brothers' studies here, we'll need to explore the means for you to continue."

"I would greatly appreciate that, sir," I replied, "as I have only an uncle, and he is in no position to offer assistance."

"Very well," Ernesti said. "While we receive help from various local charities, we also try to find opportunities for our students to earn back at least some of their tuition and board. In your case, you could work for the cantor and live in the family apartment. There is a strong precedent for students being placed so, as you may be aware, and I am confident that you will manage your schoolwork despite whatever demands are placed on you. Given your bearing and his undeniable genius and love of teaching, I believe it could be an extremely auspicious arrangement."

It all sounded very promising. I knew that others had passed through and benefited greatly from the extra music lessons Bach generously provided. I assured the rector that I was honored to be considered and asked if I might have a day to think things over.

"By all means," Ernesti agreed, standing and moving toward the door. "But please, do not take too much time. The cantor requires assistance, so I would hate to … Well, I'm sure you appreciate the urgency, yes?"

"Of course," I replied. "I promise you will hear from me soon. Good evening, Herr Rector."

After leaving Ernesti's office, I climbed the steps to the dormitory; the sounds of a horn and a singer echoed along a nearby corridor. We were fortunate that every boy had a bed to himself, but we were eight to a room, so there was nothing in the way of privacy. One student was at his desk, studying by candlelight. A few others were talking nearby. I lay on my straw mattress, contemplating my options. On the one hand, I was unsure if I wanted to be under Bach's scrutiny and held to his high expectations. On the other hand, glancing around, I imagined the improvements such an arrangement would confer.

My thoughts bounced to and fro. I could appreciate the prestige of such an opportunity, but would I live up to the demands placed upon me? Ernesti had mentioned nothing about specific responsibilities, but perhaps he wasn't sure himself. Would I be required to copy music? Run errands? I imagined taking musical dictation, writing down the notes as Bach played or perhaps sang them. That would require skills I did not yet possess. I supposed I could become proficient with practice, but would the old man demonstrate patience enough while I warmed to such tasks?

One thing was certain: Bach had strongly contemplated which student might best fill the role. I had been singled out for a reason. For myself, I knew I could throw myself into the work in hopes of meeting or exceeding the cantor's expectations. Should I prove inadequate or find my new tasks not to my liking, I could still return to dormitory life and my old bed.

I decided to discuss the offer with my brothers, whom I believed would understand and encourage me. Christian Samuel, already an oboist of merit, would later hold several distinguished posts, including membership in the Royal Court of Copenhagen. (Both of his sons would also become virtuoso oboists.) By contrast, Georg Heinrich was no musician and an unremarkable singer; when his voice broke, he left St. Thomas and apprenticed with our uncle, thus continuing in our father's footsteps. My brothers proved excited about my news, which helped to ease the decision. With their blessing, I soon reported back to Ernesti.

As it so happened, what Bach required was a fresh set of eyes. He would soon take drastic measures to regain what years of squinting in candlelight had cost him, but until then, I would attempt to ameliorate his struggles as faithfully as possible. With both confidence and humility, I can say that our time together—while all too brief—exceeded both our expectations. And despite his failing vision, Bach opened *my* eyes to a world I could never have imagined.

Chapter 2

THE BACH FAMILY APARTMENT OCCUPIED the lower floors at the south end of the St. Thomas School building. The apartment's front door opened onto the courtyard, but within the building, Bach needed only to pass through one or two doors to access several schoolrooms. Because of this, one never knew when or where the cantor might appear. Something was fitting about the school of St. Thomas—and, in turn, the church connected to it—being physical extensions of Bach's private life.

The first time I climbed the two steps from the courtyard to the door of Bach's home, I paused to consider how the course of my life might be altered once I crossed the threshold. As if by magic, the door seemed to unlatch itself a moment after I rang the bell; I would learn a mechanism on the floor above released the toggle. Once inside, my eyes rapidly adjusted to the light of several softly glowing lamps and the stove burning in the far corner. The room made for a welcome sanctuary against the frigid November air.

Four of Bach's children were gathered around a table near the stove and turned their attention from their studies when I appeared. The three younger ones were being supervised by their eldest sister, Catharina Dorothea, Bach's child from his previous marriage. I had often noticed the younger girls playing on the school grounds in the company of their mother, who had now entered.

"You must be Herr Barth," she said warmly. "I am Frau Anna Magdalena Bach. The children and I wondered which young man had been chosen to help Papa with his work." She glanced at the children, waving them forward. I instantly recognized the boy, who was one year younger than me. Though we had never met, his precocious musical talent was already recognized well beyond the walls of St. Thomas.

Bowing slightly, he introduced himself formally as Johann Christian. "But I'm called Christel," he continued, "as I share the name Johann with my elder brother, Friederich…and Papa, of course." The girls drew up next to him and curtseyed. After presenting herself, Catharina Dorothea introduced Johanna Carolina, 13, and 8-year-old Regina Susanna.

"I'm Carl Friedrich Barth," I returned, bowing my head, "and I'm honored to make your acquaintance." My eyes took them all in. "Thank you for opening your home to me."

"That will do for now, children," Frau Bach said. "You may return to your studies."

They all bowed once more and did as they were told. Frau Bach motioned me toward the stairs at the back of the room. As we ascended, she noted that while most St. Thomas students were recognizable to her family, few were known by name.

"We are certainly very honored to have you join us, Herr Barth, and doubly thankful for your willingness to serve my husband, the cantor."

"That is most kind of you, Frau Bach," I assured her as we crested the top of the staircase, "and I am equally honored in return."

Traversing a modest hallway, Frau Anna first led me to a large, open room on the northeast side of the apartment, its row of windows overlooking the spacious courtyard below. This promised to be a hub of activity since it functioned as a dining room, a rehearsal room, and a workspace. A large, handsomely carved oak table, centrally placed, held numerous instruments—a horn, a pair of fiddles, and recorders of varying sizes—set as if only recently abandoned. Perilous piles of sheet music competed for space on the tabletop, chairs, and benches. A cembalo, its frame ornately carved and laced with gold filigree, occupied one corner of the room. A cello rested casually on its lid. In the opposite corner, a majestic ceramic stove stood sentry, its stalwart body emitting luxurious heat. It proudly commanded the modest army of wooden music stands lining the far wall.

As we moved further down the hallway, I detected a faint scent of tobacco and the unmistakable aroma of freshly baked bread. We passed the open kitchen door and a handsome mahogany cabinet lined with books that sat securely behind four locking doors.

Frau Bach now led me to her husband's office suite, which occupied the apartment's southwest corner. The outer room was dominated by a broad oak writing table and a pair of keyboards, back-to-back. Quill tips, some pointed and others yet to be cut, poked out of a pewter stein at the top of the broad desk, neighbored by a crowd of black ink bottles, several nearly depleted. Stacks of musical manuscripts framed the edges of the desk, while at its center lay several pages of what I assumed was a composition in progress. I caught sight of the corner of one page, where a small marginal ink stain betrayed the hastily discarded quill at its edge. A lute and several fiddles hung from pegs on one wall, and this outer room's imposing stove stood in the far corner, fed through an aperture cut through to the hall. A pair of windows welcomed in the last light of the afternoon sun, offering a handsome view of the Pliesse River and the distant countryside beyond.

My hostess motioned me toward a smaller, adjacent chamber, Bach's composing room. Oblivious to our presence, Bach sat at a desk with his back to the open door, leaning closely into his work.

"Papa," Anna uttered gently. "Your Herr Barth has arrived."

Bach slowly lifted his head, his concentration broken. "I'm sorry, *Liebchen*?" he answered.

"Herr Barth, the young man assigned to assist you," she patiently repeated. "He has arrived."

"Ah, so he has!" Bach exclaimed, turning and standing to greet me. With an apologetic gesture toward his work, he stepped forward and motioned for me to enter. "Thank you, Mama," he said to his retreating wife, who bowed her head in acknowledgment before leaving us alone in the study.

I had already caught sight of two objects on the wall above Bach's desk: a wooden cross at eye level, and below it, an image of His Majesty Frederick II, King of Prussia. But as my attention moved to Bach's face, I realized I was seeing him for the first time without his wig. Nor was he garbed in his usual attire. The boys in my Latin class certainly needn't have worried if the cantor wore his work clothes to bed! What hair he possessed was silver-gray and closely cropped, and he wore a loose-fitting, white linen nightshirt, its edging ruffled at the collar and cuffs. A nightcap lay draped over the back of his desk chair.

"Step closer, please, Herr Barth, and allow me to get a better look at you."

As I leaned down slightly to meet his eyes, Bach's countenance now struck me as sympathetic and compassionate—a great contrast to his foreboding demeanor in the school and rehearsal room. Despite his squint, his fleshy jowls, proud nose, and full lips were altogether convivial. I found myself unable to look away.

"Herr Barth, you appear shocked to see me as nature intended. It is startling how profoundly a hairpiece alters one's appearance, don't you agree?"

I hesitated, but thankfully Bach went on.

"I vividly recall the first time Fräulein Anna—as I knew her in those days—saw me without a wig. Though I possessed far more hair at the time, I think she was equally taken aback … though what she saw must not have entirely displeased her," Bach confided with a wry smile.

"Please forgive me if I seem to be staring, Herr Bach, but yes, it is a markedly different impression than I am accustomed to."

"No matter," he continued. He picked up his nightcap from his chair and set it snugly on his head. "Given that our arrangement suits you, this intimacy will become the norm. And I must apologize for leaning in when I speak to you, but my eyes are giving me trouble. I can hardly read music anymore, and even my script has become prone to smudges. Of course, my present situation is more or less why you're here."

"That's quite all right, Sir," I replied. "I fully understand—though admittedly, I'm not entirely sure of my role. The rector did not make it at all clear, I'm afraid."

"Ah…there will be time enough to sort all that out," Bach uttered, with a dismissive wave. "In truth, Ernesti may not have been entirely sure himself. We spoke about my needs but for a moment, as I was determined not to prolong my visit with the man! But we needn't be concerned with all that presently. Tell me, Herr Barth, may I offer you a beer? I always enjoy a sip or two before bed and believe it would be a fitting way to welcome you to our home. And then you can tell me a bit about yourself, yes?"

We immediately adjourned to the dining room, where we took seats at a corner of the table free of instruments and music. Catharina Dorothea appeared soon after, bearing a tray with two steins of beer, cheese, and bread. Thanking her, Bach handed me a stein, saying it was a Gose brewed nearby that he hoped would be to my liking. I acknowledged its pleasant sour flavor and then briefly described my village of Glauchau and the death of my parents, recalled their love of music as related to me by my uncle, and, finally, how I had come to play the cello.

"I do not believe I have ever been to Glauchau," Bach replied, "although I grew up not so far away. I was born in Eisenach and come from a long line of musicians—town pipers, church musicians, and the like—all from Thuringia." Gesturing to a portrait on the wall behind him, he continued. "My father, Ambrosius, had been a town piper in Arnstadt, then a violinist in Erfurt—a 'beer fiddler,' Ernesti would have called him—and finally, in Eisenach, a trumpeter and town music director.

"My sons have headed for what they hope are greener pastures. My eldest, Friedemann, is employed in Halle, Handel's birthplace. Sadly, he seems to rub the authorities the wrong way constantly. That apple certainly didn't fall far from the tree!" he laughed. "And Carl Phillip is serving His Majesty, our old enemy, in Berlin. But I suppose one would be foolish to refuse a royal appointment, regardless of the employer. At any rate, work has largely prevented me from traveling very far from home, though as a young man, I went to school in Lüneburg, once walked to Lübeck to hear the great organist Buxtehude, and twice traveled to Berlin."

I noted that the image of Bach's father, whose dark wavy hair cascaded well beyond his shoulders, appeared a fair deal younger than the man seated before me. But rather than commenting on Ambrosius's luxuriant features, I simply remarked on the strong family resemblance before turning to the wall behind me. There hung a portrait of Bach, formally attired and holding a page of manuscript stiffly in his right hand.

"It's a remarkable likeness, Herr Bach."

"Indeed it is!" Bach answered. "It was executed fairly recently by a man named Haussmann, an excellent painter who journeyed to Leipzig, having formerly been in the service of the King of Poland. Mine was one of several portraits he made of prominent Leipzig citizens, and I was very flattered to have been asked to sit for him."

Returning to the subject of travel, I confessed that I had yet to venture beyond Saxony and would therefore be greatly interested to hear his impressions of Berlin, a city rumored to be exciting and exotic.

"With pleasure," Bach acknowledged, "though my experiences won't shed much light on the city itself. The hour has grown late, however. Such stories must wait for another evening and perhaps another stein of Gose. Tomorrow, as you know, is the first Sunday of Advent. My daughter Johanna Carolina will walk me to church as she often does, and following services and our cantata performance, you will join us at our table. Afterward, we'll repeat the cantata at the vespers service—as is customary—but when our work is finished, we'll sit and discuss my needs and your responsibilities. Have you been shown to your room?"

As I had been ushered to his study immediately upon my arrival, Bach called again for Catharina Dorothea, who would show me to my quarters before returning to clear the table. Bach then repeated his welcome and bid me good night.

Catharina Dorothea lit two candles, handed one to me, and silently led me to a bedroom on the floor above. The modest chamber contained a small desk beneath a window, a ladder-back chair, and a bed whose mattress, I assumed, was stuffed with chaff, sawdust, or straw. The only other furniture was a wooden table next to the door, fitted with a porcelain washbasin, and a copper candle holder. Spartan though these accommodations were, I knew any of my former roommates would have changed places with me in a heartbeat!

After kindly inquiring if I lacked anything, Catharina Dorothea bid me *eine gute Nacht* and departed. Placing the candle on its copper stand, I looked around again, quickly replaying the day's events before undressing. I blew out the candle and lay back on the mattress, pulling up the wool bedcover. Exhausted, I closed my eyes and fell asleep under Sebastian Bach's roof for the first time.

I rose at dawn and dressed for the morning's Advent performance. Downstairs, I found Johanna Carolina, cape and hat in hand, having just returned from St. Nicholas. Realizing her father had forgotten his breakfast, she asked if I would deliver it on my way to choir rehearsal. Happy to oblige, I placed the small sack in my coat pocket and stepped outside just as an icy wind sent my hat skittering along the footpath. I retrieved it, bent my head, and pushed past the market, its stalls boarded up for the Sabbath. Turning into Nicolaistrasse, I braved another stiff gust as I passed under the church's imposing octagonal bell tower and pulled open a door.

Though no stranger to the dimly illuminated sanctuary, my eyes were immediately drawn to the magnificent palm fronds that seemed to spout from the capitals of the Romanesque columns spanning the length of the nave. I always admired this curious ornamentation, which drew one's eyes ever higher, to the geometric patterns of greens and creams playing visual tricks along the vaulted ceiling. But my contemplation of the church's architecture was suddenly interrupted by organ music, pulling my gaze from the ceiling toward the loft.

I could not distinguish the organist from where I stood, but I was certain the bewigged Bach was seated in the loft before the imposing set of manuals. Above him, the phalanx of silver pipes, plainly visible, protruded majestically toward the ceiling. At first, he seemed to be testing the pedals and adjusting the instrument's stops. When a series of virtuosic arabesques followed, I assumed Bach was attempting to limber up his fingers, for it felt almost as cold inside the church as out. From his seat behind the lip of the loft wall, his back to the sanctuary, Bach could not be aware of my presence. And so, I stood spellbound, an audience of one.

After a quick modulation through a cycle of keys by way of a dazzling series of scales, Bach suddenly ceased playing. But once the air was clear of echo, he launched into the familiar strains of *Nun komm, der Heiden Heiland* [*Now Come, Savior of the Gentiles*], highlighting the instrument's trumpetlike clarion register. I recognized the music from the chorale at the heart of the cantata we were set to perform. Bach repeated Luther's melody a second time, now on the pedals, a register so deep as to rattle several of the sanctuary's stained-glass windows. Then a responding phrase sounded in the soprano register, as the pedalwork gave way to a fast, rumbling accompaniment. I was no expert in the art of counterpoint, but had completed enough compulsory studies to realize that Bach was treating the chorale as the subject of a fugue!

Fascinated, I listened as the pattern moved successively through the alto and tenor voices, with Bach's fingertips drawing out layers of dense counterpoint that threatened to overwhelm Luther's melody. Too soon, the chorale ran its course, and the vertiginous exposition gave way to a brief, transparent episode in which fragments of the chorale rapidly emerged and dissolved into the shifting musical fabric. Caught up in this blur of aural activity, I struggled to follow the dizzying web of accumulating sound.

The music reached a deafening climax when Bach abruptly lifted his hands and feet from the glorious instrument and plunged back in, introducing the subjects in reverse order: tenor, alto, soprano, bass. Though the structure was no less elaborate, Bach now drew upon a greater variety of organ stops, imbuing the Lutheran chorale with new, distinct personalities—the lament of a violin, the martial tones of a trumpet, the solemnity of a trombone. Finally, when this fugue had also run its course, he closed his astounding realization with a pair of massive chords. A cavernous resonance filled St. Nicholas as the fugue's final echoes floated into the vaulted canopy's embrace.

Tales of Bach's dazzling keyboard command and exquisite improvisations were legendary in Leipzig. But aside from occasionally offering a chorale prelude at the start of services, he had long ceased performing publicly. Thus, few St. Thomas worshippers would have had the sublime opportunity granted me this morning. It has remained among my life's most breathtakingly transcendent moments.

I made my way toward the loft and up the stairs; Bach turned as I approached the organ. Still awestruck by what I had just heard, I managed to wish him a good morning before setting his breakfast packet on a nearby chair.

I then confessed to having listened to the entire fugue from below. "Herr Bach, I am only sorry that your eyesight has forced you to rely entirely on your memory." Yet even as I said this, it occurred to me that although Bach had led the cantata rehearsals from the keyboard, I had never seen him use music.

Laughing, he replied, "Herr Barth, my eyesight is indeed failing me, yet God, in all His goodness, has not yet deprived me of my memory. However, what you just heard wasn't played from memory."

"But … if not from memory …," I stammered, "how did …" Could he have been improvising?

"Ah, that was but a little extemporaneous exercise. Putting this morning's chorale through its paces seemed as good a way as any to warm up these old fingers … and this old brain," he muttered, rubbing his forehead. "It is frightfully cold, even up here. Are you aware that a man named Fahrenheit has developed a means of determining temperature with mercury? I understand he came through Leipzig not long before my arrival. I wager that his invention would meet a formidable foe in St. Nicholas this morning!" he exclaimed, chaffing his arms through his coat sleeves.

I acknowledged that it was indeed cold, but was also determined to learn more about what he so casually termed an "extemporaneous exercise." So I asked where such inspiration came from. Bach's look suggested he did not quite understand my question.

"My inspiration, Herr Barth? That can come from only one place," he said, pointing toward the ceiling. "And now it's off to choir with you, my good sir!" Thanking me for bringing his breakfast, Bach waved me off. I descended the spiral stairs as if from a heavenly sphere back to earth.

⌒●⌒

Several weeks earlier, at our first rehearsal for that morning's service, Bach had brought in two cantata settings of *Nun komm, der Heiden Heiland*. We learned that he had written the first setting many years earlier, in Weimar, where he had begun composing such music for every Sunday of the year, and had written the second shortly after taking up his present post in Leipzig. We were meant to spend the next several rehearsals getting to know each of them, and then he would decide which to perform at the start of Advent.

My initial impression was that the cantatas were the work of two composers, so different were they. Though the Leipzig score was somewhat longer and included parts for oboes and horn, both were constructed of six movements and modestly scored, keeping with Advent's devotional spirit; trumpets and drums would have to wait until Christmas. Each cantata naturally bore Bach's adaptation of Luther's medieval hymn; it was in their respective characters that the two parted company.

I would describe the earlier composition as the more reflective, though it certainly wasn't without its share of drama. In particular, I thought Christ's knocking at the door, which Bach depicted with a dry rattling of pizzicato strings, was truly inspired. The later cantata, by contrast, was simply more festive. I believe that is why it was the one ultimately performed.

Rehearsals were particularly memorable. Some of the most thrilling moments came at the opening chorus, with the entrance of the continuo two measures in—and with that large *violone!*—making the hair on the back of my neck stand up.

I also remember the uncontrollable laughter that erupted at our first reading, when the tenor soloist turned blue in the face during his aria. Bach's phrases being notoriously long, his singers were often left gasping. On this occasion, even Bach had to smile. Mercifully, he modified his tempo to ensure his soloist had enough air to get through the aria. Sympathetically, though, I continued holding my breath for him.

I would be amiss if I didn't mention one other anecdote. Bach's dramatic aria for bass voice, "Streite, siege, starker Held!" ["Fight, conquer, strong hero!"], originally included a simple accompaniment for harpsichord and a single cello. But one day, he brought in another version scored for a full complement of strings. The resulting power and drama proved a sonic revelation. When the ensemble reached the end of the first verse, we stomped our feet in collective admiration. By no means did Bach need our praise, but I believe this spontaneous, joyful outburst tipped the scales in favor of the latter work.

As he often did on Sundays, Bach led the cantata this Advent morning from the harpsichord. Immediately following the close of the service, he stepped back from the instrument to make room for all to file out of the loft, though I remained behind to help him down the narrow steps. Brilliant sunshine and bone-chilling November air greeted us as we passed through the sanctuary doors.

Bach must have traversed the path from St. Nicholas to St. Thomas hundreds of times, yet he maintained a firm hold on my arm as we passed the market and eased toward his apartment. But, to my surprise, he directed me through a small gate leading to the river. I initially thought Bach's eyesight was playing tricks on him such that he had momentarily lost his way.

"Do you not wish to head back home, Herr Bach?"

"We'll be there soon enough. Let's walk a few moments longer. There will be ample time to warm up before we break bread with the family."

We followed a path along the river. The fading murmur of the nearby waterworks offered a calm counterpoint to the crackle of dried leaves beneath our rhythmic footsteps. When Bach asked if I thought he had made the right choice with the cantata, I understood that he had diverted our course to allow us a few extra minutes to speak alone. I felt confident that our performance had been compelling, but it now occurred to me that he had been unable to read the faces of his listeners.

"Certainly, Herr Bach," I replied. "Looking around, not just at your family but the rest of the congregation, the cantata appeared to have been enthusiastically received. And for me, it was a singularly thrilling experience!"

"You mean that our tenor didn't pass out?" Bach asked, amused.

"Well, I'm sure he would have appreciated a few more rests sprinkled here and there," I joked back. "But I'm speaking overall. It is glorious music. I would be at a loss to declare any movement a favorite, but I confess to finding the angelic prayer sung by the sopranos and altos particularly moving. It is all so breathtaking and inspired."

"As I told you earlier, Herr Barth, my greatest inspiration comes from above. Never forget that. When I write *SDG, Soli Deo Gloria*—To God alone belongs the glory—at the bottom of a score, I am acknowledging, with all humility, that my pen has been guided by the Spirit of the Almighty. That said, while I always attempt to honor our Creator, I also admit to the influences of others—composers whose work I have diligently studied. Certainly, there is ample evidence of that in both my Advent cantatas."

"How so?" I questioned.

"Well," Bach replied, "if you remember, I opened the earlier score—the one composed in Weimar—with a French overture, an inspiration drawn from Jean-Baptiste Lully. Though Italian-born, Lully was adopted by the French court and composed expressly for Louis Quatorze. Of course, Lully and I served very different kings," he added, again glancing heavenward. "Lully found a powerful and convincing musical means of setting the stage for his monarch's dramatic entrance, and I have drawn on his rather stately, pompous style on any number of occasions."

With Bach's hand still on my arm, I noticed he was trembling from the cold. My own teeth were chattering, so I asked if we might turn back.

"Certainly, Herr Barth. That's probably for the best." As we reversed course, he thanked me for indulging an old man in his idle thoughts. And yet, these thoughts were anything but idle to me, and I began to perceive my new role assisting Bach might afford insights of no small privilege. If this stroll were any indication, he would continue to reveal to me, quite generously, his thoughts and processes apropos of his music along with his foundational beliefs about the world around him.

Though still shivering, Bach picked up the thread of his thoughts.

"Vivaldi, that other native Italian, has also, at times, proven inspirational. Indeed, I've written several keyboard transcriptions of his concerti and occasionally infused my musical language with his own. Take the very opening of this morning's cantata, for example. That refrain, the *ritornello*, is imbued with the joyous spirit of Vivaldi's violin writing.

"And as for the more theatrical version of the bass aria—the one for the full complement of strings, which I originally composed for continuo alone—that was a nod to Herr Handel, who has also occasionally invigorated my musical psyche. That man has undoubtedly captured the continent's attention with his remarkable flair!

"So you see," Bach concluded, as we reached the steps to his apartment, "whatever I've managed to carve out of my little place in the world, forces both divine *and* natural have had an undeniable hand along the way."

Bach's avowal complete, he looked overhead, softly intoned *Laus Deo,* and crossed the threshold. At the top step, I followed his lead and glanced skyward, reflecting upon the conduit that seemed to flow between him and his Spirit above. I felt an unmistakable sense of belonging as we returned to the warmth of hearth and home. As I closed the door behind us, shutting out a billow of cold air, I thought that whatever *I* was to achieve henceforth would be largely on account of my new master and the family that had taken me in.

Chapter 3

BACH CAME OF AGE IN a house where his father's students shared living quarters with the family, a tradition he was glad to carry on. As it was, I was the only student living with Bach and his family at the close of 1749, though others came for lessons or to assist with various musical tasks. Thus, on that first Sunday of Advent, present at table were Herr and Frau Bach, four of their children, several of Bach's keyboard students, and my brothers, whom the Bachs had graciously invited.

If my siblings were in any way envious of my new station, they never indicated as much. Most likely, they preferred the after-hours company of their classmates to that of the school cantor and his family. For me, though, the Bach household felt increasingly like home, and though it was still too soon to say for sure, I sensed that Bach and his family considered me a good fit.

That Sunday's meal was a festive one. The central table, cleared of its usual musical instruments and manuscripts, had been set with wooden bowls, pewter plates, and copper flagons of wine. A pair of three-branch brass candelabras burned at either end of the table. At the center sat an Advent wreath, the first of its four beeswax candles lit; the others would be kindled on successive Sundays until Christmas when all four would burn together. After Bach blessed the meal, Johanna Carolina and Regina Susanna served delicious beef soup, warm loaves of Sabbath bread, ample roast pork with cabbage and carrots, and nut-stuffed baked apples for dessert. Bach drank from a pewter goblet that featured a personal monogram he had designed himself, the same seal I would later see stamped in wax on his correspondence. Nevertheless, I noted that he partook modestly of both wine and food since vespers was only a few hours away.

As dinner ended, Bach expressed his gratitude to all of us for sharing his table and thanked his wife and daughters for preparing and serving the meal. He then looked at my brothers and me and began to reflect on his youth. Just as our parents had died in our childhood, so too had his. Furthermore, he had likewise gone to live with a relative, in his case, his older brother, Johann Christoph.

"Christoph was already an established church organist, so it was only natural that he would help lay the foundations of my keyboard technique," Bach eagerly related before nostalgically sharing a favorite anecdote.

"Among my brother's treasures was music by some of the most famous composers of the day, which he kept locked up in a small cabinet. At night, when everyone was asleep, I would sneak out of bed and, with my little hands, reach through the grillwork and pull out the music. I feared waking the others, so I didn't so much as light a candle. Instead, I read and copied the music by moonlight. But my brother heard me playing it at some point and confiscated my copies. Maybe he thought I wasn't ready for such music, but I had already memorized all of it! He couldn't take *that* away!" Bach chuckled at the recollection.

"Well, I may already have been a hard worker," Bach continued, gazing at us all in turn, "but with discipline, each of you can accomplish as much." Instantly, I recalled his miraculous improvisation of the morning. While I fully appreciated Bach's encouragement, it seemed unlikely that any of us would accomplish a fraction of what he had.

"And speaking of work," Bach said, standing and placing his napkin next to his plate, "we still have another performance ahead of us. So, if you pardon me, I shall bid each of you a good afternoon and give myself a few minutes of rest."

The guests now withdrew from the table and thanked our hosts. The others departed but I returned to my room upstairs, fully satiated, and quickly fell into a deep and lovely sleep. Late that afternoon, I headed across the courtyard to St. Thomas Church, to join the choir for vespers.

In the evening, Bach invited me to his studio to discuss my duties. I found him seated behind his desk in the outer room of his suite, filling and tamping his pipe. When he looked up to call his wife to bring a match, as seemed to be habitual, he saw me and indicated I should take the harpsichord bench. Anna Magdalena padded in soon afterward, lit her husband's pipe, and nodded to me before leaving. Bach took a few shallow puffs and gently pushed down the first embers. As he settled back in his chair, I noted the pleasure the entire ritual afforded him.

"Herr Barth," he began unceremoniously, "my living area is overrun with my manuscripts. I have therefore determined your first responsibility will be to sort through the parts and scores piled high both in the dining room and throughout my study, and decide what belongs where." He took a deep pull on his pipe and exhaled before continuing. "Johann Bammler, my former assistant, is working through some of my larger works in the school library nearby—passions, oratorios, and the like—but nobody has yet sorted out the chaos under my own roof."

Stray parts were to be reunited with their scores, he said, most of which could be found in the library where Bammler was working. When a set was complete, I was to make a note of it. But if I came across an incomplete work, I was to copy any missing parts from the score to make a full set.

"Have you done much in the way of music copying, Herr Barth?"

I told him that, regrettably, most of my musical writing had been compulsory coursework, such as the counterpoint studies from Fux's *Gradus ad Parnassum*.

"Ah yes, old Fux will certainly put you through your paces. The good Lord knows how much time I've spent with him! Well, you will learn as you go. Please just be meticulous. I can't emphasize how much time is lost correcting errors during rehearsal. Merely playing or singing the correct notes is work enough!"

He set his pipe down and went to a cabinet that contained supplies I would need. He first handed me several quills and a razor-sharp penknife. Next came two bottles of ink, a rastrum for drawing parallel staff lines, a pouch of sand to dry the ink, and finally, a short stack of thick trimmed paper. He said to simply inform him of any lack of materials in the future.

"Regarding how to proceed, look for Herr Bammler. He has been at it for quite some time and will probably be your most helpful resource."

Bach returned to his chair after showing me a leather satchel and instructing me to keep my supplies in it. I remained anxious about this assignment but assured him I would take my responsibilities seriously. Bach shook his head and reclaimed his pipe.

"I have complete faith in you." He smiled, but I wasn't sure if it was because of his trust in me or the pleasing flavor of the tobacco. Thinking our business for the evening was complete, I stood to fill the satchel and take my leave, but he gestured for me to resume my seat. We sat in silence for a moment, as a cloud of pipe smoke drifted lazily to the ceiling.

"Herr Barth, I could certainly use another reliable cellist in my orchestra for the upcoming Christmas services. If it should please you, I shall see you get parts to practice. In return, I shall offer you private lessons, provided you are willing and can commit to the work. With your efforts and my tutelage, I am confident you will be ready in time."

I hastened to reply that I felt sure I was up to the challenge and thanked him for entrusting me with his music and his willingness to teach me.

"Oh, and Herr Barth, one last thing before you go. As you are fast becoming a family member, would you be overly offended if I dispensed with formality, at least within my home? I should much prefer to call you by your Christian name."

Trying, poorly, to conceal my incredulity at this gesture of kinship, I answered with some emotion that nothing would please me more.

"Excellent!" he declared. "When my children are unavailable, please continue to accompany me to church and rehearsals held beyond the school walls. And please, Herr Barth … er … Carl … keep me apprised of your organizational tasks. I trust all this will occupy you enough for the time being."

I told him, in all sincerity, that I was honored to attend to his needs and wishes—to serve as his eyes—and that I would commence sorting through the music in the dining room the next morning.

Supply satchel in hand, I wished him a very good evening and closed the studio door behind me. On my way to my room, I retrieved a stack of music from a chair in the dining room and tucked it under my arm. Once inside my own quarters, I set the pile of music on the table beneath the window and collapsed onto my bed. Bach had offered to dispense with formalities, making me feel even more ingratiated, but now that I was alone, I wondered if he was placing too great a stock in my abilities. I was woefully untested as a cellist and quite inexperienced as a copyist. With heavy eyelids, I drifted off, wondering if I could live up to my master's expectations. Or my own.

I quickly fell into a routine: school in the mornings, rehearsals and practice in the afternoons, time with Bach's music before bed, or whenever I could fit it in. After I had made my way through the first batch, I carefully tied it up and took it to the school library, where I sought out the section dedicated to Bach's scores. It was up to me to discover what was what and where on any particular shelves. Although there was no true organizing principle, it quickly became evident that the music for keyboard and smaller ensembles occupied one set of shelves, and orchestral works and concertos were heaped on another. The choral music commanded an entire wall all its own.

My immediate duty was to replace missing parts from Bach's cantatas, but as I stood before the crowded shelves, I had no idea how to locate any particular work. At a nearby table, I caught sight of Johann Bammler, Bach's former prefect, so I begged pardon, introduced myself, and consulted him by describing my present task and asking how I might go about it.

He looked around to be sure no one was within earshot and then burst out laughing. "My young man, locating anything in this library is the journey of a lifetime. I wish you Godspeed! There are probably 300 or so cantatas huddled over there," he said, pointing to the wall crowded with choral music. "To locate a particular cantata, you'll need to search each first page for the words of the opening chorus. If you're lucky, your desire will be granted within an hour or two. Otherwise, you might be here for days. Herr Barth, I would seriously consider bringing candles, some bread and cheese, and a feather pillow next time!" Grinning at me, he clasped his hands in mock prayer before settling back to his work.

In the following days and weeks, heeding Bammler's good-natured counsel, I became increasingly adept at my labors without losing too much sleep. As I worked through the myriad piles in the apartment, gaining comfort with the tools in the satchel and my competence as a copyist, I settled into a pleasant rhythm. Most notably, I became ever more familiar with Bach's music.

Late one afternoon in the library, as I was sifting through yet another set of parts, I noticed a stack of music, seemingly misplaced and already tied, pushed to the rear of a shelf. I pulled it out, set it aside, and continued my work until dark. When I quit for the night, I took the unknown bundle to my room. The first few pages appeared to be odds and ends, stray parts that could have belonged to any number of compositions. I imagined them having been hastily thrown together years ago, perhaps in preparation for one of Bach's moves. But as I worked my way down, I discovered a title page that read:

> *6 Suites for*
> *Violoncello Solo*
> *without Basso*
> *Composed by*
> *J. S. Bach*
> *Maitre de Capelle*

A collection of solo cello music followed—Preludes, Allemandes, Courantes, and more. I quickly counted six suites, each in a different key, all in Bach's hand. Beneath each was a duplicate version penned in a hand very similar but most assuredly that of a copyist.

Despite my familiarity with Bach's work, which was far greater now than when I had begun these labors, I could make only a trifling sense of what was in front of me, so little did it resemble any of the music I had codified. Spellbound, and deeply curious, I decided to head to my master's studio and inquire about it. But alas, I had lost track of the hour; the household had already retired. I resolved to simply place the two sets of music on Bach's desk, with the following note:

> *Herr Bach—*
> *I came across this music in the library,*
> *tucked amongst stray instrumental parts.*
> *I kindly await your instruction as to its*
> *proper location.*
> *I remain your humble servant,*
>
> *—C.B.*

Little did I know how much time would pass before Bach would enlighten me about what I had found.

I was seated in my room several nights later, copying out an oboe part and imagining my brother's beautiful interpretation of it, when Frau Bach softly tapped on my door. With a candle in one hand and an obvious musical manuscript in the other, she apologized for the intrusion and politely asked if she could speak with me. I welcomed the opportunity, as she and I had not yet conversed beyond daily pleasantries.

She began by inquiring if I felt comfortable or lacked anything. I replied, most sincerely, that all was well and I was truly grateful for her family's warmhearted generosity. Then she said that Herr Bach had spoken to her about the Christmas service and performance, expressing his hope that I would play cello.

"I am relieved," she said, "that Sebastian will lead only this service during Christmastide. In years past, he would have directed performances on each of the major feast days through the season! Just on Christmas Day, I can recall his having led a cantata at seven o'clock Mass at St. Thomas, another at a nine o'clock service at St. Paul's, and yet another at vespers at St. Nicholas. Then another cantata at both early Mass and vespers on the Feast of St. Stephen, the Second Day. And on the Third Day, the Feast of St. John, still another cantata at early Mass! Even on Sundays, he was literally sprinting from one of Leipzig's churches to another. And they call the Sabbath a day of rest!"

Frau Bach understood, as perhaps no one else did, her husband's seemingly inexhaustible capacity for work. Still, she was clearly of the opinion that too much had been expected of him.

"Because of the demands placed on Papa, whether teaching, composing, rehearsing, playing the organ, or leading the music at services, the one task he delegated to others was copying parts. I did my share over the years, so I prepared these for you." And she handed me several music pages.

"My husband has chosen what is to be performed on Christmas," she went on, "and he wanted to be sure that I copied a few of the more challenging portions of the cello part for you. He said he hoped you would be prepared to play these for him in the next day or so. He also offered you the use of one of the cellos. He truly believes in your abilities."

I remarked on how closely her elegant script resembled that of her husband. "Well, we've been married for twenty-eight years! Some would say that over time you begin to resemble your spouse. But in this case," she said with a smile, "I suppose it is our musical notation that has become nearly indistinguishable." She then rose to take her leave. Expressing my deepest thanks, I told her I hoped to make the cantor proud of my work as a copyist *and* a cellist.

"I am certain you will succeed admirably on both counts," she said and bid me a pleasant rest.

I now pushed aside the oboe part and laid out the pages Frau Bach had brought. Holding the candle above the music, I stared at the notes but struggled to make sense of the individual fragments. I recalled the programmatic pizzicato "knocking" from Bach's Advent cantata, rehearsed weeks earlier, when I had realized that effect might be best appreciated when heard in context. The pages before me offered no such aid, only the following information: *Coro*, in ⅜ time, several staves of passagework, and an aria of considerable length, marked simply *Adagio*. Further understanding of the composer's musical intentions would have to wait. It was enough to see what Frau Bach had copied for me, and share her confidence that I would earn the master's approval.

Over the next few days, along with classes and choir rehearsals, I gave myself up to Bach's music, practicing in the warmly heated ground floor room where I had first met Frau Bach and the children. From this distance, I anticipated little chance of disturbing Bach in his studio upstairs. Each time, I would light candles on either side of the music stand and tune the cello generously loaned to me, then attempt to animate whatever musical impressions the notes seemed to imply. The tempo indication of the aria, *Adagio*, seemed curious, but I believed the performance would ultimately depend on Bach and his soloist's breath control. In my diligence, I began working it through at various speeds. I took a similar approach with the music marked *Coro*, though I suspected the tempo would be faster. How fast, or at what dynamic, would depend on the chorus.

Fully engrossed, I did not hear Bach's footsteps until he reached the bottom of the stairs. I looked up to see him standing in his nightshirt and cap, pipe in hand. "Pardon me for interrupting, Carl, but you're playing an incorrect note. Let's have a look."

He approached the music stand and leaned in very closely. "Here," he said, pointing at the page. "You're playing a G natural, but the harmony here is A minor. Thus, the note is G sharp." Embarrassed, I apologized. "No matter," Bach answered, "it will be obvious once the keyboard supplies the harmony. I propose we play through it together tomorrow. That way, we shall clear up any other potential errors."

I thanked him, intimating how helpful that would be, wished him a good evening, and returned to my practice, ever more attentive to the details.

The following day began a series of private lessons that would continue through Christmas. We met several times a week in his studio. Typically, he would sit at the harpsichord and accompany me, sharpening my skills as he fleshed out the harmonies. At other times, he picked up his violin to demonstrate the subtleties of one bow stroke or another. When I confessed I had been unaware that he played the violin, Bach explained that he had learned the instrument during childhood and that his versatility had proven indispensable when he served in Weimar the first time.

"I was but a lackey when appointed to the duke's *Kapelle,* and I had to earn my stripes as both a violinist and keyboardist playing with different ensembles. While keyboard skills are invaluable to a composer, a certain level of competency on the violin is particularly helpful in the role of music director. Admittedly, it has always held a certain allure because of its vocal qualities. That is why I chose it as the vehicle for the *tombeau* I composed following the death of my dear first wife."

I revealed that I had heard only whisperings about her unexpected death. Bach sighed deeply before continuing.

"After about a half-year in Weimar, I left for several other posts, though I didn't remain anywhere very long—I either quickly became disillusioned or ran afoul of the authorities. In Arnstadt, the town council accused me of luring an unknowing maiden into the choir loft, yet that maiden was hardly unfamiliar! She was my second cousin, Maria Barbara, and I planned to marry her, which I did several months later.

"Arnstadt's provinciality quickly made it clear that we needed to move on, so I returned to Weimar, this time as organist and music director of the ducal court, a position much more suited to my temperament. The three years I remained were very productive indeed, especially as I composed a great deal for organ and orchestra during my tenure. But then Prince Leopold, in Köthen, wanted to hire me away as *his* music director. The position in Köthen held great attraction, for I knew the prince to be a passionate musician, and I had become rather miserable in Weimar. So, I pressed hard to be released from my contract. Too hard, evidently, for my obstinacy landed me in jail!"

My expression must have betrayed my surprise, yet I held my tongue as I imagined my master confined to a cell.

"Admittedly, in my case, being a prisoner of the duke wasn't as unpleasant as one might think. Had I been a hardened criminal, I would have been dealt with severely, but as a member of the ducal court, with some measure of celebrity, I was granted certain benefits. I had a little room to myself, and the guards not only allowed visitors and honored my nightly request for ale but also supplied me with paper, ink, and quills—surreptitiously, of course.

"So, rather than pacing to and fro within those four walls—what they humorously referred to as 'the justice room'—I made fair use of my time by composing a series of keyboard studies in every key. True, I lacked an instrument, but I nevertheless pursued my goal. That project eventually grew into the two books I came to call *The Well-Tempered Clavier*. I take no small pride in claiming them among my finest pedagogical achievements, particularly in light of the circumstances in which they were created.

"Anyway, the authorities soon realized how stubborn I was. If possible, they were more distressed than I about my continued presence in their city! So after about a month, I was discharged—dishonorably, I might add—from both the jail and my duties in Weimar, and allowed to leave with my growing family. It proved, in every respect, a very fortuitous change."

Bach told me about his employment in Köthen, particularly the occasion of accompanying the prince to Carlsbad to take the waters. Upon returning home, Bach learned that his beloved wife of thirteen years had died and been buried while he was away.

"As you might imagine, it was a tremendous blow. In my grief, I set about composing that tombeau I spoke of, a set of variations—a chaconne for violin alone. You might say it is an elegy of sorts." Bach paused, and out of respect, I looked away. Then he went on. "Admittedly, writing for a solo violin presented great challenges since much of what I wanted to say was not limited to a single line of music. What I had in mind would have been far more easily dispatched on the keyboard. But as this was music born of my sorrow, I remained steadfast. And as you now know how I liken the violin's sound to that of the human voice, I determined it was the most fitting means of conveying the grief that consumed me."

With these last words, spoken sorrowfully but without self-pity, Bach hesitated and averted his gaze. He soon turned back to me and added how fortunate he was to have been granted not one but two spiritual partners as wives.

"Certainly, I would never have accomplished half so much had I not later met and married my dear Anna. Well, enough about all that, Carl," he said, pointing toward the music. "It's time we resumed our lesson." And so we did.

Several afternoons later, I chanced to mention to him a particular frustration, confessing that I sometimes grappled with my perceived notion of the cello as limiting, particularly in its role as a solo instrument.

"How so, Carl?" he queried, as if bewildered. I attempted to explain that unlike the keyboard, which could assume both melody and harmony, the single line of a cello was entirely dependent on others. It could assume either melody or harmony, but not easily both, though I also knew this to be true of the other string instruments.

After a moment's reflection, Bach explained that the limitations of expressing a single line—whether harmony or melody—are merely what we imagine them to be. He then reminded me that developing a singing style on any instrument, regardless of its role, was essential.

"And I can think of no better instrument than the cello, save perhaps the fiddle," he said with a wink, "to pursue such an objective." He then addressed the cello's critical position within an ensemble, cautioning me not to overlook its significance as it pertained to music theory.

"Do not forget that the cello is our thoroughbass, our *continuo*. It anchors a composition's harmony *and* rhythm, thus serving as the perfect foundation for a musical composition. Carl, the pursuit of music is to enrich the mind and soul and to glorify God. Your instrument, the cello, is the bedrock of that ideal!"

Suffice it to say that, until then, I had never considered the spiritual role of the cello nor heard anyone describe the instrument in such an elevated manner. I have often recalled that moment, just as I have frequently reflected on all my lessons with Herr Bach. Whatever my limitations, either as a cellist or as a consequence of the embryonic stage of my musical maturity, I never found my master to be anything but encouraging. Moreover, I genuinely believe he enjoyed our shared hours as much as I did. Indeed, those weeks before the Christmas season marked the true beginning of my musical journey—as a student of Bach, as a cellist, and as a musician.

Chapter 4

In mid-december, Bach began to instruct me in the art of musical embellishment—in particular how nuances, which he called "affections," can stir the listener's passion. Whenever Bach demonstrated for me, whether on violin or keyboard, he instinctively drew from each musical phrase its innermost feeling. Simply by stressing certain notes or leaning into dissonances, he elicited an astounding range of emotion that never failed to move me. Near the conclusion of one lesson, I told him that I yearned to transmit such profound musical expression myself. Bach was abundantly reassuring.

"I know you, Carl, as a young man with deep feelings! With time and practice, you will gain a greater understanding of harmony and phrasing, which will inform your ability to express such affections to a listener. I must add, however, that while some possess an abundance of such understanding or show great potential in this vein, such as you do, others lack it entirely."

Lingering on this train of thought, Bach began to reflect on his life in Köthen.

"My employer, Prince Leopold, about whom I have spoken, not only loved music but profoundly understood it, which in my experience is a rare trait among the nobility. Leopold was an extremely capable harpsichordist, violinist, *and* gamba player. More than that, he grasped music in the ways we've just been discussing, and it was my honor to serve and compose for such a man. I was doubly fortunate that the prince ruled over a Calvinist court, allowing me to turn my attention to secular music while in his service. The prince and I developed a marvelous rapport, not because he comprehended what I *did* but because of what I *said* as a musician.

"But then, alas, there was my dear prince's wife, Princess Frederica Henriette. Unlike her cultured husband, she possessed no grasp of music whatsoever. She was a real *amusa*—a dunderhead. I could have looked beyond her musical illiteracy, which is no sin. But boundlessly worse, she appeared to disdain music outright. And me as well! Regrettably, the prince began to trim back the musical activities at court, for which I suspected she was directly responsible. Consequently, I thought it best to begin considering other options. And when I learned of the death of the esteemed Leipzig cantor, Johann Kuhnau, I threw in my lot."

Given Bach's extraordinarily versatile talents, I asked if his appointment had been a foregone conclusion. "To the contrary!" he exclaimed. "I certainly knew my strengths, but as I had kept mainly to the region around my birthplace, few were aware of me or my music. Besides, Telemann, who possessed a towering reputation, was vying for the position, along with several other formidable musicians. But as luck would have it, each man withdrew his candidacy for one reason or another. So the post ultimately fell to me.

"I was also fortunate that the Prince of Köthen remained my champion, perhaps to spite his wife. He signed my dismissal papers and allowed me to continue using my title of Royal Kapellmeister. And then, as soon as I signed my contract, the 21-year-old *amusa* died! My poor, bereaved prince all but begged me to remain, but this time I felt compelled to honor my contract. And so here I am, in Leipzig.

"Naturally, I hoped this position would be free of strife and conflict, but I was sorely mistaken. And thus we come to Rector Ernesti."

When I told Bach tactfully that the rector had alluded to their discord, Bach sighed heavily, signaling there would be little more musical instruction that day. I gently laid my bow on the music stand and sat back in my chair.

"To be sure, the rector is a brilliant man," Bach said, measuring his words. "He is far more widely read than am I, and his work is highly respected. Furthermore, he is unwaveringly committed to the *humaniora*. But as for music, while Ernesti might not outright disdain it, as did Leopold's wife, neither does he understand it. It is said that when he passes by the room of a student practicing the violin, he is apt to barge in and ask the hapless boy if he intends to become a beer fiddler later in life. I hope he has never said as much to you, Carl."

I chose not to repeat Ernesti's remarks about Bach or the complex nature of his music. Instead, I simply replied that the rector had treated me only with respect. Upon hearing this, Bach nodded.

"Still, for all his erudition, our rector possesses no understanding of our noble art. You yearn to transmit deep musical emotion, but it will be lost on the likes of him." Bach gestured impatiently in the direction of Ernesti's apartment. "The fact that he fails to regard the humanities *and* music with the same reverence remains an enduring source of aggravation."

With some trepidation, I mentioned that Ernesti had recounted how honored he was to serve as godfather to two of Bach's children. Bach nodded, then stood and stepped toward the window, as he often did at moments of contemplation. I observed his silhouette, set off by the changing light of day, and wondered how he might respond. Perhaps he was concerned that further discussion about his relationship with the rector would be a violation of confidence.

"We were still on excellent terms when Herr Ernesti became godfather to my children," he said, turning back toward me. "But that all changed when he appointed a prefect without my consent. The position was mine to fill—after all, I am the one who must keep four churches supplied with singers year-round. Worse, the man Herr Ernesti appointed was a bungler, incapable of accurately beating musical time! How could I entrust music lessons and choir rehearsals to someone so unfit? I countered by allocating the duties to a prefect of my choice. And what did Ernesti do? He forbade all the boys, on pain of whipping, to give obedience to the prefect I assigned!"

Bach went on to tell me that in his frustration, he had filed complaints with the city council and then with the consistory. Ernesti held firm, Bach countered, and on it went until Bach filed the matter with the court of Dresden. The court ultimately ruled in Bach's favor, but the sordid business had erased collegiality between the litigants. To make matters worse, the story was widely circulated within the halls of St. Thomas.

"To be sure, Carl, I am not proud of the ordeal. God knows I can be very stubborn, and I've long pushed back when I believe I've been wronged. But had Herr Ernesti consulted me about his appointment, or better yet, left me in charge of it, we could have avoided locking horns."

At this point, Bach took a deep breath and apologized for carrying on. It seemed clear to me that unburdening himself, even to his newest student, had been a relief for him. This was, however, the last of such conversations. In every lesson going forward, he confined himself to mentoring and challenging me as a cellist and musician.

─────✑─────

When Bach first brought the orchestra together to rehearse the cantata, only two weeks before Christmas, the event proved particularly gratifying. To this point, my familiarity with the music encompassed little more than what Frau Anna Magdalena had copied for me. Now, I was experiencing the music's broader design, and because of my rapid development under the composer's tutelage, I could contribute at a significantly higher level. At Advent, when I sang as a choir member, the cantata we performed was more in keeping with the reflective spirit of the holiday. But this grand cantata, *Christen, ätzet diesen Tag* [*Christians, Engrave This Day*], was lavishly scored for strings, oboes, bassoon, trumpets, and timpani. The closing chorus, with its celebratory pomp and inspired counterpoint, proudly proclaimed the joyous festival fast approaching.

The chorus would join us in rehearsal once the orchestra had fused into a tight-knit ensemble. And so we set to work. Bach sat at a portative organ with the players amassed around him, strings closest, then oboes and bassoon, with the timpani to the rear. To heighten the overall effect on Christmas morning, Bach instructed his trumpet players to stand on opposite sides of the ensemble in the loft, fully visible to the congregation below. With the orchestra tuned, Bach stood and signaled the downbeat, immediately setting the festive tone. The entire orchestra struck a C major chord, launching a joyous call and response between the oboes and trumpets, and all followed along in spirited, triple-meter time. In a less-than-polished voice, and to our amusement, Bach sang the various vocal parts. Even though the chorus had yet to join us, it was evident that Christmas would be welcomed in grand style.

We were only two cellists, and the principal was an older St. Thomas student far more adept than I. Still, given my diligent preparation under my master's guidance, I felt confident seated next to him and the presence of my brother, seated nearby as the first oboe for this performance, only added to my comfort. I only hoped he wouldn't encounter any mistakes in the music I had copied out for him weeks earlier. Within an hour, Bach had taken us through the entire score; fortunately, all parts were free of error. The orchestra progressed rapidly over the following days and was soon joined by the chorus.

Then, one week before Christmas, everything changed. As I entered the loft and threaded my way through the company of instrumentalists and singers preparing for rehearsal, I noticed Bach standing to the side in private conversation with Ernesti. I hoped my master was not again being reprimanded, but neither man seemed angry. Then Bach moved away from the rector and walked directly toward me.

"It seems our principal cellist has become violently ill," he murmured. "He is not in any significant danger, for which we are all grateful, but it appears unlikely that he will be able to join us for the cantata."

I looked from Bach to Ernesti, and again at Bach, concerned for my colleague's welfare and my own. Placing his arm on mine, Bach calmly continued.

"Carl, I know you have not studied the continuo solos. Fortunately, there are only a few in this cantata, and with my help, we shall have you ready in time. Placing you in this position is not what we anticipated, but it is in such circumstances that one's mettle is truly tested. Blessedly, you will have the pleasure of accompanying your brother's oboe solos in the third movement, the duet for soprano and bass." Now he patted my shoulder, a gesture perhaps intended to put us both at ease. "We shall find another cellist for the section. Can I depend on you?"

How could I refuse? By now, I knew the music well and had the advantage of having heard my partner play the solos several times. I did not relish the additional responsibility but understood everyone was looking to me. After a moment's contemplation, I gave the cantor his answer.

"Herr Bach," I said with as much assurance as I could muster, "I'm honored by your confidence in my abilities and will attempt to rise to the occasion. And let us hope my colleague's health improves come Christmas!"

Bach thanked me and then shared the news with the orchestra. His announcement was met with the shuffling of many feet in support, for which I was silently grateful.

"Now," Bach continued, "I propose today we begin with the third movement so Herr Barth can find his bearings." I turned to my brother, who winked and smiled. The boy soprano and bass soloists then stepped forward, and upon Bach's signal, we began. With Bach at the organ, my brother and I began to shape the graceful aria's opening. Gradually, my nerves settled, allowing me to savor the experience. Assuming the continuo role under my master's command, grounding the singers and accompanying my brother, for the first time I felt that I was truly making music for and with Sebastian Bach.

Over the next several days, Bach helped me refine the aria's bass lines. From behind a harpsichord in his study, he guided me through the movement's nuances, demonstrating when to move to the fore and when to recede, when to add weight to dissonances and depth to the phrasing, and when to simply keep time. Then, the evening before the final rehearsal, Christian Samuel was shown to Bach's study, where he told me that Herr Bach had summoned him only shortly before. A moment later, Bach entered with Frau Anna.

"Gentlemen, while Carl has assumed his new role splendidly, to help put him even more at ease, I thought it would be beneficial to go through the aria, just the four of us. Since our soloists cannot be here, my wife has graciously consented to join us. She sings a fine soprano, and I am confident you won't be disappointed." Frau Anna blushed before we commenced to play.

Although I attempted to remain focused on the bass line I had worked so hard to polish, it proved impossible not to be distracted by what was happening around me: Bach gruffly singing the bass vocalist's lines and filling out the harmonies at the harpsichord, Frau Anna filling in for the soprano soloist with astonishing eloquence and sweetness, and my brother's exquisite oboe solos, which granted still more depth to Bach's rich musical texture. I found myself fully in the moment, soul, and mind, surrounded by glorious music and people I cherished.

Those minutes remain among my most treasured musical memories. When we had finished, Frau Anna was the first to weigh in. "Well, your Barth brothers make it easy for us, do they not, Papa?" she smiled, affectionately stroking her husband's shoulder.

"They do indeed," he affirmed. "Christian Samuel, I cannot imagine those solos being played any more expressively. And Carl, I apologize for throwing you into the middle of everything, but you have acquitted yourself splendidly. Bravo!"

I bowed deeply, first to Frau Anna Magdalena, then to Herr Bach, and finally to my brother. We all adjourned to the dining room, where we raised a glass to Bach's cantata and Frau Anna's "fine soprano." And before anyone took a sip, my master turned directly to me and wished me luck on Christmas morning.

Chapter 5

In Glauchau, the Christmas season always begins the first week of December, on the eve of St. Nicholas Day. Our family tradition was to polish and place our boots outside our bedroom door. The following morning, we would awake excitedly, hoping to find them filled with sweets. However, Leipzig, and the Bach household in particular, followed the practice of Martin Luther. Adults would exchange gifts on Christmas Eve, and the *Christkindl,* or Christ Child, himself would bring presents for the children.

As the holiday approached, I sometimes joined the family for evening strolls around the lavishly decorated central market. With Frau Anna on Bach's arm, the two girls would often hold each of my hands as we toured the festive stalls. Here was found everything, from wooden kitchen utensils and evergreen wreaths to delicious roasted nuts and *glüwein,* the seasonal spiced wine of which Bach and Frau Anna were particularly fond. Having wandered off on my own one evening, I chanced upon a vendor of writing tools. Beyond the usual offerings—penknives, inkpots, storage containers—I was mesmerized by the exotic woods and rich leathers of the various boxes and satchels, inkwells cast in silver, bronze, and ribbed glass of lovely colors, and porcelain pounce pots for the ground cuttlefish bone that hastened the drying process. I was imagining what such tools would feel like in hand when the Bachs found me. As the girls tugged at my arms, I bid the vendor a splendid holiday.

We welcomed Christmas Eve with the mouthwatering aroma of roasting chickens, turning on their spits above charcoal beds in the great kitchen fireplace. The feast began with beer soup, followed by the chickens, already carved and set on a platter alongside braised cabbage and poached eggs. For dessert, we were treated to *Stollen*, an extravagant fruit bread stuffed with raisins and candied orange peel, flavored with marzipan, dusted with powdered sugar, and served only once each year. Bach's guests for the evening were all accomplished musicians well known to the family, for the holiday was to be celebrated with music after we had adjourned from the table.

One decidedly unmusical guest was also present: Herr Johann Ernesti. Inviting the rector into their home from across the hall was certainly the charitable and seasonal thing to do, as he lived alone. Accordingly, both cantor and rector conducted themselves with exceeding cordiality. No one unfamiliar with their history would have suspected their strained relations.

Ernesti did corner me after dinner, ostensibly to ask if everything was in order with the Bach family, and if my duties were to my liking … or perhaps too demanding. Unhesitatingly, I assured him I felt comfortable and welcomed, and was learning a great deal under Bach's wing. Furthermore, I allowed that though I was kept very busy, the work was highly rewarding.

"*Wunderbar!*" he exclaimed. "Herr Bach tells me you are well on your way to becoming a fine cellist and an accomplished copyist, which I'm very pleased to hear. I hope the arrangement continues to be mutually beneficial." I then thanked him, with all sincerity, for having encouraged me to accept the position.

With full stomachs and good cheer, we watched the children open their gifts. The dining room table was then pushed to the side, to make room for the cembalo carried from the corner. Chairs and music stands in place, the company commenced to play and sing well into the night. I did my share of both, first caroling and then joining as the cellist for various trio sonatas.

Bach's poor eyesight precluded him from playing chamber music, though he appeared more than content to sit and listen. He had kindly selected for us music by composers of whom he was particularly fond—Telemann, some Italians, and even trios by his sons Carl Phillip and Wilhelm Friedemann. I was delighted by the sight of my master and Ernesti seated side by side, and I relished overhearing Bach relating some of the finer details of the music to him.

Bach's spirits that night were exceptionally high, and those hours in the company of his family and friends were among the most joyous I would experience during the months I lived there. Near the end of the celebration, several guests pleaded with Bach to play for us. He thus requested his Stainer violin, then honored us with the fugue from his Sonata in G minor, which he said he had composed in Köthen.

From the opening notes, I was swept up in the range of emotion Bach drew from his music, the phrases yearning one moment, resolute the next, and then showing a sudden turn of melancholy. This piece astonished me with its fluid counterpoint and Bach's seemingly inexhaustible powers of invention. How did he glean such poignancy—from a fugue, no less, and one composed for a solo fiddle?

I have often reflected upon that evening's performance by my master. If asked how he had achieved such a wonder, I suspect Bach's response would have been akin to Galileo attempting to unravel the mysteries of the cosmos for a curious child. But I was far from alone in my amazement. All the guests were held in rapt attention, even Ernesti, who despite himself, sat spellbound, an unsuspecting prisoner of Bach's art and unfathomable genius.

When the festive evening came to an end, all that was left was to wish one another *frohe Weihnachten*—Merry Christmas. Friends, some more than a little tipsy, departed contented and exhausted, promising to reconvene bright and early for Mass at St. Thomas.

The Christmas cantata came off effortlessly. The band was in a celebratory mood and my brother Christian Samuel's oboe playing was as beautiful as ever. I experienced some nerves over my debut in such a prominent role, but Bach had thoroughly prepared me for the moment and once we began, I found the experience exhilarating. After the service, as I helped Bach down from the loft, it was obvious that our performance had worked its intended effect. Children marched toward the doors, mimicking the festive trumpets, and outside in the late December chill, congregation members waited to congratulate us.

Still, though I left the church with my soul uplifted, performing the Christmas cantata in the St. Thomas loft did not spark the same exhilaration I felt upon playing the aria with Bach, Frau Anna, and my brother a few days earlier. As I returned to the Bach apartment, I briefly considered asking my master if he shared my sentiments, but decided to forego such queries about the spiritual significance of a musical experience.

In time, however, I came to believe that for Bach, the most profound meeting place between the musical and the spiritual was found neither in church nor in leading a performance, despite the legitimate satisfactions he derived from both. Rather, I sensed that my master was at his most spiritual when absorbed in composition or immersed in improvisation. Indeed, some of his thoughts about these matters would be shared with me in time. And while I have little doubt that our ad hoc reading of the aria was also memorable for Bach, especially as the occasion involved his dear wife, I gradually realized that I simply did not possess the same religious fervor that dwelt at the core of his being. To Bach, music and God were inseparable. To me, music was and would continue to be miraculous in and of itself.

Later that Christmas Day, I returned to the St. Nicholas loft to sing in the choir for vespers. Bach and his family now sat among the congregation. Afterward, we walked home and enjoyed a light repast of sausage, bread, and wine. Instead of bidding me a good rest after the day's exertions, however, Bach and Frau Anna asked that I remain in the dining room. She left momentarily before returning with a short stack of music and placing it on the table between her and her husband.

"Carl," Bach began earnestly, looking first at me and then at his wife, "Anna and I did not present you with a gift during last night's festivities, as we wanted to do so privately. We have both found your presence in our humble apartment a blessing. You are not only thoughtful, serious, and compassionate but industrious. Furthermore, circumstances beyond anyone's control put you in a challenging position for the cantata, and we're both very proud of how well you distinguished yourself. And so, with all that behind us, we wanted to give you a token of our affection and appreciation."

Bach now asked me to step to the cembalo, once more in the corner of the room, where I would find a package placed on top. Unwrapping it revealed a large dovetail box of dark German spruce, with the initials "C.B." exquisitely etched into the lid. As I returned to where they sat, my benefactors motioned for me to set the box down and open it. I carefully lifted the lid to discover the box was a writing desk! The lid's underside served as a sloped writing surface, below which chambers of various sizes were fitted: square ones at either end, containing respectively a full glass inkwell and a pounce pot, and a longer compartment in between, which held several fresh quills and a handsome penknife.

"A copyist needs proper tools and a proper place to store them," Bach observed. "Merry Christmas, Carl."

Speechless, I could only look at them.

"We saw how taken you were at the market stall," Frau Anna explained, "and thought you should have your own implements. We pray this gift will remain with you for many years and accompany you wherever you go."

"And may you experience more of the world than we have!" Bach added.

Looking back down at the writing desk, I ran my hands gently over its smooth surfaces and, closing the lid, admired its lovely workmanship. I entertained a fleeting thought of sitting aboard a coach, this precious object in my lap, headed toward some enchanting destination. Just how far my travels would one day take me, all on account of my master, was beyond the scope of fantasy.

Still, I struggled to find words. "It is, without doubt, the most beautiful gift I have ever received or owned. I am honored by your generosity, Herr and Frau Bach …"

"There is no need to say more, Carl," Frau Bach kindly interjected. "Your expression says all we need to know. Now, as to this music …"

She turned the stack toward me, and I immediately recognized the solo cello music I had found in the library weeks earlier. Given everything that had happened since, I had completely forgotten about it. Anna Magdalena carefully pushed the pages toward the center of the table, and my master described how he had composed these six suites during his time in Köthen.

"Most were written for a four-string instrument like yours, Carl. Occasionally, I asked one of our fine court cellists to play a passage or two to ensure everything was in order. But the final suite, as you undoubtedly noticed, calls for a cello with an additional string. The prince's outstanding collection contained several curiosities, including a five-string *violoncello piccolo*. It was somewhat smaller than most cellos but featured an added E string. I had never encountered such a thing but soon fell under its spell because of its extended range and unique timbre. Sadly, although the court musicians were all excellent, none could play the instrument proficiently. So I have yet to hear the work performed as I intended."

Bach placed his hand gently upon Frau Anna's. "Thankfully, in Köthen, I also had the fortune to be surrounded by first-rate singers. When we met, Anna Magdalena was not only the gifted soprano with whom you are now well acquainted, Carl. She was also the first woman fully employed in Prince Leopold's court and its highest-paid musician—other than myself! As you might imagine, I was as impressed with her voice and musicianship as I was with her charm," he added with a swift wink. "She also proved my most trusted copyist, in time."

Frau Anna now steered our attention to the pages before us. "As with much of Sebastian's music, I made copies of all six cello suites. But somewhere between Köthen and Leipzig,

Sebastian's original autograph and my copy disappeared," she said, pointing at the one I had recognized as Bach's script and then at her own. "Now that you have found them, we wondered if you might like to make a personal copy."

"Naturally, if they meet with your approval," Bach said lightly.

I stared at the music and recalled my initial impression of the dusty pages when I had no understanding of their significance. Nor had I ever played any music for solo cello beyond the studies assigned by various instructors. Nonetheless, I was eager to try my hand at it.

Unlike my stammered gratitude for the writing desk, words now came easily. "I am deeply flattered that you are entrusting me with such a project, and humbled by your confidence in my abilities," I told my hosts, carefully thumbing through the pages before looking back up at them. "These suites intrigue me beyond measure, and it would be my honor to devote myself to their study. Though given their obvious demands," I added, "I can only hope one day to do them justice."

I now recalled my master's words about the value of a solo cello, spoken in response to doubts I had expressed weeks earlier. "Herr Bach, I'm embarrassed to have spoken as I did. At the time, you said nothing about this music. Instead, you unveiled a larger picture, stressing the importance of developing a singing style *and* the cello's harmonic and rhythmic role within a musical work. In this collection, I sense this *is* the larger picture, and it appears to be truly magnificent. Might you know if they are the only works of their kind?"

"In Köthen," Bach answered, "I was told of an Italian cellist named Domenico Gabrielli who performed his own solo music. I never heard more about the man or his compositions, but I am nonetheless certain that what lies before you is unlike anything previously written. And while I crafted the suites according to the same basic plan, each is a world entirely unto itself.

"Carl, your instinct about their demands is certainly accurate, what with their precarious string crossings, intricate chords, rapid passagework, and the like. Still, I humbly believe that whatever time and energy you dedicate to them will be repaid with ample dividends. Along with your new writing desk, we hope these pages will provide you with many years of companionship."

"Carl," Frau Anna suggested, "perhaps take Papa's autograph upstairs and return my copy to the library? Please place it with the other instrumental works from Köthen, where this music should have been all along. Take whatever time you need to copy the original, and shelve it in the library alongside mine when you've finished. Now that these scores are back with us—thanks to you—we shall know where to find them."

I suddenly realized that Frau Anna, like her husband, had dispensed with the formalities of my name. I met their eyes, trying to communicate my contentment, and again thanked them aloud for everything they had done for me. At this point, my hosts stood to wish me a blessed Christmas and a restful evening before retiring. But I lingered, savoring the moment before blowing out the candles and gathering up the treasures entrusted to me, giddy with excitement about the glorious musical journey ahead.

Chapter 6

I THREW MYSELF INTO THE CELLO suites at every opportunity over the ensuing weeks. Despite the ongoing demands of schoolwork and rehearsals, I also continued to whittle down the piles of music in the apartment, of which but a few remained. Late afternoons found me in the library copying parts, and evenings in my room getting to know my six new musical companions.

On that first night, I imagined I was a brigand, making off with a cache of jewels and returning to his lair to sort through the treasures. Yet, these treasures would take time—perhaps years—to reveal their worth. I carefully paged through the manuscript, omitting no detail and keeping in mind that, as my master had said, each suite adhered to a similar overall design. Indeed, like the curtain rising on an opera, each was ushered in with a Prelude endowed with a distinctive mood. There followed, in turn, five dances of different national characters—earnest, weighty Allemandes from German lands, sprightly Italian Courantes, reflective Spanish Sarabandes, stately French Gavottes, Minuets or Bourrées, and, finally, jaunty English Gigues. Yet it was undeniable—and evident even without cello in hand—that every movement was unique. One trait united them all: their breathtaking creativity.

I recalled Bach speaking about the particular difficulties of the Fourth and Fifth Suites, so they naturally aroused my greatest curiosity. When I arrived at the Fourth Suite, I immediately noted that the Prelude somehow correlated with the opening Prelude of Bach's *Well-Tempered Clavier*, with waves of arpeggios spawning captivating harmonies.

The Fifth Suite offered a similar abundance. The work had been ingeniously conceived with the instrument's top string tuned down one step, and in my mind's ear, I could easily discern the sweet, delicate sound of the viola da gamba. Bach had cast the Prelude as a French overture, which put me in mind of his descriptions of Lully and the court of Louis Quatorze. As I followed the progress of the stately, measured introduction, I envisioned the royally attired Sun King imperiously entering a fantastically appointed ballroom, his costumed subjects deferentially posed, and an orchestra of gambas mirroring the monarch's rhythmic steps. But it was not until the introduction gave way to a fugue that I gasped in amazement. Such ingenuity! How was it possible to envision, much less craft, such music with only four strings?

Recalling Bach's Christmas Eve performance of the solo violin fugue, I marveled anew. How long would it take me to learn such a piece? Glancing further into the suite, I caught sight of the C minor Sarabande. Though it appeared uncomplicated, I sensed deep sorrow within, which in turn brought to mind the death of Bach's first wife.

Upon first sight of the Sixth Suite, scored for an instrument of not four but five strings, I began to feel dizzy in the now-flickering candlelight. Bach had assuredly tapped the cello's potential with his first five compositions, but the added E string propelled the composition forward in a way that was as much unorthodox as logical. I felt like a door had been thrown open, revealing entirely original territory! But a cello of five strings—where or when would I ever come across such an instrument?

All told, my wondrous first tour through the manuscript revealed a magnificent trajectory. It was evident that Bach had gifted me—and the wider world—something precious and of unending value. For myself, these compositions would prove to be lifelong companions whose friendship and meaning would continue to blossom over time.

It took only a few nights for me to copy out the first two suites in their entirety. And because my master's ears remained sharp as ever, Bach occasionally came from another room or floor in the apartment to offer a suggestion or two as I practiced. Clearly, he was most pleased to hear his long-lost music resuscitated.

A few weeks into the start of the new year, my master proffered advice about the challenging bowing patterns of the first movement of the collection, a G major Prelude. At other times, he helped with the intricacies of phrasing by showing me how he sometimes compressed ideas to create forward momentum. But mostly, Bach left me to my discoveries—and struggles—as I slowly unlocked the wonders his music beheld.

As I thus cultivated my cello skills, I participated more frequently in the orchestra for Sunday morning performances and sang less often with the choir. I was still called upon to sing when an extra baritone was required, as such voices were in short supply. Still, my preference was unquestionably to have my cello in hand, as my preoccupation with Bach's suites had heightened my desire to improve as quickly as possible.

During the first several months of 1750, I remained consumed with schoolwork, rehearsals, performances, and helping Bach as needed. By mid-January, I had finally cleared the apartment of all the stacks of music and restored a dozen or so cantatas to wholeness with complete sets of parts. I also remained acutely aware of my master's increasing struggles with his vision and growing reliance upon the help of others and knew that instructions for my next assigned task would not be long in coming.

Early one afternoon, as I practiced before the stove on the ground floor, Bach's daughter Johanna Carolina appeared, begging my pardon for the interruption. Her father was asking to see me in his study.

"Of course, at once," I responded. I placed the cello in the corner and followed her upstairs, where I found my master at the desk of his outer studio.

"Good afternoon, Carl. I requested your presence as I believe it is time to move on to the next phase of your duties here. You have done an impressive amount of organizational work, but the persistent problem now is that much of my current work remains unfinished." Bach gestured toward multiple pages spread over the desk and manuscripts stacked along its edges.

"I simply can't see well enough to continue alone. My wife and I have followed your progress and remain impressed with your diligence and the refinement of your copyist skills. In short, Carl, I would like to enlist your help preparing some of my works in progress for publication."

"Herr Bach, I am honored, but I haven't any experience with …" I began, but he immediately cut me off.

"Carl, before you answer, I propose we take a stroll. The temperature is not so cold, and I think a little exercise would do this old body some good."

Bach sensed my apprehension, and with some relief, I agreed that a walk would be welcome. We slipped into our coats and hats, and with my master's arm in mine, we headed toward the fashionable Brühl. As we maneuvered around fountains and carriages, I waited for him to initiate further conversation. Soon enough, he returned to the subject of his eyesight, admitting that he was now mostly reduced to making out solid shapes in the light and was all but helpless in the dark. As for putting music down onto manuscript paper, he had to lean in so close to the pages that the posture had become debilitating.

Nevertheless, Bach seemed in good spirits, and as we neared the Brühl, he requested we stop before *Zum arabischen Coffe Baum*—The Arabian Coffee Bean—which he claimed was one of Europe's oldest coffeehouses. Though he could no longer make out the façade, he drew my attention to its trademark Ottoman passing a steaming cup to a cherub.

"Look carefully, Carl. The image signifies one of the Orient's great contributions to European culture. We've yet to repay the favor! And now that I recall, I don't believe I've ever noticed *you* drink coffee when we have served it at home!"

I replied that I had neither developed a taste for the drink nor braved the smoky atmosphere of the city's coffeehouses to acquire such.

"Well, my young man, I suggest you develop a taste for both as soon as possible! These are some of life's great pleasures—along with a glass of nightly ale. And I know just the place to get you started."

We walked to nearby *Katherinenstrasse* and entered *Zimmermannsches Kaffeehaus*—Café Zimmermann—which occupied the lower two stories of one of the neighborhood's most impressive buildings. I immediately noted the absence of any women.

"I'll have to take your word for it," Bach commented as we made our way to the second story, "though I do recall the presence of the fairer sex at the downstairs performances."

We found an empty table in the hazy, boisterous room. A waiter rushing past us paused when he recognized Bach and quickly strode to our side.

"Herr Cantor, it has been far too long! I trust you have been well?"

Bach stated that he was in good health, aside from his eyes. "I'm sorry I cannot make out your face, but your voice is familiar, Herr ..."

"Adler. Jacob Adler, at your service," the waiter formally replied. He turned to me and proudly recounted having served the café's clientele for over two decades. Then, addressing Bach, he fondly recalled the lively concerts my master had been known to lead downstairs.

"I relished them as well, Herr Adler," Bach responded. "And among my most tasteful memories is that of your delicious coffee. Might you indulge us, with sugar and cream for my young friend?"

"With pleasure, Herr Cantor." Adler quickly turned on his heels and made for the kitchen. I immediately inquired about the downstairs concerts, for I was surprised to hear of performances in such a setting.

"That was a delightful time," Bach began. "About five years after coming to Leipzig, I took over the prestigious Collegium Musicum, a private society of musically gifted university students that Telemann himself founded. During the winter, we performed here, downstairs, for the public, women included. And in the summer, we performed in a coffee garden behind St. Nicholas."

"It sounds splendid," I responded, "but I imagine such events added considerably to your already exhausting workload."

"True enough," Bach agreed. "I directed and composed many works over my eight years with the Collegium—orchestral suites, secular cantatas, various concertos, and so on. However, some of the most memorable were not the *ordinaire* concerts, but rather the *extraordinaire*. For instance, we once presented an evening birthday concert for the Elector of Saxony, Augustus the Strong, that involved some three hundred students bearing torches! The frequency of *extraordinaire* concerts only increased with the son of Augustus, Frederick Augustus II, beginning with the festivities surrounding his accession. I never ceased to execute my duties faithfully, but the Collegium came to demand too much of my time."

Adler soon returned with two cups and the condiments. These he placed before us before filling each cup from a steaming brass coffee pot, which he left so that we could pour additional draughts as we liked. The beverage, which I initially sampled without cream or sugar, was rich but too bitter for my taste. Bach suggested I add a spoonful of sugar and a touch of cream, and with my next sip, I took to it at once. Bach appeared equally delighted, so we sat silently, enjoying the warmth of our drinks and the thrum of activity around us. I could make out bits and pieces of vigorous discourse and animated debates from nearby tables. Other patrons sat in peaceful introspection, alone, poring over newspapers pulled from racks in a far corner. Still others studied chessboards, solo or in pairs, contemplating their next moves.

The swirling air was thick with the intermingling aromas of pungent coffee and fragrant tobacco smoke and I quickly relaxed in the establishment's agreeable atmosphere. Between sips, Bach soon returned to his prior narrative.

"My Collegium duties were eventually taken up by a colleague, although I remained closely associated with the society and even resumed my involvement for several years until the death of Gottfried Zimmermann—this café's founder," he said, glancing toward the ceiling. "By that point, Leipzig concert life had begun to change considerably, especially with the founding of the Grand Concerts, which took place at another venue and drew audiences of hundreds. These were far from the intimate affairs with which I had been involved."

For a moment, my master's attention drifted. But the return of Herr Adler brought him back around. The pot was now empty, and Bach withdrew a leather coin purse in an attempt to pay, but Adler refused to accept anything from "one of our town's most illustrious citizens."

"That is much too kind of you, Herr Adler," Bach said. "Well, let's hope it won't be so long until the next time, and then you *must* accept my money."

"Of course, Herr Bach, the next time," Adler politely demurred before bidding us a pleasant evening. Neither man could have guessed that this visit to Zimmermann's would be Bach's last.

With my master again on my arm, we headed home by a roundabout route. Walking past the *Rathaus*, Leipzig's city hall, Bach drew my attention to the bell tower, recalling how his Collegium musicians had once trumpeted fanfares thence for the Elector of Saxony. He then regaled me with a colorful account of the Prussian army's occupation of Leipzig. This tale began with the long struggle between Prussia and Austria, the first of a series of Silesian Wars with which I would one day become all too familiar. That which Bach recounted had the two powers battling for the disputed region of Silesia, which lay between them.

Fighting for Austria, the Saxon army eventually joined the Habsburgs in a final attempt to stem Prussian aggression and gain some of its territory; in 1745 their combined forces marched toward Berlin. They were nearly at the Brandenburg border when the Prussians, who had shadowed the enemy, launched a surprise attack. The confused Austrian army—Saxons and Habsburgs alike—scattered before the Prussian onslaught, and the Saxon threat collapsed.

"On that Christmas of 1745," Bach explained, "Prussian forces under 'Old Dessauer'—as Frederick the Great's general was known—walked into Leipzig without resistance. Perhaps we owe it to the brave surrenderers that our city remained intact!

"Anyway, Prussian soldiers were everywhere ... some two thousand of them," he continued, now with a broad sweeping gesture. "Their existence placed considerable strain on our little town. Leipzig, however, was not the goal. The Prussians wanted Dresden. So Dessauer soon departed for the Saxon capital, where he converged with Frederick's army, occupied the city, and brought matters to an end—temporarily at least."

Bach paused for a moment in recollection of those chaotic times. "One wonders if things would have turned out differently, had we been commanded by someone as talented as Frederick. Anyway, eighteen months later, another Saxon"—Bach chuckled, lightly tapping his chest with his thumb—"passed through Frederick's gate, this time at the king's invitation."

Given the time spent in Zimmerman's and walking about town, I thought my master might be ready to return home, but he surprised me.

"To the contrary! I find it quite pleasant and the air at dusk invigorating." So we walked on in the quickly fading light, as Bach recounted his trip to the palace of the King of Prussia and how the *Musical Offering* came to be.

Chapter 7

"Given that I went to Prussia in the wake of the Prussian invasion, at the king's invitation," Bach continued, with no small amount of pride, "some probably regarded the trip as a foray into enemy territory. Whether or not others perceived it as a peacekeeping or suicide mission, it surely raised the eyebrows of officials from the locals to the Elector!

"I traveled in the first week of May 1747, in the company of my son Friedemann; even then, my age rendered such a journey too arduous to attempt alone. Our instructions were to travel to Potsdam, where Frederick maintained a magnificent summer residence, Sanssouci. We arrived on a Sunday evening, exhausted after two all-but-sleepless days and nights in bone-rattling coaches, and were just settling in when there came a knock on the door. 'Herr Bach, His Majesty, the King, will see you now …'

"So summoned, we were allowed but a moment to change from our travel garb and brush our shoes before being whisked through the palace corridors. I believed I could make out music at the end of a hallway, and before long, we were being led across a magnificent ballroom. Frederick stood resplendent at the far end, flute in hand, surrounded by several musicians and perhaps a dozen listeners, all exquisitely dressed. Behind the seated ladies, their gentlemen partners stood like statues. I also recall a few children seated quietly off to one side. The king turned, and I distinctly heard him quip to those nearest him, 'Ladies and gentlemen, old Bach is come.'

"As Friedemann and I drew closer, I could make out several members of Frederick's entourage, including the flutist Quantz, with whom I had once played; the Graun brothers, one of whom had been Friedemann's teacher for a time; and my son Carl, whom I embraced warmly. Following the formal introductions, I was escorted to a series of lavishly decorated rooms containing splendid fortepianos built by my old friend Gottfried Silbermann. At the king's behest, I improvised on each of the instruments, and after this 'pleasure' of playing four or five of them, he informed me that well over a dozen more were installed throughout the palace.

"To be honest, I'm still unsure if His Majesty wanted to hear me play or listen to me gush over his prized collection. My best guess is that his goal was to convince me that my usual instrument, the harpsichord, was an inferior, antiquated specimen. Which, considering his reference to me as 'old Bach,' seems to be how he regarded me as well!"

With that cynical quip, Bach at last indicated that we should return home for a hot meal. Frau Anna met us at the door and voiced concern about our having been gone so long, but my master assured her that he was well and had been in capable hands. Shedding our coats, we walked upstairs to warm ourselves before the kitchen fireplace, then joined the others in the dining room for cabbage soup and *Schwarzbier*. Afterward, having bid the younger children goodnight, I accompanied Bach to the outer room of his study. Bach sat at a harpsichord, lit his pipe, and took a deep, satisfying draw. A moment later, we were back in Potsdam.

"I believe the king's true objective in bringing me to Sanssouci was to demonstrate his superiority. Make no mistake, Carl! Frederick was no blockhead. Beyond his genius on the battlefield, he was also an exceptionally educated man who preferred to speak the French of his frequent guest Voltaire rather than the lowly German of his father … or me, for that matter. And he had been taught flute by none other than Quantz himself.

"So there I was: a 63-year-old musician with no university education, exhausted from travel and performing like a trained monkey before His Majesty and his coterie of illustrious musicians. Because I had already tried out several of Silbermann's pianos, His Majesty requested I improvise a fugue based on a subject of *his* invention."

Intent on recreating the scene for me, in imitation of the king, Bach haughtily cocked his chin and adjusted his ruffles with exaggerated flair. He then played what he called the *Thema Regium*, "Theme of the King," a series of some twenty-one notes whose peculiar design featured a pair of precipitous jumps and a slithering descent that threatened to unmoor the tonality of the entire subject.

"*Voilà*, that's what he gave me! Really! How is such a thing suitable for a fugue subject?" And Bach slowly replayed the royally mandated sequence, meticulously stressing its bizarre characteristics.

"This is a theme designed for failure, and I believe His Majesty was counting on precisely that when I sat down to do his bidding. I could hardly conceal my irritation when I took my place at the keyboard. I had the nauseating feeling of being ambushed and wondered if other musicians in the room were in on their king's little joke. I remember thinking the Saxons must have felt this way when the Prussian army jumped them without warning!

"I should add, Carl, that this was hardly the first time I had been asked to flaunt my skills before powerful people. Years earlier, at the home of a leading minister of state in Dresden, I was invited to enter into competition with the great French organist Louis Marchand. We were to execute, *ex tempore,* several musical tasks. But at the last moment, Marchand failed to appear! He had fled that very morning by special coach. The man had a sterling reputation as an excellent player, yet evidently thought better than to try his hand—or hands—against mine.

"So here I was, sitting before the King of Prussia and an expectant audience. Secreting out, by any means, was not an option. Shrugging off all thoughts about my predicament, I plucked out His Majesty's theme, imagining the possibilities I could develop from it, before setting about unfurling the most worthy fugue I could muster. With the introduction of each new voice, I remained ever vigilant to avoid any musical dead ends. Nonetheless, my thoughts strayed to the image of Theseus slowly unfurling his thread and slaying the minotaur before finding his way back out of Daedalus' maze."

I sat in shocked silence. All anyone in Leipzig—save Frau Anna—knew about Bach's trip was that he performed for the king and returned a conquering hero.

"At long last," he continued, "I wound my way to the final resolution and lifted my hands from the keyboard, perspiring all the while. Naturally, I assumed this was the end of the evening's entertainment and expected that I would now be allowed to return to my quarters for some long-overdue rest. But the final chord still reverberated within that cavernous room when the king, clapping his hands, exclaimed, '*Tres formidable, Monsieur Bach, tres bien*! *Vous êtes en effet un magnifique improvisateur.* Bravo, Bravo!'

"And then, placing his forefinger near his temple and striking an innocent pose, Frederick continued. 'Herr Bach, I'm wondering … might it be possible for you to improvise a six-voice fugue on the same subject?'

"I froze. Had I heard the king correctly? Truly this was a nightmare from which there was no waking. Granted, with sufficient time, I surmised I could compose something quite worthy of Frederick's outrageous request. Doing so on the spur of the moment was another matter entirely.

"And so, I answered, with all humility, 'Your Majesty, I must beg your pardon, but it is with the deepest regret that I admit such a task is beyond my abilities. Perhaps had I come better prepared …'

"'Ah, I see that there is indeed a limit to Herr Bach's wizardry,' Frederick exclaimed, smugly glancing at his entourage. 'Very well then, my dearest Bach, how about improvising something of your choosing?'

"This offer hardly tempered my indignation. Did he equate my art to a circus stunt, like a juggler tossing another ball in with the five already airborne? Unable to catch Carl Phillip's eye, I couldn't help but wonder if he was privy to this contemptible farce. Nevertheless, having no choice in the matter, I honored His Majesty's request for an extemporaneous, six-voice fugue on a subject of my choosing. And thus, the evening mercifully came to an end."

"Bravo, Herr Bach!" I cried, forgetting in the intensity of my admiration that Frederick had said the same. "So you triumphed, no doubt astonishing the king and his court with your powers of invention?"

"Perhaps, my dear Carl, perhaps. Frederick, however, was not yet quite finished with me. Early the next morning, he summoned me to perform on the organs at each of Potsdam's churches. Granted, I had gained sufficient rest and was allowed to play the music of my choice on those glorious instruments. I still stung from Frederick's attempted humiliations of the previous evening, yet there we were, like old chums, touring about his city so he could revel in my private performances."

Bach had risen from the harpsichord to pace about and gesture for effect. He now dropped back onto the bench, exhausted. I took this opportunity to mention Bach's portrait of Frederick, which I had noted the first time I entered his inner study. I asked him why he displayed this work in his most private room, especially in light of the travails he had just shared with me.

"Ah, that is a fair question. I was set to depart Sanssouci the day after touring Potsdam's churches. But to my dismay, there was no further word from the king, much less a gift or token upon taking my leave. Not even a royal servant availed himself to convey His Majesty's gratitude or wishes for a safe return to Leipzig! Friedemann and I simply boarded the carriage and set out for home.

"Just beyond the gates, my son noticed an artist selling portraits of Frederick the Great, so I ordered our driver to stop. My eyesight now prevents me from making out the image's finer details, but I recall it as not merely an impressive likeness but rather one that captured His Majesty's insolence. My son, who had sympathetically witnessed my embarrassment for the king's amusement, also did not understand why I would wish to acquire such a work, but I had my reasons.

"I hung Frederick's portrait on that wall to symbolize something far greater than the image itself. Surely you noticed that he is positioned well below the cross. When I am seated at my desk and pause from my work, I have only to look at where that painting hangs to remind myself that all of us, even kings, must answer to our Creator. But it also represents something more personal: that even the most humble servant can rise higher than one who rules over him.

"The hour is late, Carl, but I hope you will indulge me as I share one more chapter from my Prussian story," Bach said. I nodded for him to continue. "With the portrait purchased, wrapped securely, and stored in the rear of the carriage, I began contemplating how best to exploit the potential locked within the king's exasperating theme. First, I reworked it ever so slightly in my mind. From there, however, I struck upon a fascinating and challenging idea: rather than base a single composition on the *Thema Regium*, I would construct an entire collection. In other words, I would nurture Frederick's theme until it grew into something of truly royal dimensions!

"I worked nearly unabated here at home, stopping only to catch a few hours of sleep. I even took meals at my desk. No doubt the stress and strain further depleted my eyesight, but within two weeks my design had come to fruition."

Bach now stood, retrieved a stack of music, and beckoned me to take a look. "Herein lies my answer to the king's challenge—my *Musical Offering*, fashioned of fugues, canons, and a trio sonata for flute, violin, and continuo. In Potsdam, Frederick had requested a six-voice fugue. I believe the results of my labor far exceeded anything he could have envisioned."

As Bach described the work's scheme, he separated the manuscript's portions on the desk. "I cast the fugues as *Ricercars*, by which I mean they are composed in an improvisatory style. The first is built of three voices; the second, six."

Bach leaned in closely, squinting, and drew a finger along several details on his autograph copy. I could see the voices unfolding in intricate counterpoint and began to appreciate Bach's wisdom in declining further improvisation when the king had demanded it.

"And one more detail," Bach went on. "Take note of the title heading." He flipped back to the first page. "Here I devised an encrypted Latin acrostic:

Regis Iussu Cantio Et Reliqua Canonica Arte Resoluta,

that is, 'At the king's demand, the song that is the fugue,' the first letters which spell out R-I-C-E-R-C-A-R."

Bach now turned to another portion of the composition, a series of canons. "Here is where I truly put the king's theme through its contrapuntal paces. The first canon is in retrograde, the next in unison, then contrary motion, augmented contrary motion, and so on. I also added a pair of Latin inscriptions in the margins of the king's autograph. Here, where the notes increase in length, I wrote, *Notulis crescentibus crescat Fortuna Regis,* 'May the king's happiness grow like the augmented notes.' And here," Bach said, pointing to another passage, "where the canon ends a step higher than it began, I wrote, *Ascedenteque Modulatione ascendat Gloria Regis,* that is, 'As the modulation ascends, so may the king's glory.'"

My eyes wide, I asked what the king had thought about Bach's miraculous gift. "Alas, no words of gratitude were forthcoming. Nor was there any indication that the king ever played it, much less laid eyes on it. I must add that the king's silence on the matter was all the more disquieting, given that a trio sonata with flute lay at the very heart of my *Offering*. Knowing the king's proficiency on the instrument, I hoped at least that inclusion would have made a favorable impression. As things are, the gift may be buried somewhere in the royal library, waiting to be unwrapped. And that, Carl, is where the saga finally comes to an end."

When I set down the cello earlier that evening, I had expected an imminent proposal from my master about how I might aid him with another musical project. But by now I had completely forgotten my anticipatory unease, which in retrospect seemed trivial as well as unwarranted. Bach had unguardedly shared with me the most personal aspects of his fabled meeting with Frederick the Great, and I silently vowed to commit every detail to memory.

Years later, when I became more familiar with the *Musical Offering*, I realized that his improvisations for the king had been among the last performances of his life and that the *Musical Offering* included the only music Bach ever composed for the fortepiano.

As I prepared to leave, Bach thanked me for my patience in listening to an old man's stories. "Tomorrow, Carl," he added, his characteristic energy restored, "I shall show you how one constructs a proper fugue subject. And then we shall see how you might help me further."

"It is I who should be thanking you, Herr Bach," I replied, and wished him good night. Reeling from it all as I prepared to retire, I sensed that I was becoming an increasingly meaningful presence in the Bach household, though precisely why eluded me. The next day, I began to understand.

Chapter 8

Two events from the final week of January 1750 stand out. The first was the onset of bitter cold. The morning after my excursion around the city with Bach, I awoke to windows coated with frost. What until then had been merely chilly weather became numbing, and the temperature continued to plummet throughout that day. By evening, the apartment had become so cold that we had to place buckets of water before the kitchen hearth to keep some from freezing. The upstairs stoves were fed as usual and continued to exude warmth throughout the day, though we could not spare fuel enough to stock the large fireplace on the ground floor. And although Johann Christian and I made for an effective team hauling wood, woe to him whose turn it was to step outside and gather more.

My other vivid memory is of joining Bach in his study on the first evening of this cold spell. I paused for a few minutes in the doorway as Bach sat with his back to me, playing what sounded like dense contrapuntal studies. At first, I could distinguish a similar subject at the beginning of each, despite the introduction of new textures and voicings. Eventually, though, I lost my way on account of the music's complexity, my shortcomings, and the debilitating cold, which made it highly challenging to focus on something as ephemeral as music.

In time, Frau Anna marched past me and lifted her husband's hands from the keyboard. Waving me in, she remonstrated, "Sebastian, Carl has been waiting to see you!"

"Oh, do come in, Carl," Bach agreed.

I apologized for the intrusion.

"Nonsense, young man. We have work to do, and I was simply trying to keep my fingers warm."

"Indeed, Herr Bach," I shivered. "This is the most extreme cold since I came to Leipzig."

"I'm sure you're correct," he answered. "We are now securely in winter's grip. Well, no matter. As long as the worst of it remains outside, we shall persevere. Here is one of the works I wanted to discuss with you."

Bach reached to the side of the keyboard, picked up a heft of pages, and dropped it onto the instrument's music rack.

"These are a series of variations, you might say, all based upon an exploration of the same basic fugue subject—though one that differs significantly from that quagmire Frederick pushed me into." Pulling away the title page, Bach revealed the opening of what he referred to as the first *Contrapunctus*.

"The subject, which naturally appears at the start unadorned and unaccompanied, has a distinct melodic and rhythmic profile," he explained. "It is arguably also a bit serpentine, but this subject is designed to evolve. Simply playing it along with its inversion creates a nuanced harmony. That effect is at the heart of what I set out to achieve."

Bach now played the opening subject against its inversion. I instantly found the combination compelling. I also noted that its concluding phrase made for a logical cadence, though

I could not immediately discern the larger musical significance of the exercise.

"Did you set out to best your *Musical Offering*, Herr Bach, once you had posted it to Potsdam?" I inquired.

"In truth, I began this project years before Frederick developed an interest in—or shall I say, curiosity about—my abilities. I intended to create a manual on the art of counterpoint by producing an exhaustive study of possibilities born of a single idea."

He then walked me through the manuscript. First were the simpler fugues, most of which I could discern on sight. Next came each subject, first in combination with its inversion and then set against additional themes. As the music grew more complex, the elusive mirror fugues ensued, in which both subject and countersubject unfolded in mirror image—miraculously, as it seemed to me—followed by a series of canons at multiple pitch levels.

"And here, Carl, is the very last fugue," Bach announced, as he reached the final pages. "I present the theme in combination with others, including one constructed from my name. See if you can spot it."

I leaned in and, near the beginning, caught sight of the original subject's inversion in the bass. Further down the page, I noted the appearance of a new theme introduced by the alto voice, and as I read on, I located where Bach had combined the two ideas. Finally, I spotted it: B–A–C–H, announced by a series of bold half notes in the tenor line! Remarkably, all three subjects were soon brought into play, one against the other. But after a few more notes in the tenor voice, the music ceased. Empty ledger lines filled the remainder of the page.

Eager to see the closure of this brilliant confluence, I quickly flipped the page, only to find the verso completely blank.

"Pardon me, Herr Bach, but the fugue … it breaks off midstream," I said, pointing to the curious final notes on the recto.

"Ah, yes. I had yet to decide what path it would take when I began reworking some of the earlier fugues. Then came Christmas and New Year, which kept me too busy for additional work. But I've recently decided to prepare this volume for publication and am thus impelled to bring matters to a close."

"May I ask what it is to be called?" I inquired.

"Well, I remain as undecided about that as I am about how to button up the final fugue. Perhaps *Compendium Contrapunctus*, although that sounds like a dull pedagogical primer, even to my ear! Or maybe something with more aesthetic appeal, such as *The Art of Fugue*. Do you find that too pompous?"

As I worked my way backward through the manuscript, replacing the pages in their proper order, I began to grasp the significance of what lay before me. Yet I couldn't help but wonder how these magnificent ideas might come to life for a listener. Would it even be possible to comprehend such an intricate design, even with repeated hearings? As to the substance of the work itself, it represented a most extraordinary achievement. Regardless of what Bach called it, I was certain it would endure for generations.

"In my humble opinion, Herr Bach, I find *The Art of Fugue* a most handsome title," I finally replied. "Admittedly, I can hardly fathom the extent of your accomplishment, but what you have revealed to me appears nothing shy of Promethean. If others find the title pompous, so be it!"

"Well, whatever it's worth," Bach responded, "it will have been a useless exercise should it go unpublished. And to avoid that outcome, I shall require the help of several sets of eyes and hands." He now picked up the manuscript and carried it to his desk, setting it down carefully.

"The project, alas, will be fairly tedious. We shall set up shop in the dining room, for the table is large enough to allow everyone to spread out their work. A new version of the score must be prepared, with each section checked and rechecked, by others, naturally. I am bringing in several students to help and hope I can also count on you to prepare the final copy for the engravers."

So this was to be my next undertaking. I assured my master I would be honored to participate in such a monumental endeavor.

Bach's assessment of the weather proved portentous, for Father Winter was reluctant to release his hold on Leipzig. Thankfully, the stove in the corner of the dining room remained stoked, and throughout much of February and well into March of 1750, the Bach apartment was transformed into a hive of activity. To prepare *The Art of Fugue*—the title ultimately ascribed—for publication, stations were set up around the large dining table, each dedicated to an individual contrapunctus or canon. Initially, I felt overly conscious of my inexperience, but I quickly realized that everyone engaged in the pursuit felt similarly. Soon, we all settled comfortably into our work.

Each movement was meticulously copied and rechecked by several sets of eyes. Bach himself came and went. Meanwhile, he could be heard at the harpsichord, experimenting with possibilities for the B-A-C-H motive. The half-step configuration of this strange musical gesture stood out in high relief against the project's bold, main subject, yet the more Bach mined its potential, the further its destination seemed to recede. Across the hall, we wondered if the cantor would ever settle upon a solution for his final fugue.

Those many weeks now seem a blur, but winter did give way to spring. With Easter soon upon us, *The Art of Fugue* was set aside. We now prepared for Good Friday, with rehearsals for Bach's *Johannes Passion* taking precedence over all other activities. Happily, I was recruited to help fill out the cello section for this glorious work.

Two days before Easter, the solemn observance was ushered in with the dawn tolling of Leipzig's massive bell, the Gloriosa. Within an hour, all the musicians and singers had settled into the loft of St. Thomas. Only the composer was not present, for he was no longer up to leading a performance of such length. In the sanctuary below, the candles were lit, and the city's archdeacon stood ready to officiate as celebrant.

Fortunately, Bach's *Passion* was in the capable hands of one of his most trusted subordinates, and the performance came off extremely well. The choir, bolstered by additional voices of university students, never sounded better, and the orchestra—the largest with which I was involved during my time at St. Thomas—outdid itself. After the service, we all commented that Bach, nestled in a pew surrounded by his family, had never appeared healthier.

Chapter 9

During that Holy Week, our congregation might have included a traveling surgeon of considerable repute. John Taylor rolled into town on 26 March 1750, a Thursday, seated comfortably in a white luxury coach pulled by a pair of handsome horses. I cannot say why the surgeon arrived just before Easter, which meant it would be several days until he could ply his trade. Perhaps Leipzig was a logical stop on the way to Berlin—his next destination, as I would soon discover—and the holiday was simply a minor inconvenience. Or perhaps he wished to use the time to ingratiate himself.

Whatever his reasons, there was no mistaking his arrival. I did not personally witness the initial appearance of Taylor's coach, which featured prominent images of the human eye on each side, underscored by the motto *Qui dat vivere dat visere,* "Giving sight is giving life." But the grand entrance, epitomizing as it did the man's extravagant and flamboyant airs, attracted no small amount of attention.

On Saturday evening, 28 March, Taylor presented the first of two lectures at the university. I could not attend, as I was rehearsing for Easter services. But news of Taylor and his guarantees of sight restored circulated as quickly as a summer plague. Having been informed of the celebrated doctor's presence by a city elder, Bach requested I attend the Tuesday lecture on his behalf. As I had only one service to play that morning, I was happy to comply.

John Taylor cut an impressive figure from the stage, radiating unbridled confidence in his shoulder-length wig, stylish clothing, and abundant jewelry. Though English by birth, his German was flawless, which I took as a mark of sophistication and worldliness. The *pièce de résistance* of his costume was the cross of precious stones on a fine chain about his neck, which brilliantly reflected the light from the hall's chandeliers.

He trumpeted the myriad titles bestowed upon him by the sovereigns he claimed to have served, though this level of detail seemed gratuitous. Still, for all his hauteur and bluster, it soon became evident that he commanded a deep understanding of ocular anatomy, disorders, and diseases, and possessed a wealth of experience with the latest ophthalmic surgical procedures. In particular, he declared cataract surgery to be routine, so frequently had he performed it.

Taylor had barely concluded this second lecture before the nearest audience members began rushing the stage. As I was seated toward the rear of the hall, he was impenetrably surrounded before I could draw near. I recognized several city officials among the legion of potential patients, but most appeared to be simple, modest folk hoping for affordable curatives. As I waited my turn, I noted his striking, elongated face set off by a broad forehead and deep-set, gray-green eyes. A prominent, aquiline nose contributed to his aristocratic countenance, as did full, sensual lips that curved slightly upward. Taylor was of medium height and build, yet the full effect was of someone much larger and more imposing.

After speaking to each supplicant in turn for several minutes, the doctor removed his coat and placed it on a nearby chair. I then decided to leave a message rather than tarry further. From the small journal in which I had jotted notes for my master, I carefully tore out a page, scratched out the request, and moved to the chair to slide the missive into Taylor's breast pocket.

> *Most gracious and honorable Chevalier—*
> *Herr Sebastian Bach, Thomaskantor,*
> *kindly requests an evaluation at his St.*
> *Thomas residence*
> *at your earliest convenience.*
>
> *Your most humble and obedient servant,*
> *C.F. Barth,*
> *Apprentice to the Thomaskantor*

Late that afternoon, I was observing activity in the courtyard from one of the dining room windows when to my surprise, I saw Taylor's unmistakable carriage pull up. I carefully observed the coachman spring from the driver's box and proceed to the apartment steps to ring the bell. The driver quickly returned to the coach, opened the door, and proffered Taylor his hand. The Chevalier alighted from the carriage dressed in an emerald-green velvet coat, a paisley vest, and black breeches. Brushing off his sleeves, he retrieved a black leather bag from the carriage before dismissing his driver. The conveyance had scarcely departed when Frau Anna appeared at the door of Bach's outer studio with the surgeon in tow. Bach, who had been seated at his harpsichord with his back to the door, stood and turned when he heard voices behind him.

"Herr Cantor, please permit me to introduce myself! I am Doctor John Taylor, Chevalier," he announced with a half-bow and flourish. "It is my understanding that you have requested an examination."

"Indeed," replied Bach, motioning for Taylor to approach. "My eyes are causing me pain and I am now nearly blind."

Frau Bach and I watched anxiously from the doorway as the surgeon opened his bag and withdrew a curious silver candle holder. Attached to this unusual tool was a thin metal strip that ran up the candle's length, to which was affixed a small, adjustable mirror. Taylor slid the mirror along the strip, up to the candlewick, and screwed it into place before inquiring about Bach's age.

"Sixty-five," Bach responded curtly.

"Very well, very well," Taylor said. "And may I ask if you take a pipe or imbibe alcohol?"

"Both, and with pleasure," Bach answered.

"Ah, quite right, quite right," Taylor murmured. "Let's have a look, shall we?"

With a bejeweled hand set off by the ruffle protruding from his shirt sleeve, the surgeon lit the candle and stepped toward Bach, holding the instrument aloft. Whether because of the shadowy surroundings or the sober circumstances, Bach appeared uncomfortable and vulnerable, waiting to be examined.

Taylor peered first into Bach's left eye and then the right. He pondered momentarily, blew out the candle, and set the instrument on Bach's desk.

"Well, Herr Cantor, my cursory examination reveals rather extensive cataracts in both eyes. I'm sorry, how old did you say you are?"

"Sixty-five."

"Hmm, yes. Herr Cantor, cataracts are cloudy intrusions that gradually appear upon the eye's lens. These are, without doubt, the likeliest cause of your vision loss and are quite common among those who smoke and drink, though I suspect your cataracts are also the product of your age and years of extensive eye strain. But the clouded lenses are dislodged easily enough, allowing light to enter unobstructed once again. I have performed the procedure hundreds of times with great success."

Bach nodded tentatively, though he did not respond to the Chevalier's claims. Taylor gestured for his patient to return to the harpsichord. The light in the room was slowly fading, so Taylor lit the candles at either end of the keyboard's music rack and opened the volume resting between. "Please," he said, touching the score, as Bach sat, "I would like to observe how well you read music. Typically, I would use a book, but given the circumstances …"

Bach leaned in and squinted, his hands hovering above the keys. Even from my station behind him, I could make out the unmistakable patterns of the First Prelude of his *Well-Tempered Clavier*. This was glorious music, hypnotic even, and it never failed to remind me of a boat rocking amidst the play of waves. However, the notes Bach played were from the Twenty-Fourth Prelude, the very last of the set. Over a gently walking bass, Bach sensitively interlaced two lines in the right hand with such delicacy as to all but betray the subtle double counterpoint. The music took on a subdued, resigned quality, perhaps reflecting his state of mind.

I knew, therefore, that Bach now played from memory only and, like a devious schoolboy, was attempting to deceive his interlocutor. At the conclusion of Bach's misleading demonstration, Taylor exclaimed, "Bravo, Herr Cantor! That was exquisite—though, if you will pardon me, I had a bit of difficulty following the music's essence. Admittedly, I am no connoisseur. Was that something you have played often?"

"Not for quite some time," Bach answered. "However, since you struggled with that portion, I'll spare you the fugue that follows," he added wryly.

"As you wish," continued the doctor. "But Herr Cantor, it appears you see rather well."

"Herr Doctor, I have been led to believe that you are a very competent and knowledgeable surgeon, but do you play or read music?" Bach asked, motioning to the keyboard.

"Neither, I'm afraid. Regrettably, the surgical arts and the incumbent travel have deprived me of sufficient time for such pursuits."

"I see," Bach continued. "So you would be unable to ascertain if I was playing the music before me?"

"Ah, I grant your point, Herr Cantor."

"I composed that music myself," Bach said, closing the volume, "albeit many years ago. In general, I have little need to see what's in front of me when I play nowadays. Almost everything is either from memory or improvised."

Bach then inquired if the doctor at least enjoyed music. "When granted the opportunity to hear it," Taylor admitted. "In particular, I find the music of my fellow Englishman, Mr. Handley, quite charming."

"Handley?" Bach inclined his head slightly to one side.

"Herr Doctor, are you speaking of Handel?"

"Ah, yes indeed! John Frederick Handel. Capital stuff."

"George," Bach responded, clearing his throat.

"Pardon?"

"George. More accurately, Ge-org," Bach intoned slowly, emphasizing the German pronunciation. "The truth is, Herr Doctor, your Mr. Handel was born *Georg Friedrich Händel*. He came of age in Halle, not so far from here."

"Truly? He is a Saxon?" Taylor exclaimed.

"Technically, Halle sits just beyond our borders, within the Duchy of Magdeburg," retorted Bach. But yes, Handel is a native German speaker."

"Well," Taylor smoothly responded, "he has certainly adapted well to my country. Even the king has taken a fancy to him! Are you perchance familiar with anything he wrote?"

Bach shrugged briefly, and I grimaced at the surgeon's lack of tact. As if taxing his memory, Bach mumbled something under his breath, straightened his back to perfect stiffness, and hammered out *The Harmonious Blacksmith*, one of Handel's most popular pieces. Taylor immediately assumed an animated expression, and exclaimed at the theme's conclusion, "Yes! Yes! I know that one. Capital! Capital!"

"Of course you do," Bach quipped, abruptly pulling the lid over the keyboard. "Doesn't everyone?"

"Yes, yes, I'm sure you're quite correct," the doctor replied in soothing tones. Then, in a return to his authoritative air, Taylor queried Bach about his general state of health.

"My constitution has been exceedingly hearty, a fact I attribute to my unwavering faith in God and my nightly glass of ale. I'm proud to say I've rarely spent a day in bed on account of illness, although I do recall being laid up with a fever some years ago, an illness which regretfully cost me the chance to meet your Mr. Handel."

The surgeon, who had now removed a magnifying glass from his bag to examine Bach's eyes more closely, pulled a chair in front of his patient and urged Bach to continue.

"It was during one of Handel's return visits to Halle, and though I planned to make the short trip, I was unable to travel. So, I sent my son Friedemann, who invited the great man to Leipzig. Handel, unfortunately, declined. I also recall another opportunity years earlier. I was living in Köthen when I learned

Handel was in Halle. As it was only a half day's journey, I set out at once but was told upon arrival that he had only just departed. Pity then, that we have never met."

"Well, Herr Bach, perhaps the opportunity will still present itself," Taylor said, again peering into each of my master's eyes. "In the meantime, I can remedy your cataracts with an oft-used procedure called couching—that is, should you be willing to entrust yourself to me. If so, I shall return tomorrow afternoon, following other procedures to which I am already committed, and remove them both. I propose operating in this room, which should have sufficient light by the time I arrive. I shall also require someone to steady your head while I work—preferably not a family member."

Bach turned to look in my direction. "Carl, would you be willing to assist the good doctor?"

"I would, of course, be honored," I replied. Even then, however, I felt a prickling sense of unease.

"Capital!" interjected Taylor. "If everything meets your approval, we can discuss details and my fee."

Frau Anna and I then left Bach alone with the Chevalier.

Following the doctor's departure, apprehension grew with each passing hour throughout the apartment. Taylor had declared the procedure to be commonplace, but Bach uncharacteristically wandered from room to room, silently, his tension painfully obvious. I cannot speak to my master's feelings toward the Chevalier, but I suspected his antics at the keyboard were an attempt to denigrate the surgeon's superior air. This would have been well in keeping with his character as I had come to know it. Or perhaps playing music of his own choosing allowed Bach some foothold in his precarious state. Whatever the case, he could not now conceal his grave concern.

Shaken by the rapid sequence of events and more than a little apprehensive about the role I had agreed to take on, I soon retired to my room, where I became lost in thought. The thrill of the Easter performances, where my master appeared hale and happy, remained fresh in my mind, yet his future now seemed disturbingly uncertain. Hoping to find some distraction, I turned to the Second Suite in Bach's manuscript, believing its D minor tonality would resonate with my solicitude. I had just tuned my cello when there came a light knock at the door. I turned to see Frau Anna, absent her customary cheerful bearing.

"Might I have a word with you, Carl?" she shyly inquired.

"Of course, Frau Bach, please …" I said, quickly setting down my cello, then standing and gesturing for her to come inside. She sat awkwardly at the end of the bed and, as I returned to my chair, began to speak in a hushed, unsteady voice.

"I'm so sorry to interrupt you, but I must confess to being deeply concerned about tomorrow. I haven't shared my fears with Sebastian, but what the surgeon is offering—for lack of a better way to put it, to simply wash away the fog that has all but blinded my dear husband—seems too good to be true. According to my piety, which you have surely noted by now, I first place great faith in Almighty God and then let earthly labors do the rest. Between us, and I know I may rely on your confidence, I don't put much stock in miracles as such.

"Beyond the healthy delivery of my children by God's grace, and perhaps my husband's creativity, I cannot say I have encountered anything in this world that I would call truly miraculous. And, harsh as it may seem upon such short acquaintance, John Taylor strikes me as arrogant and his claims sound dubious. What are your thoughts, Carl? I'd very much like to hear them."

"Frau Bach," I answered, "God knows, not only since this evening's examination but throughout the time I have lived among your family, neither the cantor's welfare nor the deterioration of his eyesight have been far from my mind. The latter has been difficult for me to witness, as I am certain he is in pain, though he rarely complains. And I wonder, 'What if the deterioration grows worse?'

"But then, an acclaimed traveler with well-known expertise in the ocular arts steps through the door, confident in his ability to cure my dear master. The doctor seems to be promising improved sight, though all we know of his prior successes—and, for that matter, his failures—are what he has chosen to announce. I can attest to the fine impression he made at the lecture hall, and we agree that he seems to be highly knowledgeable. Admittedly, his arrogance, as you say, chaffs at me too. Nevertheless, if his surgical skills are commensurate with his claims of knowledge of ocular science, then I think we have little choice but to trust him."

Frau Anna, listening intently, bore an expression so heartbreaking that my own fears increased, though I knew not whether I was abating or worsening her concerns. I rambled on.

"I imagine that at worst, nothing will change and your husband's eyesight will diminish further. But if the doctor succeeds, Herr Bach may regain his sight, or at least some of it. Given that he has so little left, I wonder if what can be done should not be done. Like you, I cannot speak with any certainty.

"I do know this, however: Whatever the results, Frau Bach, I shall be here to help in all ways possible. I am honored that you consulted me, though the matter is far beyond my experience. I regret I cannot further assuage your fears."

"Carl, your honesty is much appreciated. We're all crossing a narrow bridge. God knows, if something dreadful should transpire, I cannot begin to think what we might do. But as you say, it seems that the greatest hope for Sebastian is for us to place our faith in the hands of the surgeon and the surgeon in the hands of God. I can only hope Doctor Taylor would not undertake such a procedure if he had concerns about the outcome."

I acknowledged that I harbored the same feelings.

"Thank you for taking the time to speak with me. Please do carry on. I shall enjoy hearing whatever you are about to play. It will no doubt provide comfort."

I gestured toward her husband's manuscript of the Second Suite.

"These pages have brought me limitless pleasure, and with every pass, I'm more deeply impressed with what Herr Bach has managed to create. Of two things, I'm certain: I shall never tire of his music, and I shall forever strive to do it justice."

Anna Magdalena nodded, sighing heavily. I picked up my cello, inhaled deeply, then intoned the first three pitches of the Prelude, a yearning triad that seemed to inquire—speaking straight to the tenor of the household on this somber night—whither now? I broke off long enough to glance at Bach's devoted wife before regaining my composure and beginning again. Almost instantly, I became fully immersed in the journey of sound. It was a miracle I experienced every time I sat down with my master's music.

Chapter 10

Until the arrival of John Taylor on Wednesday afternoon, 1 April, scarcely a word passed anyone's lips within the apartment. Bach remained secluded; I knew not where. The rest of us moved about as if on eggshells.

This time, the Chevalier came smartly dressed in a saffron-colored vested suit of wool-silk poplin, set off by a white frilled collar. He was carrying his leather bag which I presumed contained his surgical kit and supplies. As I had agreed to assist him and Frau Anna was sitting with her husband, I greeted him at the front door. His first instruction was for me to help his driver convey the surgical chair from the rear of the carriage to its destination upstairs. Brushing past the doctor on my way out, I could not help but notice a series of red flecks on his collar—traces, I assumed, of an earlier appointment.

By the time we brought in the chair, Taylor had already positioned himself at the writing table in Bach's outer study and pushed aside various papers to create adequate space for his bag and its contents. He then spread a silk kerchief and placed upon it several instruments, including a small sterling case and two tiny vials. Last, he drew the curtains wide and positioned himself with his back to the window. The light of day would fall on Bach's face during the operation.

The surgical chair, crafted of English oak, was unusually designed. Its shallow depth and unusually high seat allowed the doctor to more easily look into his patient's eyes, and he could steady his arms on its leather-padded armrests. Carved into the chair's high back was England's Great Seal of the Realm, above which was lettered "Oculist to His Majesty, George II" and below, a motto similar to that painted on the doctor's carriage: *Qui visum vitam dat* — Who gives sight, gives life.

Taylor called for his patient, who entered on his wife's arm with obvious trepidation. The two men greeted each other and promptly settled into place: Taylor in his contraption and Bach in front of him in a ladder-back chair.

"Herr Cantor," Taylor began, with a stiff, authoritative air, "the procedure I'm about to undertake, while far from unbearable, is not without its share of discomfort. As I explained during my examination, couching has been around since the days of ancient India. As I said, I have performed this procedure hundreds of times with brilliant results. The process requires a small incision in the cornea, the transparent lens of the eye." Stepping to a harpsichord, he depressed a key and continued, "The incision is but a fraction of the width of this piece of ivory."

Taylor reached for his silver case, its cover etched with *fleur-de-lis*. He opened it to reveal a red velvet lining that held three identical carp's tongue needles. Taylor related how these had been crafted to his specifications by Paul de Lamerie of London, whom he regarded among the continent's foremost silversmiths, and pulling one from the case showed us its thin, flat blade. It looked about a half-finger's length, with a fine ridge running down the middle, like a sword, and tapered to a fine point at one end.

Taylor replaced the needle and showed us another tool that featured an ivory handle and a delicately scooped tip of metal, cast at a right angle. During the procedure, the bent tip would allow the doctor to hold the instrument below or to the side of the patient's eye. The Chevalier continued detailing the steps of his process, seemingly as much for my edification as my master's.

"Once I have made the incision, I shall use this tool to slowly work the cloudy lens down and away from the center of the eye, towards the vitreous cavity—the corner of the eye," he said, pointing to his own, "thereby clearing the obstruction.

"In his medieval ophthalmic manual, Benevenutus Grassus of Jerusalem states that the cataract should be held away from the pupil for four *paternosters*, long enough to be sure it has been fully detached. To be quite frank, I'm no longer certain I can remember it well enough to recite it even once," Taylor chortled. "Please pardon me, Herr Cantor, for I understand you are a deeply pious man. Rest assured, the phlegmatic matter will remain securely off to the side, beyond your field of vision, and will disappear with time.

"This is laudanum, a tincture of opium," the surgeon said, lifting one of the vials. "It's a fast-acting agent that will numb your senses and help you relax." He set the tincture down and raised the second vial. "I shall administer these contents when our procedure is complete. They are a more highly concentrated opiate and will help you sleep. I shall leave a vial behind for Frau Bach to use as she thinks fit," and he turned briefly toward the doorway, to be sure she had heard.

Removing the cork from the laudanum vial, the Chevalier handed it to Bach. He then turned again to Frau Bach and explained that the poultices he would apply to the patient's eyes after the operation must not be discarded until he could open them without discomfort.

"I also follow Jerusalem's post-operative directions about keeping the patient prone in a dark room," Taylor continued. "Herr Bach, you must not attempt to look at any light for eight days, and your good wife should dress your eyes with the beaten white of an egg, twice daily and twice nightly. The poultices should be returned to the eyes after these ministrations until you are able to open your eyes as normal. At the end of the eight days, you may leave your bed.

"Our ancient author, by the way, maintains that the patient should make the sign of the cross before he rises," Taylor finished, flashing a quick smile at Anna Magdalena.

The doctor again addressed his patient. "Herr Cantor, your eyes will be highly sensitive to light during your recovery. The cataracts have blocked much of it for years, but they will readjust quickly. And while they will never again be as sharp as when you were much younger, you will see well enough to get yourself to church and a chamber pot!" Taylor paused to gauge whether this ill-fitting jest, which seemed well rehearsed, had hit its mark.

"*Cum Deo auxilio*," was Bach's only response. "With God's help."

Taylor signaled that he was ready to begin. Frau Anna came and kissed her husband on his forehead and whispered something in his ear, which Bach lovingly acknowledged. As she left the room, Taylor asked my name and instructed me to take my place behind my master.

"Herr Barth," pronounced the doctor, "I traveled for some time with an assistant, an ox of a man who wrapped his victims—er, I mean patients—with the strength of a vise. But the good man has up and left for England! He was intent on fighting for the British East India Company. Messy times over there, as I understand—a trade war with the French, or something of that nature. All of which is to say, Barth, you must hold your master's head with the firmest grip possible. No matter what happens, *he must not move*. Am I understood?"

I nodded.

While Taylor waited for the laudanum to take full effect, he removed a sheet of paper from his black bag and set it on the table. Using one of Bach's quills, he began composing what I assumed was a repetition of the instructions he had already communicated. Shortly thereafter, determining his patient was ready, he spoke again.

"Herr Barth, here is your position," wrapping one of my arms around Bach's forehead and the other around his jaw, like a wrestler pinning an opponent. "It is essential that neither of you move during the procedure, which will not last more than a quarter of an hour."

Nodding again, I tightened my arms about my master's head. His breathing had slowed and he did not acknowledge my touch; clearly, the sedative was doing its work. Taylor then pulled Bach's right eyelid forward and fastened a small clamp to it so it could not close. Once the clamp was screwed down and the lid immobilized, Taylor took up the carp's tongue needle, and with a deft flourish, swept the tip of the glinting blade across his sleeve.

What Taylor had described as "couching" no doubt required a supremely steady hand, beyond that of the finest jeweler or scribe. But as Taylor lowered his right elbow onto the armrest, I noticed a slight tremor in his hand—his operating hand—at which he began to scratch vehemently. Worse, he began to scratch other parts of his person as well—mostly his upper back and head.

I could scarcely believe it, but the man was obviously struggling with his *own* eyesight as he repeatedly moved closer to my master, shook his head, and then backed away. In the very moment before the first incision would be cut into Bach's right eye, Taylor drew his hand back yet again. But this time he glanced up at me with a furtive expression. Abruptly, he stood, dropped the needle onto the kerchief, and almost leapt for the door. I heard him traverse the hallway and descend the staircase as if pursued.

Puzzled, I released my hold on my master's head and walked quickly across the hall to the dining room window. From above, I saw Taylor hastily approach his carriage but wave off the coachman. He opened the door himself and withdrew a small wooden box, which he placed on the running board before removing a vial similar to those now on Bach's writing table. I observed as he hastily pulled the stopper, drained the liquid within, and returned the empty vial to the box. Next, the surgeon withdrew another vial and slipped it into his pocket before crossing the courtyard back to the apartment.

As I returned to Bach's studio, I chanced to look upon the freshly written note I had assumed were instructions from Taylor to Frau Bach. But instead, it bore the following notice:

Ber. Priv. Zeit.

> *This Saturday past, and again last night, the Chevalier Taylor gave public lectures at a concert hall in the presence of a considerable assembly of scholars and other important persons. The concourse of people who seek*

> ***his aid is astonishing. Among others, he has operated upon Kapellmeister Bach, who has recovered the full sharpness of his sight ...***

The notice claimed success for a surgery still to be performed! From the distance of years, I understand that at this moment I was debilitated by the utter chicanery unfolding before me. I was too young to know how to intervene and too uncertain of myself to know what to say even if I had tried.

Still, I mentally noted the brazen lines before stepping back to my master's side. Bach sat somnambulant; by contrast, my senses were astir. Yet I could not fully comprehend events as they were taking place. Nothing in my life had prepared me for this moment.

When Taylor reappeared, now all business, he retrieved the carp's tongue needle and resumed his place before my master, indicating for me to brace his head once again. I remained trained on the doctor's hand for signs of tremor as he again brought up the small blade to Bach's right eye. None were evident. But, to my horror, his right elbow slipped forward off the armrest and the blade struck the corner of my master's eye!

Bach uttered no cry, but his head jerked back so violently that I lost my hold and was hit squarely in the chest. As Taylor lowered the blade, he snapped with curled lips, "Barth, you *must* hold my patient's head immobile. I cannot work like this!"

I had not been at fault, but bit my tongue and secured my master's head as Taylor dropped the needle into his lap, reached for some gauze, and daubed the blood running from the corner of Bach's eye. Once the area was clear, he made the proper delicate incision—hand steady, this time—before flushing the eye of fluid and exchanging the needle for the ivory-handled tool. I watched as Taylor placed his left thumb beneath Bach's eye, worked the curved tip up and under the eyelid, and appeared to manipulate the cataract. Though Bach was still barely conscious and thus quite pliant, I cradled his head as tightly as was in my power.

After what seemed to be well over a quarter hour, Taylor declared that he would free the left eye. Before commencing, however, he stood and turned to face the writing table. Though shielded from me, he scrabbled as if inside his coat; when his head tilted back, I could only believe it was to gulp the contents of the second vial. The Chevalier then resumed his seat, and again I remained silent.

Work on the second eye went significantly faster and mercifully without interruption. Taylor, apparently satisfied, stood and wiped the curved ivory tip on his sleeve before placing it back in its case. Next, he produced the two poultices he had mentioned from his bag, along with a length of white gauze bandage. After placing the poultices across my master's eyes and gesturing impatiently for me to move aside, he wound the gauze to hold them in place.

Stepping back from his handiwork, Taylor now asked for Frau Bach and directed her to usher the patient to his room. With the study cleared but for the two of us, he shut the door and turned to me.

"Herr Barth, I'm sure you did your best, especially considering your inexperience, but your master has suffered some damage to his right eye. It will be wise to watch for any signs of trouble, such as fever or seeping of fluids."

It seemed beyond reason for the doctor to suggest that the injury had resulted from *my* neglect. Whatever damage my master had suffered was a direct result of Taylor's own error. But the Chevalier was not yet finished. Tugging off one of his heavy gold rings, he held it up for just a moment and turned it so it glinted in the late afternoon light. Then he grabbed my right hand and, pressing the ring into my palm, thanked me in flattering tones for my assistance.

With any presence of mind, I should have flung his cursed gold to the floor. But Taylor, calculating that no such threat was forthcoming, swiftly gathered his supplies into his bag. Perfunctorily clapping me on the shoulder, he stated that his driver would be up immediately to help retrieve the surgical chair. I felt incapacitated as I fixed my gaze on the ring in the palm of my hand. Time, it seemed, stood still. When I looked up, John Taylor was gone.

Chapter 11

THE FAMILY, AND I AS well, monitored my master night and day and liberally administered the opium tincture in the hope he might bide easily. Previously, I had no occasion to enter Herr and Frau Bach's modest bedroom with its writing table, chest of drawers, and pair of hard wooden chairs. On the wall above their bed hung a lone cross. Bach, so frail in his voluminous white nightdress as to seem almost lifeless, sank into the mattress. As the doctor had ordered, we kept him prone in the dark room.

Frau Anna, the children, and I took turns at Bach's side, vigilant for the slightest sign of alarm or discomfort and bathing his eyes according to instructions. The apartment, generally filled with voices, the laughter of Bach's children, and music—always music—was preternaturally quiet. The only audible sounds were those of Bach's shallow breathing and the incessant grinding of machinery from the nearby waterworks.

By Sunday, the fourth day after the surgery, Bach had regained some lucidity. Yet he complained of pain in his right eye and by the following morning he had begun perspiring heavily. We all knew that Frau Anna's report of unusual heat when she placed her hand on her husband's brow was a fearful sign.

Still, she slowly unwound the gauze and peeled away the poultice from his left eye. Bach blinked several times, reporting that the movement caused him no pain, and said vision in that eye had indeed improved. Our joy was short-lived, however: Bach's right eye was cloudy, and reddish mucus had collected in the corners. Only I understood this as the effect of the trauma he had suffered at Taylor's hand. Yet how could I reveal the doctor's terrible incompetence, when I would also be confessing my own failure to intercede?

My guilt intensified until Frau Anna seized my hand and pulled me beyond her husband's earshot. "May God help us, Carl, it's as I feared. The doctor—please fetch him at once. And implore him to hurry!"

I was already on the street before I realized I had no idea where Taylor might be, or if he remained in Leipzig. My initial thought was to race toward the university, so I passed through the market and swept past St. Nicholas Church, frantically inquiring of everyone I encountered if they had, perchance, seen a white carriage in the vicinity. The guard at the east gate assured me that no one had crossed through on his watch and then, seeing my distress, kindly checked his log. No record was to be found of such a coach departing through that gate, but I knew there were other gates and other guards.

Rather than take more time to exhaust this strategy, however, I turned back and raced toward the coffeehouse Bach and I had visited. Perhaps the Chevalier could be found in that fashionable neighborhood. Sure enough, just off the Brühl, I spotted his white coach in an alley behind an inn. Having learned from the innkeeper that the room I sought was the first at the top of the stairs, I bounded up and knocked frantically. There was no answer, but I continued to pound at the door with growing urgency. I thought I could make out the sound of voices. And after what seemed an eternity, the door swung open.

Taylor stood before me dressed in a silk banyan tied about the waist. He glanced behind him as if to ascertain that he was alone in the room.

"The cantor urgently requires your services, it is a matter of the utmost importance!" I cried.

"I'm sorry, Herr Barth, but I am packing. I plan to depart for Berlin at once. Patients there await my services."

"You cannot abandon my master like this," I retorted, pointing toward St. Thomas. "His eye, the one struck during the procedure, has turned cloudy, and he is feverish. There must be something you can do. If you don't come, I ..."

Taylor, red-faced, cut me off. "Barth, you are dismissed," he growled. "Run along. I have done my best for your master and now have other matters of importance to attend to." Without further word, Taylor abruptly shut the door.

Dumbstruck, I turned away. The events of that dreadful day ran through my head as I stumbled back into the alley. I passed the horseless coach, in which the doctor would soon depart ... finely dressed, perhaps with his instrument bag on his lap as I had once dreamed of traveling, holding the precious writing desk gifted to me by my master and Frau Anna. And then, as in an explosion of thought, I saw in my mind's eye the document scribbled out by Taylor as Bach sat next to him, becoming insensible from laudanum. The Chevalier was going to Berlin, and the abbreviations at the top of that nagging document—*Ber. Priv. Zeit.*—referred to *Berlinische Privelegirte Zeitung*, a Berlin newspaper!

I now dashed to the Café Zimmermann, but a few steps away. Taking the stairs two at a time, I raced past tables and waiters to the corner rack of periodicals. It held at least two dozen newspapers; most were from German cities although as I riffled through them I noted some from Paris and even London. My search was soon rewarded with the most recent edition of *Berlinische Privilegirte Zeitung*. My hands shook as I flipped its pages, crumpling them in dread, and desperately scanned its columns.

And there was Taylor's eerily familiar notice, now in its entirety, in print for all to see and believe. Taylor's dispatch was dated 1 April, the date of my master's surgery. The article read:

> **This Saturday past, and again last night, the Chevalier Taylor gave public lectures at the great concert hall of Leipzig in the presence of a considerable assembly of scholars and other important persons. The concourse of people who seek his aid is astonishing. Among others, he has operated upon Kapellmeister Bach, who by a constant use of his eyes had almost entirely deprived himself of their sight, and that with every success that could have been desired, so that he has recovered the full sharpness of his sight, an unspeakable piece of good fortune that many thousands of people will be very far from begrudging this world-famous composer and for which they cannot sufficiently thank Dr. Taylor. Owing to the numerous engagements the latter is obliged to discharge in Leipzig as a result of this great success, he will not be able to proceed to Berlin before the end of this week.**

Even before the first disastrous incision, Taylor was planning to use my master's good name to burnish his own reputation and, ultimately, enrich himself. And he must have expected to be in Berlin—or, at least, en route—by the time the poultices and bandages were removed and the true state of things discovered. But why had the Chevalier lingered in our town? Could it have something to do with the visitor I had heard in his room at the inn?

My actions were now as hasty and decisive as my silence and immobility had been in Bach's study. I turned to race back toward the stairs, nearly colliding with Herr Adler and the cups and saucers he bore. "How is Herr Bach?" he called after me. But, determined to keep moving, I only replied, "As well as expected." Waving the paper, I shouted, "I am in need of this, thank you!" and raced by, averting his gaze.

Moving past the innkeeper without a glance, I again banged on Taylor's door. And now, the great physician stood rigidly before me, lips pursed, glaring with decided impatience.

"Herr Doctor, I ask you again to make haste to my master's apartment. If you refuse," I announced, rattling the newspaper's front page so he could not mistake it, "I shall dispatch a truthful account of my own."

Before he could interrupt, I shook the article and hastily continued.

"Chevalier, here is your notice about Bach's *successful* operation. I saw it on the desk that day—words you drafted even *before* you commenced to operate! And I saw much more than that! I saw you imbibe at your carriage and again during the operation. I saw you cause grievous injury when your arm slipped and your needle sliced into my master's eye."

I was beginning to speak more calmly, having caught my breath. "This procedure was anything *but* successful. As I stand before you now, and shall someday stand before Almighty God, do not underestimate me. If I must, I shall send word to Berlin about everything I witnessed. All of it!"

Taylor appeared stunned by my outburst and the evidence I clutched of his perfidy. Seeming to assess his predicament he peered up and down the empty hallway and then, without warning, grabbed my arm, pulled me inside the room, and slammed the door.

"Young man, how dare you threaten *me*! Do you know nothing of my reputation? I am renowned, far and wide! Who will believe you? Should anyone presume to question the details of Herr Bach's surgery, I shall simply respond that you, a mere schoolboy, panicked and, ignoring my careful instructions, lost your grip on the cantor's head. No one will doubt that any ill effects are the result of *your* negligence."

I was fully calm now as well as bold with conviction. "Dr. Taylor," I responded, "I observed you very closely and am confident in my recollection. I witnessed you down some sort of potion, most likely the same sedating tincture you gave to my master, who trusted you. I saw your hand tremor and your incessant scratching. I noted how you struggled with your eyesight. Most of all, it was *your* needle that struck my master when your arm slipped from the chair. Perhaps you require the potion, as I perceived a change in your bearing afterward when you operated on my master's second eye."

In a final act of desperation, I looked at Taylor directly. "What will the good people of Berlin think of your reputation when they learn the truth about that day?"

Flushed and stammering, Taylor furiously shoved me back into the hallway and slammed the door. I stumbled backward, trembling: never in my life had I spoken this way to anyone. By the time I reached the bottom of the stairs, though, I was already mentally drafting a newspaper notice of my own. And I kept the Berlin paper with me, tucked under my arm as I ran home to St. Thomas.

Frau Anna and her younger daughters, waiting at the door, said nothing when they saw I returned alone. As we made our way to Bach in his bed of fever, I attempted to explain my failed encounter with Taylor. But, as they knew nothing of the oculist's botched procedure or my failure to halt it, I fell silent when we reached the bedroom.

Frau Anna and the children rushed to my master's bedside but I sat down, crushed by the weight of my guilt. My heart broke further as I helplessly watched the pathetic scene before me. Still, even through the depth of my sorrow for my hosts, my thoughts strayed back to the oculist, as I attempted to stitch together the various threads about his visit to Leipzig. Upon recalling how his name had been emblazoned on advertisements across the city in advance of his arrival, it occurred to me that the local papers must have carried notices similar to what I had read in the *Berlinische Zeitung*.

Despite my weary state, Taylor's modus operandi was coming into sharp focus. He would arrive in a given town as heralded, stage a lecture or two promoting his expertise, offer his services, and schedule appointments. With his work complete, he would strike out for his next port of call, thus handily avoiding the consequences of his ineptitude. His dependency on opiates fleshed out the sordid story.

To our surprise, Taylor rang some hours later. He was immediately escorted to the bedroom where Bach remained motionless and feverish, his right eye covered. When Bach faintly inquired who was there, Taylor replied it was he, the Chevalier, wanting to have a look. Taylor made a brief examination and called for a fresh bandage to be placed over my master's right eye.

Beckoning Frau Anna into the hallway, he spoke softly. "Regrettably, your concern is warranted. The left eye is healing nicely, but the right appears worrisome. I must drain it and then treat it with a solution, a laxative that will be brushed onto the eye directly. I also propose bleeding him to draw out the ill humors." Glancing back at the candlelit room, he continued. "I shall return at first light, but please know, Frau Anna, that will be my last call."

"Herr Doctor, I must consult my husband," Frau Anna replied. "Please, if you would be so good as to wait?" Their ensuing conversation was inaudible, but he gently squeezed her arm. She returned to us and informed the doctor that Bach would expect him in the morning.

I walked Taylor to the door, informed him that the vial he had left was depleted, and lost no further time before offering him his gold ring back and asking, with all the humility I could command, how much of the precious tincture such an exchange might afford. Taylor pulled a single vial from his bag.

"It's all I can spare," he said pointedly, thrusting it at me. "Use it prudently. And you will not mention the ring again." He then turned, pulled up his collar, and disappeared into the night.

As promised, Taylor arrived just after sunrise and was shown to Bach's bedside. Assessing the surroundings, he determined to operate there in the bedroom and directed that the small writing table be cleared and placed next to where Bach lay. He instructed us to lift the patient's head to receive the required dose of laudanum.

"Herr Bach," he murmured, "to whatever degree you remain aware of the procedure, I beg you to resist any temptation to move once I commence. Your young friend will help you to stay still. Am I understood?"

Bach weakly responded in the affirmative. While waiting for the sedative to take effect, the ritual of the previous week was repeated. Taylor removed a silk kerchief from his bag, placed a carp's tongue needle and a small brush upon it, and gestured for me to prepare to take hold of my master's head. This time would be easier, I realized, because Bach was lying down. I could apply my body weight if necessary, though I prayed it wouldn't come to that.

Once Taylor deemed the patient sedate and I was in my place, he made a pair of tiny incisions to drain the right eye of mucus and blood. Bach's body writhed in pain despite the opiate but he strained not to move his head.

As I held him immobilized, I had the sensation of submitting him to some barbaric torture. Unable to stop myself, I began to sob and grimaced to keep my tears away from my master's face. After a time, the doctor set down his knife and poured some liquid over the brush, which he then wiped across the affected eye. Bach winced from the sting of the solution. Taylor swiped the brush across Bach's other eye as well—"for good measure," he loftily imparted.

The excruciating part of the procedure was mercifully over. The rest, albeit grim, would be routine. Over Bach's moans, the doctor next withdrew a small, opaque jar from his bag and tweezed forth a leech. He carefully held the squirming parasite against the inside corner of Bach's right eye, where it greedily attached itself. While the creature had its fill, Taylor wiped his needle on his coat sleeve, placed it back in its case, and dropped it, along with the brush, into his bag. Finally, he plucked the leech from my master's face and returned it to its caliginous home.

With Bach now asleep, Frau Anna and I walked Taylor to the door.

"There is nothing more to be done," the doctor murmured, looking first at Frau Bach and then at me. "The cantor has my best wishes for a complete and speedy recovery."

The Chevalier donned his hat, bowed slightly, and crossed briskly through the courtyard to his waiting carriage. It was the last I would see of the oculist for nearly twenty years.

Chapter 12

THE FOLLOWING WEEKS WERE LADEN with anguish. Bach labored mightily, beset with fever, debilitating headaches, and dizziness. He initially maintained that his left eye could detect some light and make out vague shapes, but his right eye remained severely damaged. Delirium came and went.

On Tuesday, the day after Taylor's second surgery, I stole away from the Bach apartment, hoping a visit to Zimmermann's might disclose more information about the Chevalier. I immediately noted that the white carriage was no longer parked behind the inn and suspected he had finally departed Leipzig. A quick perusal of the Berlin papers revealed nothing. Returning a few days later, I stumbled upon the following announcement in a subsequent edition of the *Berlinische Privilegierte Zeitung*. Taylor's dispatch was dated 4 April, though I presumed it too had been similarly crafted in advance.

> Several people have so far called each day to seek the Chevalier Taylor's help. Among the many ladies and gentlemen of various ranks and ages to whom his skill has afforded council and consolation, his cures of the *medico* Dr.

> Koppen, of Kapellmeister Bach, and of the merchant Herr Meyer have been so particularly successful as to do him honor. The many patients who call upon him have caused him to postpone his departure until Tuesday next, when he proposes to leave for Potsdam, with the intention of reaching Berlin the following day.

It confirmed Taylor's departure earlier that day, but whether he had truly lingered on account of those wishing to see him, I could not say. Nevertheless, the oculist continued to tout success, even as Bach lay in crisis across town. Unsurprisingly, there was no mention of a second operation. I now experienced a sickening sense of self-doubt. Taylor had followed my bidding at the time, and his compliance had been my goal. But even so, should I have notified the Berlin papers of his deeds?

Any preoccupation with Taylor or his future, however, was far superseded by my immediate obligations within the Bach apartment. While we continued tending to my master at every turn, letters were dispatched to those of his children living abroad. His son Carl Phillip was the first to respond, anguished at the report and relaying his prayers for his father's complete recovery. Quite unexpectedly, he also shared news about the oculist: shortly after Taylor's arrival in Berlin, the king had decreed him forbidden to work in the capital ever again, in the wake of debacles there.

Meanwhile, Frau Anna grew more and more distraught. Though she maintained a stoic temperament in her husband's presence, she often admitted her fears to me, even as she had done on the eve of the first surgery. I mustered some bearing to comfort her each time, assuring her that I too feared the worst.

At those moments, although my inner torment did not abate, my sense of kinship with the family heightened.

In the time I spent alone, I continued to turn to my master's cello suites. Frau Anna asked me to play them for her now and then, and I always obliged. By June, I had all six copied. I was most familiar with the first three, to which I devoted the majority of my practice time. But I had also begun to acquaint myself with the Fourth and Fifth Suites, despite their challenges. The Sixth would have to wait, for it required a cello with five strings, and I still had no idea where such an instrument could be located.

Whenever I played but a single passage from any of these works, I resolved that, with enough time—doubtlessly measured in years, if not the full span of a lifetime—I might become proficient on all six. To that end, I longed for further study with my master but became resigned to such a wish remaining unanswered. I was left to take solace from Frau Anna's assurance that Bach derived pleasure in hearing me play while confined to his bed.

By mid-June, Bach had no sight at all in either eye and the rest of his health declined almost by the day. Whether this was a consequence of Taylor's second visit, I cannot say; I knew only that every physician we summoned professed helplessness, including the most prominent doctor from the university's Faculty of Medicine. As each came and went, the hallways of the school grew more loudly abuzz with concern for the cantor's future. I also learned that the St. Thomas administration, believing he could not survive much longer, had begun considering applicants to fill his place.

On 20 July, Bach suffered a stroke. Two days later, Christoph Wolle, Archdeacon of St. Thomas, administered the sacrament.

It was shortly thereafter that my master called on me.

Without Bach supervising preparations of *The Art of Fugue*, the enterprise had naturally come to a halt. I and my fellow assistants from the school cleared the Bach dining room of manuscripts, paper, ink, and other effects. Yet, in his lucid moments, the composer remained consumed by this, his final project. One such day, as I took my turn at his bedside, my master confided that he now knew how to bring the opus to a close and asked for my assistance. I was to retrieve *Wenn wir in höchsten Nöten sein* [*When in the Hour of Greatest Need*] from the school library, where he said I would find the music among his chorale preludes for organ.

I had long hoped to serve my master's creative process, but I had never imagined doing so while he lay dying. Bach's words now seemed to seal this doom. "Tomorrow," he uttered, with difficulty, "please bring it to me. What I have in mind will, in all likelihood, be my final effort."

Bach's instructions puzzled me and I wondered if, in his delirium, he was confusing a chorale scored for voices with an organ chorale. But I found the brief one-and-a-half page work precisely where he said it would be. As I pulled the score from the shelf, I immediately understood that Bach had long ago taken the traditional chorale melody and expanded it into a four-voice work for organ.

The next morning, the cembalo was brought from the dining room and set near the foot of Bach's bed. Through slightly parted curtains, a thin shaft of light illuminated the instrument; the rest of the room remained shrouded in darkness. With no more preparations to be made, I gently informed Bach that I had the music in hand.

"Please, Carl, sit at the keyboard and play it for me," Bach whispered. I thought I could hear him mumbling as I did so. When I finished, he told me that in a dream, he recalled the old melody sung to different words, "Vor deinen Thron tret ich hiermit." He then asked me to fetch the book of chorales from the glass-door bookcase in the hallway.

I made haste to return, and he asked that I read that chorale aloud. As I recited the poignant text, I fully comprehended why this hymn spoke to my master in this hour:

> Before Thy throne I now appear,
> O Lord, bow down Thy gracious ear
> To me, and cast not from Thy face
> Thy sinful child that sues for grace.
>
> Grant that in peace I close mine eyes,
> But, on the last day, bid me rise,
> And let me see Thy face fore'er—
> Amen, Amen, Lord, hear my prayer!

For all that I had suffered with Bach's family as we watched my master's once-hearty constitution crumble, it was at this moment that I truly comprehended the truth: he would soon be leaving us all. My tears sprang, unbidden, and unchecked because I knew he could not see. Ever the patient teacher, Bach had wanted me to read *Vor deinen Thron* for my own sake, as much to bring me comfort as to grasp the prayer he had in mind. Still, I failed to understand Bach's larger plan.

"Carl, I am blind and in pain," he said. "I pray my situation does not continue like this much longer. But whether or not music surrounds me in the afterlife, I must use whatever time is left to me on this Earth as best I can. So, with your help, we shall improve upon my old organ chorale that you just played.

You will begin by writing *Vor deinen Thron tret ich hiermit* atop a page of manuscript paper. It will be the title of our work. What I have in mind should provide a satisfactory conclusion to my contrapuntal treatise … and my life."

My master's breath had grown shorter during this speech, so through my tears I suggested we could begin after he had taken some small refreshment. But shook his head and spoke again.

"Carl, I have neither enough time nor energy to tarry with the fugue encompassing the letters B-A-C-H, with which I planned to conclude my contrapuntal treatise. Perhaps Carl Phillip, in Berlin, will one day manage a satisfactory conclusion, for he is among the few who understand the art of counterpoint well enough to do it justice.

"I also suspect,"—and here, Bach managed a weak chuckle—"that my son may have been the one who devised that devilish theme put to me by his employer, for Frederick could not have done so alone! So, having solved that puzzle, I shall challenge him in return.

"I would like to rework some of the details of my old chorale, naturally with your help. When finished, we shall have a calm, satisfying conclusion for *The Art of Fugue*. The difference in materials will not matter so much. It will be a bit like finishing off a complicated cantata with a simple chorale everyone can sing."

I now looked down as I scribbled the new title as instructed. But when I looked up, Bach had drifted off. Carefully, I closed the instrument lid, approached the bedside, and gently touched his outstretched hand. "Sleep in peace, master," I whispered. Frau Anna came in then, to relieve my watch, and I quietly withdrew.

Our reworking of the four-part chorale lasted much of the week, but only for brief bouts, for Bach's sleeping hours now dominated. When he was both awake and sufficiently alert, we moved forward a measure at a time; with speed, I wrote down his desired alterations to the voice leading, the melody, or the rhythm, striving to record every note before he faded back into slumber or delirium. Sometimes, he asked to hear the effect of a particular change and inquired what I thought.

Witnessing the unfolding of Bach's ideas in this intimate fashion brought me untold satisfaction, even though he wasn't genuinely composing anew. My greatest wish, as my master's light inexorably dimmed, was that we would reach the final bar.

Just before the Sabbath, his will prevailed. I played through the recomposed chorale as he lay propped against his pillows, sightless eyes half open. "Herr Bach, I am honored to have assisted you in the compositional process and so grateful that you have entrusted me with that privilege. But please forgive me as I ask why you have devoted the remainder of your strength to it?"

"Carl, please come closer. What you ask is important." Accordingly, I moved from the harpsichord bench at the foot of the bed to one of the chairs near its head.

"My boy, I have strived my entire life for musical perfection," Bach confessed, his words labored. "Such perfection, I fear, I have rarely attained. Still, I trust the Lord has not been entirely displeased with what I have fashioned, since always I have done so in His honor and for His glory.

"In health, I struggled with the final fugue based on my name; in sickness, I have struggled to finish what I can. I give thanks to God for providing the answer, which came to me in a dream. As always, I needed only to do His bidding. And for helping me to carry it out, I am deeply indebted to you."

I began to object, but he stopped me. "Please, Carl. I wish to impart something that I hope will remain with you …

"During our lessons, I have noted your interest in my obsession with counterpoint—fugues, canons, and the like—when such techniques have long fallen out of fashion. The reason, I tell you now, has to do with this same quest for perfection.

"I know why much of the younger generation's music finds so many admirers, for it is easy on the ears and rarely challenges the listener. But I believe that this newer style, for all its immediate charm, lacks gravitas … lacks a certain soul. I, too, have occasionally conceived of melodies beautiful for their own sake. But in my musical world, perfection requires purity. And such purity, I believe, is to be realized only through counterpoint—that is, music that draws upon itself. Nothing less and nothing more is required of it and for it.

"Perhaps it's better put another way," he mused, and I rejoiced that his voice grew a bit stronger. "We formerly had a brilliant scientist, Winkler, on our faculty. He understood the world like few others, save perhaps Newton. For all their formidable knowledge, both men regarded science and religion as operating in consort with one another. For me, this is the essence of counterpoint.

"As you know, music is my connection with the Creator. And counterpoint, with its inherent logic, connects heaven and earth. It embodies the meeting place between the spiritual world, that which is unknowable, and the scientific, that which is known. In short, fugues and canons represent the supreme order of musical creation, the means of uniting our humble art with the cosmos."

Again I attempted to interrupt, fearing that my master would exhaust himself beyond recovery. But once more he waved me off and continued, though I was obliged to lean in ever closer to hear him.

"I once told you that I had worked hard and that anyone who worked as hard could achieve as much. The truth is, I know God blessed me with an innate ability. To honor that gift, I believed I was required to communicate music's essence—its soul—as I understood it. That soul, at least in my small corner of the world, was counterpoint …

"Carl, I thank you. Rarely have I divulged so much about my art to anyone. Somehow, together, we have found our way to the end. And now, I must rest."

These were the last words Bach spoke to me. Before long, he fell into a coma.

On the eve of Tuesday, 28 July 1750, I was in my room, attempting to practice, yet I could not focus on the pages in front of me. I gave up and had just blown out the candles on my music stand when Frau Anna came to tell me that her husband had passed from this world.

Activity in the Bach apartment, frozen during my master's final weeks and hours, now agonizingly thawed. Funeral arrangements were made and urgent notices were dispatched, to family members and myriad others, carrying the grievous news. These *communiqués* related that Bach had recently been operated upon by John Taylor, the well-known English oculist, and closed thus: "The loss of this uncommonly able man will be greatly mourned by all true connoisseurs of music."

Bach's funeral proved an understated affair, in the sober Lutheran tradition. Ernesti himself delivered the eulogy, which was brief. In it, he acknowledged the past differences between rector and cantor, yet maintained that Bach had demonstrated the highest values of the school. He scarcely needed to add that my master would be sorely missed.

Over much of his professional life, Bach had participated in the funerals of others; now, a modest procession, including his widow and his children, several town dignitaries, the small St. Thomas faculty and student body, and church members, followed his casket through the Grimma Gate to the city's common burial ground beside the Johannes Church. Bach was laid to rest with neither a stone nor a cross to mark the site.

The family quietly mourned in the days afterward; before my eyes, Frau Anna seemed to age precipitously. Rooms in the adjacent apartment, however, bristled with activity as plans to install Bach's replacement moved forward. In light of her late husband's long service to St. Thomas, Frau Anna was granted a half-year to vacate. Yet she received no pension; thus, the support of her remaining household fell entirely upon her and she was obliged to liquidate much of the estate: silverware and pewter, furnishings and books, instruments, and even some of her late husband's manuscripts. Of the proceeds, she kept one-third and divided the rest equally among Bach's children. She would be severed from Johann Christian, whose uncle in Berlin would become his guardian. Catherina Dorothea and the younger girls, Johanna Carolina and Regina Susanna, were to remain with their mother.

Frau Anna occupied a profoundly important place in my heart. My musical aspirations were bound up with her husband, but her kindred presence had almost equal meaning. I beheld her grief with nearly as much sorrow as I endured my own. Her husband of thirty years had been everything to her, and though she had at first forged her own path with talent and fortitude, once married, she had dedicated herself to him entirely.

I stayed with the family throughout their final months in the apartment and did all I could to aid her, including helping prepare the final inventories of Bach's music. I regretted that I was hardly in a position to help her financially, but one day, amidst my sorrow, I suddenly remembered the ring pressed upon me by John Taylor. After visiting a jeweler for an appraisal, I found a quiet moment to sit with Bach's widow and express my concern for her future. I told her about the ring and that its sale had brought me twelve Reichsthalers. I said I would prefer to purchase one of her husband's cellos rather than see it pass to a stranger.

Knowing the ring to be worth nearly double the value of either instrument, I now placed all the currency before her. Initially, she refused, but after a moment, she excused herself and left the room, promptly returning with a carefully tied bundle of manuscripts.

"Carl, I cannot deny that I am in need of funds," she began. "I envision significant hardship ahead and know it will be necessary to sell still more of my late husband's autographs to survive. But I also cannot deny the value of the assistance you gave to him, or how important you were to him as both pupil and trusted aide. When we depart from this place, you must take the cello of your choosing, in Sebastian's honor, and as my gift, you will take his manuscript of the cello suites. He derived deep pleasure hearing you play them, even in his darkest hours."

Through tears, I tried to express the depth of my gratitude, not only for these gifts but also for having been allowed, for too short a time, to live as part of her family. I told her I would always treasure and practice the suites. I also promised to leave the copy I had made in the school library, next to hers.

In the months and years after Frau Anna vacated the St. Thomas apartment, I visited her often at her residence on *Hainstrasse*. I never failed to bring my cello—Bach's cello—and play a suite or two for her pleasure. I last saw Anna Magdalena Bach nine years after her husband's untimely demise. She died the next year, in 1760, having been sustained by the charity of Leipzig's city council.

My compassion and affection for Frau Anna were steadfast and unending, but my grief at losing my master was staggering. To me, he had been not only a mentor and father figure but also a paragon who taught me the wonders of music—its possibilities, impossibilities, and place in the cosmos. Mine were lessons I held tight, and I continue to meditate upon them to this day.

I remained at St. Thomas for several more years. When my time at the school ended, my gaze turned towards Leipzig University, where I enrolled as a student of theology and philosophy. There, I was to encounter new ideas, build lasting friendships, and live an entirely new existence. Those halcyon days proved among the most illuminating and fascinating of my life. Nonetheless, during periods of reflection, when my thoughts invariably turned to the precious time I had spent with Sebastian Bach, thoughts of John Taylor would occasionally intrude as well. Though it was not until my university studies were concluded that those disquieting memories decidedly re-emerged, before long, the Chevalier became enmeshed in the fabric of my life, and my fixation to resolve my enmity profoundly altered the trajectory of my future.

PART II
FRIENDSHIP

Chapter 13

AT THE CENTER OF LEIPZIG, on a street named *Neumarkt*, stands one of the city's most remarkable houses: *Die Große Feuerkugel*, The Great Fireball. The name derives from an incendiary projectile, launched in a battle waged three miles north during the Thirteen Years War, that demolished a portion of its edifice. Once rebuilt, the residence was occupied by a wealthy merchant.

The proud façade of The Great Fireball stands directly across from Leipzig's central market. Imperceptibly to passersby, it connects at the rear to several buildings that in combination frame a generous courtyard. These venerable brick neighbors embrace dozens of apartments and cramped garrets, whose location and affordability compensate for their lack of comfort or charm. Because of their proximity to the university and the town center, these apartments consistently drew a steady stream of university students. I was among them. And the garret I took upon leaving St. Thomas, offering barely enough space at its center to clear the top of my head, was to be my new home.

I remained active with the church, as its Sunday performances provided me with necessary income. The majority of my focus, however, was directed northeast toward the university, whose idyllic setting within the city provided an escape into a world of intellectual and spiritual curiosity.

As it happened, Johann Ernesti had also moved to the university, having been appointed chair of the theology department. The former rector remembered me fondly and invited me more than once to his office to discuss my studies and reminisce about Bach.

Of those with whom I was privileged to study, none was more inspiring than Johann Gottsched, among the most distinguished members of the university faculty. His gripping lectures on poetics and ancient philosophy often incorporated medieval epics he had translated himself. Given that he was intent on writing a complete history of the German language, many of us found keeping up with him quite challenging. During the hours Gottsched commanded our attention, however, we regarded literature as the essence of our existence.

Life beyond the university was something else entirely. Not long after my schooling there had begun, a foreign entity breached our walls and, like the plague, one could do little but try to survive it. Abroad, there seemed no end to the desire for global power and expansion, but wars in the New World among Britain, France, and Spain, affected us little. The voracious Prussian appetite for dominion over the German states, however, was very much our business. To complicate matters, Austria, a Saxon ally, was once again intent on wresting Silesia from the Prussians. Leipzig, straddling as it did the Saxon border, found itself directly in the path of an advancing Prussian army—just as my late master had once described to me. Frederick's troops marched in during August of 1756. I was twenty-two.

We who called Leipzig home, thirty thousand in number, had felt crowded even before the soldiers arrived. We were also accustomed to the seven thousand or so visitors who came twice annually, from as far as Russia and Greece, to throng our famous Easter and Michaelmas fairs. Within our city's walls, the timber houses of the middle class and the stone dwellings of the more affluent, some as many as six stories high, sprouted and squeezed along our narrow streets. Our markets teemed with shoppers and bakers, butchers, cobblers, textile merchants, and other vendors of all kinds.

Publishing houses also abounded. The nation's first scholarly periodical, *Acta Eruditorum*, had been founded in Leipzig nearly a century before my enrollment at the university; now, the city produced voluminous German-language materials, from books, journals, and poetry to drama and translations. We also boasted a score of booksellers, ten of which lined the *Grimmaische Strasse*.

As the seat of one of Europe's oldest and most esteemed universities, where none other than Leibniz had studied and his father had lectured, Leipzig represented a hub of intellectual and enlightened thought. Frederick's soldiers, who naturally contributed little to this status, merely added to the population. The bulk of the Prussian military juggernaut soon pressed on to the southeast, Leipzig having never been their intended target. Still, occupying troops remained, and stayed for years.

As contentious and shifting political alliances swept much of the continent, my classmates and I attempted to stay abreast of events as best we could. In reality, though, we had more than our share of problems at home. I do not mean to suggest that the occupying soldiers behaved with habitual violence but their continued presence created tremendous hardship nonetheless. Vast revenues, cash that otherwise would have supported local businesses, were extracted to feed, clothe, and billet them. Saxons conscripted to fight for Prussia depleted

Leipzig's workforce as well. Even our currency was debased, a ploy I later learned had been undertaken by Frederick and his court financier, Daniel Itzig, whereby inferior copper discs supplanted the precious metals of our prewar coinage.

By day, I endured tense encounters with the ubiquitous soldiers. By night, I contended with the drinking, revelry, and occasional fights of my fellow scholars. Moments of tranquility, quietude, or respite grew scarce. I found the rogueries of the fraternal organizations not intolerable, for after all they were students. By contrast, it was best to avoid the soldiers whenever possible—that is, except for one. Some two months into the occupation, I heard him play for the first time.

Before the war and occupation, evening entertainment in Leipzig might have included opera or theater. Our vibrant cultural milieu extended to temporary performance venues in warehouses, markets, and gardens, so great was the thirst for entertainment. Conscription, however, had all but emptied our stages of local talent. Public concerts were now a thing of the past, save for those that accompanied church services. Most remained private affairs with subscription costs prohibitive to all but nobles and the wealthier merchants. Of course, some amusements of a coarse, vulgar nature were patronized by the occupying troops, but the good Christians of Leipzig—including those students of my circle—did not participate in or even acknowledge them.

These limitations left me with few places to pass the time. I made an occasional visit to Auerbach's tavern, a stone's throw from The Fireball, and I was a frequent patron of Zimmermann's, which held strong memories for me, and where I was happy to peruse the stocked newspapers or lose myself in games of chess. Indeed, the latter became a source of increasing fascination. It appealed greatly because of the logic it demanded, which I likened to the art of counterpoint. At the coffeehouse, I had multiple opportunities to observe the matches of accomplished players.

Among those I found particularly fascinating was a cherub-faced youth I assumed was only a few years older than I. He seemed to dispatch his opponents both customarily and with ease. His name was Gotthold Ephraim Lessing, and onlookers rhapsodized *sotto voce* about his intelligence as they followed his brilliant matches. I encountered him myself at Prussian headquarters of all places, and we soon became friendly enough for him, as a chess master, to instruct me in some of the game's finer points.

One never knew who would appear at the top of Zimmerman's staircase in search of a match: peddler, theologian, student, soldier, writer, or bookseller. Occasionally, one even encountered Jewish merchants who journeyed to Leipzig for its fairs. Some spoke only enough German to ply their trade, but the language of chess was universal. The game established a fraternal order all its own, with counts and cobblers alike powerfully drawn to its sixty-four squares, like iron filings to a magnet.

Along with the camaraderie it cultivated, chess offered an appealing, if fleeting escape from school and work. Its concise rules, primarily determined by the moves permitted to each piece, meant that its rudiments could be quickly learned. Yet, the infinite strategies bound up with those deceptively simple moves could feed a novice manna for a lifetime. Chess opened a door to me, and I hurtled through it with abandon.

At Zimmermann's and around the university, I sought out players at my level, of which there was no shortage. During those first months, I played for the sheer pleasure of being at the board, incurious of any deeper appreciation for strategy. As my skills refined, however, I sought out players of greater prowess, and the competition awakened an insatiable hunger.

It was in October of 1756, two months into the Prussian occupation of the city, when I began scouring bookshops for chess manuals. Early one evening, I came across two curiosities in the *Grimmaische Strasse:* Stamma's *Noble Game of Chess,* a recent work from England that would inspire me to improve my facility in that language, and a much older volume entitled *Chess or the King's Game* by Gustavus Selenus. The proprietor informed me that the Selenus (a pseudonym for Augustus, Duke of Brunswick-Luneburg) was the only German-language book about chess he had ever encountered. It had been published here in Leipzig during the previous century in translation from the Italian of a still earlier work by the Spanish master Ruy López. This name I had heard whispered around the café tables, in reference to a series of opening moves, yet regarded such strategies as beyond my grasp. Now, clutching the battered volume, I was reinvigorated to advance my gamesmanship.

Dusk was settling as I headed home with my new treasures. I had just passed The Fireball when the unmistakable strains of the *Well-Tempered Clavier* stopped me cold. Immediately I doubled back to the front of the house, which I observed from the market. As was well known, the Prussian general staff had appropriated the historic residence shortly after their invasion, and a steady stream of soldiers marched through its majestic front doors day and night. This evening was no different, except for the musical accompaniment.

Beyond my ongoing dedication to Bach's cello suites, which I practiced in my garret at every opportunity, I seldom encountered his music during the first years after his death.

Even at St. Thomas church, it was rare for anyone to program his instrumental compositions or cantatas. Moreover, until this moment I had never heard my master's keyboard music played by another soul. It was also evident that this performer possessed an impressive technique and a keen understanding of Bach's music. I stood spellbound, delighted yet anxious. The keyboardist, I felt certain, would soon emerge.

Distant shouts and laughter emanated from the direction of the university. A lamplighter stopped to kindle a lantern before going on about his rounds. And still, I lingered. As memories of the Bach family apartment returned, I recalled my master seated at his harpsichord, playing this very music for John Taylor at their first meeting.

When the music ceased, I awakened from my reverie. Yet, when no one emerged from The Fireball during my wait, I reluctantly concluded that my master's interpreter would remain a mystery. I returned to my garret, where I dropped onto my narrow bed and imagined the keyboardist inside the great house. As I drifted off to sleep, the anonymous figure slowly melded into that of Bach, who played for me under the pitched roof.

I heard him again less than a week later, this time as I was passing St. Nicholas church, whose doors were flung wide to welcome the air of an uncommonly warm afternoon. The unmistakable sounds of Bach's organ music enveloped me just as I reached the church fountain. Eagerly, I stepped inside, taking a seat near the rear of the sanctuary whence I could just make out the crown of the organist's head in the loft. Officiates moved silently through the transept or the chancel, and visitors came and went, intent on prayer or supplication. I kept my seat, determined to meet Bach's interpreter.

After the better part of an hour, the music ceased, and the gentle click of footsteps descending the winding staircase echoed off the vaulted ceiling. At the bottom, a Prussian officer cradling a stack of music turned and moved through the nave toward the doors behind me. I stood and slid into the aisle to intercept him.

"Excuse me, my good sir," I stammered, "but if I'm not mistaken, this is the second time I have heard you playing the music of my former master."

The soldier, who until then had failed to notice me, stopped suddenly and looked up. His expression suggested I had surprised him, though it was unclear what confounded him more—my discomfiting address or that someone was familiar with the music he had been playing.

"Pardon me?" was all he said.

"The music ... that was Sebastian Bach, was it not?" I reiterated. The officer stood a head shorter than I, though he appeared of a similar age. He glanced down at the music.

"Yes, indeed, it was," he cautiously responded. "Your master, did you say?"

"That he was," I answered with considerably more confidence. "I was among the great man's last students. May I inquire if it was you whom I also heard playing inside The Fireball on Neumarkt several days ago? I distinctly heard the music of Bach."

The officer then acknowledged that he had been playing that night, and I confessed how I had stood mesmerized in the street, so struck was I upon hearing Bach's keyboard music for the first time after many years. I added that it had been here, in this sanctuary, that I first heard Bach improvise on the organ the officer had just played.

His expression softened in the presence of another admirer of this sublime music, and he courteously gestured to follow him back upstairs, where we could speak privately. We sat near the organ, among chairs scattered about from the previous Sunday's performance. He began first, quietly asking me who I was and if I was a musician.

"My name is Carl Friedrich Barth. I have been in Leipzig since entering the school of St. Thomas years ago. I play the keyboard and am a trained singer, although my passion is cello. I came to live with Bach and his family during the last year of the composer's life and thus recognized his music. Currently, I'm pursuing other studies at the university and letting a garret just behind Prussian headquarters, and that is how I happened upon you playing from the *Well-Tempered Clavier*."

The officer's blue eyes expressed both sensitivity and intelligence. He sat motionless but fully engrossed as I spoke. When I finished, he looked toward the organ as if trying to imagine Bach perched upon that same bench, then thanked me for approaching him.

'My name is Josef August Graun," he added. "Perhaps you've heard of my father, Johann Gottlieb, violinist and concertmaster at the Prussian court?"

I shook my head.

"No matter," he continued. "My uncle, Carl Heinrich, is arguably the better known, but both have hitched themselves to the musical life of Berlin. Naturally enough, my siblings and I all studied music, but I was determined to pursue a different path. I had just embarked on a course of law when the war broke out."

"How did you come to Leipzig?" I asked.

"I requested the posting once the Prussian army had established the occupation. The truth, however, is that I wanted to study and copy as much of Bach's music as time allowed. In Berlin, I learned under Bach's son, Carl Phillip, who spoke with such love of his father. Despite my career path, I remain a devoted keyboardist and my admiration for Bach's music is profound. So, I put in for Leipzig, not simply to gain residence somewhere well removed from the field of battle. Here I knew I could dedicate myself to my musical pursuits when not detained by official duties."

We were interrupted by a commotion at the foot of the stairs. I glanced over the loft's edge and saw several musicians. A rehearsal was about to begin, so I asked Josef if he had the time or inclination to continue our conversation elsewhere. He replied that he was eager to learn as much about my former master as I was willing to share, but that he first needed to report at headquarters.

"I should be free again after sundown," he said. "Let's plan to meet in the back corner of Auerbach's Tavern. I'm sure we can find a quiet table at that hour and before my uniform begins to attract undue attention."

We cheerfully shook hands and descended. I went first, passing the orchestra's early arrivals, several of whom I recognized and greeted on the way down.

⁓

Josef Graun appeared at a most fortuitous moment in my life. Before my brothers and I went our separate ways, we remained close, but I had made little time to develop deep friendships with others. Nor was I immune to the allures of women, several of whom had caught my eye. But until quite recently, my focus was bound up with other pursuits. Meeting Josef signaled that my priorities might be changing.

Perhaps it was a matter of timing, or that a singular character like Josef Graun had crossed my path. Regardless, I had begun to sense the need for something neither my university acquaintances nor the camaraderie of chess or music could offer. And a poor student like myself was hardly an ideal suitor for the daughters of Leipzig's better families. As it happened, Josef was to prove not simply the first of my close male confidants but also the most significant and enduring of my life.

As Josef predicted, early evening found Auerbach's relatively calm, an atmosphere that would change soon enough. I secured a table in the corner of a small room off the cavernous cellar, where Josef found me a quarter of an hour later. The tavern was a favorite of university students. They would fill every inch of the place, but until they started to arrive, we had the room to ourselves.

A waiter lit the stubby, half-burned candle stuck to the tabletop, then presented us with a decanter of wine and a pair of pewter cups. We initially sat in silence, watching the liquifying wax at the candle's wick. As it gradually overflowed, a single bead traveled along a well-worn path until it reached the table's edge, then wept onto the sawdust-covered floor.

My tablemate asked how I had come to live with Bach. I shared some of my experiences in his household and my work for him as a copyist. I also spoke briefly about Bach's lamentable surgery.

"What I witnessed reflected most poorly on the surgeon's calling and, regrettably, his character as well. I should have done everything in my power to remove the doctor from the house. Bach's eyes were indeed failing. But he was otherwise robust, and in retrospect, I am sure he could well have lived many more years. Perhaps he would still be alive today! One can only imagine what he might have composed."

Josef listened intently and paused before responding. "If I may ... I don't think the burden of your master's death is yours to bear." I interrupted, citing Taylor's lecture and how foolishly impressed I had been.

"No doubt you were," Josef countered. "Even I was aware of Taylor's appearance in Potsdam. He had many friends in positions of influence and took care to create a dazzling impression everywhere he went.

"But listen: King Frederick had been warned that the Chevalier might be acting as an English spy, and so informed the surgeon that if he so much as touched one of his subjects inside the city walls, he would find himself at the end of a rope." So this was the "debacle" Carl Phillip had referred to in his letter!

"Six hours later," Josef went on, "Taylor was gone. I heard he was followed by a train of coaches filled with people clamoring for his services. In any case, submitting to such an operation always entails risk. I'm sure Herr and Frau Bach weighed the matter carefully." Indeed, Frau Anna had confided their dilemma to me, as well as her trepidation.

"From what you've said, Herr Barth, even through your modesty I can tell you were a great comfort to your master in his final days and weeks. And, frankly, I'm envious of the intimacy you developed with him and his family. You might be interested to know," he continued, "that Bach's son Carl Phillip was invited to Berlin upon the recommendation of my father and my uncle, for both were well acquainted with the young man's keyboard virtuosity. I heard Carl Phillip play often, and, as I said, he also served as my teacher for a period. He repeatedly mentioned his father's brilliance, so I can only imagine what an honor it must have been to have had such a personal kinship with him and to have experienced his music-making up close."

Embarrassed, I glanced again at the candle. The melting wax was now spiraling in several directions. "I heard Bach often in the apartment," I said, "but among my everlasting memories is one that took place in St. Nicholas, where you played earlier today." And then, I described to Josef the transcendent experience of listening to Bach improvise and how divinely inspired it seemed.

"It was miraculous. Truly." He nodded, and I sensed with great comfort that my new friend fully grasped the essence of my astonishment.

Shifting the conversation, I was curious to hear of Josef's acquaintance with His Majesty Frederick the Great, given how much time he must have spent at court. "Of course! My father became part of the *Kapelle* while Frederick was still crown prince, so I practically grew up in his house—or rather, houses. He was like an uncle to my siblings and me, which we accepted as a privilege.

"Of course, as always in such cases," Josef said, lowering his voice, though we remained the sole patrons within the room, "many of his subjects were less than enamored. Granted, he had a complicated childhood, beginning with a fraught relationship with his own father, Frederick Wilhelm …

"It is said that while Frederick I was still king, he accused his son and a close friend of treason and threatened to have them both executed. Can you imagine? In the end, he spared young Frederick but forced him to witness his friend's beheading! Who could say what the after-effects such a misfortune must have had? Nevertheless, with favorable tutelage and his father's lessons in statecraft, Frederick grew into a fiercely intelligent leader. As a result, he has proven himself the far more capable of the two men, despite his thorny tactical methods."

As Josef had remarked about my privilege living in the Bach household, I felt similarly about his connection to the king. So it was with some trepidation that I phrased my next question: "If I might ask, Herr Graun, what is your role here in Leipzig?"

"My orders are ostensibly to recruit Saxons for our army, but as you may appreciate, your Leipzigers are in no rush to sign up and fight against their own. Most of those we enlist are miscreants who have stepped across one line or another. They can spend time behind bars, pay a fine—which, not uncoincidentally, few can afford—or march.

"In truth, my official work is not the least bit interesting. But as I told you earlier, my desire to come to Leipzig had nothing to do with the war. My father also studied here. Given his interest in the city and my infatuation with Bach's music, I chose to take advantage of the opportunity. Certainly, my most cherished moments here have been in the St. Thomas library and at the keyboard."

I felt no small measure of relief upon hearing that Josef had no military inclinations but instead favored artistic pursuits. Thus, I was glad for the conversation to return to Bach. I asked him about the music he was carrying when we met in the church sanctuary.

"I borrowed that material—preludes and fugues mostly—from St. Thomas and was actually on the way to return them when you spoke to me. The school has been exceedingly generous letting me spend time with their old cantor's music, but as a member of the occupying force, I know they see little choice in the matter. Still, they've become accustomed to my visits, and by appearances at least, they address me courteously and seem to respect my dedication to Bach's compositions.

"I even managed to secure a keyboard for our headquarters," he concluded. "That's what you heard me playing when you passed by last week. And as you also discovered, I try to find time for some organ playing at one of the churches, if the instrument is available."

We had finished our wine, and as the room was beginning to swarm with noise and smoke, we settled our bill and headed upstairs. As we walked, I told Josef about my discovery in the St. Thomas library of Bach's solo cello suites, and how I had come to own the original manuscript along with one of his cellos.

"I beg of you, please, bring the music and your cello to my headquarters!" he interrupted. "It would mean a great deal to hear them both! Of course, if you'd be willing."

I responded that it would be an honor to share the music with someone as interested in Bach as I was. We were standing before The Great Fireball, Prussian headquarters, bidding one another adieu, when Josef added, "I also have something to show you when you come, something I am sure you, above all others, will appreciate. Until next time?"

I smiled and headed for my garret, grateful for the possibilities of this new friendship. Admittedly, I was not completely free of internal conflict, knowing as I did of my master's hapless journey to Potsdam and his mistreatment by Frederick, a man Josef might consider family. But as it so happened, I needn't have been concerned.

Chapter 14

Several weeks later, on a cold November afternoon, I ascended the steps of The Fireball, cello in one hand and Bach's suites in the other. Josef and I had seen one another several times but had only recently managed the promised rendezvous at Prussian headquarters. Josef ushered me past the immense drawing room, large enough for an entire orchestra and audience; his chamber upstairs proved far more modest.

Upon entering, Josef's reverence for Bach was in full view. The harpsichord, appropriated from St. Thomas, stood at the room's center, surrounded by stacks of musical scores, most bearing the name Bach. As he had informed me, some had been borrowed from the school library, others brought from Berlin. A cot occupied one corner with a row of bookcases positioned close by, crowded with manuals and stacks of maps. A window overlooking the street offered a gracious panorama of the market opposite, while nearby stood a large table strewn with so much correspondence that some spilled over onto a wooden music stand.

"Welcome to my estimable quarters, Carl," Josef announced with mock pride and a sweep of his arm. Like the Bachs, he had chosen to dispense with the formality of my Christian name, which wholly gratified me. "If you could only see where I typically played the keyboard in Berlin, you would pity me now, although admittedly, my Leipzig home possesses a quaint charm! Please, make yourself comfortable."

"How can I? It's only *twice* the size of my place," I laughed, pointing toward where my garret lurked across the courtyard. "My friend, I'm honored to be within one of the city's landmarks. It's a house I've long admired."

I unpacked the cello, tightened the bow, and took my place on the harpsichord bench while Josef cleared the music stand and placed it before me. He dropped onto his cot as I flipped the pages of Bach's manuscript until I came to the Third Suite. I had made this selection with care, for its resolute key of C major and the triumphant nature of its Prelude seemed most befitting for a Prussian army man. I trained my attention on the page and launched into the music's majestic opening, occasionally glancing in Josef's direction as I made my way through each movement. My host appeared entranced, eyes closed, but sprang to his feet when I dispatched the Gigue's final C major chord with an exuberant flourish.

"Bravo, Carl! Never have I heard such marvelous cello music. And you say there are five more of them?"

I set the cello down and handed Bach's manuscript to Josef. As he eagerly perused it, I drew his attention to various details of the notation, including the re-tuning indicated for the Fifth Suite and the Sixth Suite, which had been composed for an instrument of five strings. I added that while I had made a copy of the complete set, now housed alongside the copy Frau Bach had made, I had neither access to a five-string cello nor had ever seen such an instrument. So the sixth remained inaccessible.

"Did Bach play cello, Carl?"

"He never said, and I never thought to ask. I played for him often, but when he wished to demonstrate an idea, he did so on the violin. He played remarkably well, so I believe he might have spent time with the cello at some point. I do know that when he composed the suites, he was employed in Köthen and had very accomplished players at his disposal."

Josef finished thumbing through Bach's autograph and handed it back to me. "I grew up hearing some very impressive cello playing at the Berlin court, but never music like this. It is a truly magnificent gift, Carl. No wonder this music has become an indispensable part of your life."

As he continued, he bent to reach for a stack of music on the floor alongside the harpsichord. "I also have something to share with you. You may find it nearly as interesting."

I followed him to the table, where he shoved more papers aside before reverently setting down the thick bundle. The handsomely engraved title page bore the following inscription, which I read aloud:

MOST GRACIOUS KING!

It is with deepest humility that I herewith dedicate to Your Majesty a musical offering, the most noble part of which stems from Your Majesty's Own most August Hand. It is with the most awesome pleasure that I recall the very special Royal Mercy when, some time ago, during my visit to Potsdam, Your Majesty's Self deigned to play me a Theme for a Fugue upon a clavier, and simultaneously most graciously charged me to carry it out in Your Majesty's Most August Presence ...

My breath caught in my throat. I skipped several lines until my eyes landed on the following:

> *... intent to glorify ... the fame of a Monarch whose greatness and strength, as in all the sciences of war and peace and also especially in music, everyone must admire and honor ... may Your Majesty deign to dignify the present modest labor with a gracious acceptance ...*
>
> *Your Majesty's most humble and obedient servant,*
>
> *The Author*

Leipzig, 7 July, 1747

Dumbstruck, I could read no more. Before me was the *Musical Offering,* prefaced with my master's dedication to the king! Bach had not even affixed his own name to the document. Once more, this time with incredulity, I read his words: "It is with the most awesome pleasure that I recall ..."

I stepped away from the table.

"Josef," I began, slowly at first, "my master sent this music to your king after visiting Potsdam. He shared the entire saga of his disheartening trip to Frederick's court with me. I am certain it was among the most bitter pills he ever swallowed."

I walked slowly back to the table and was leafing through the music when Josef asked if I would share what Bach had told me about his experience.

"Every page of this music was borne of Frederick's challenge to my master," I promptly replied. "Having often heard praise of Bach's remarkable improvisational abilities, the king invited him to the palace and presented him with an intricate musical subject, upon which Bach was requested—in a manner of speaking—to extemporize a three-voice fugue. Bach readily complied, after which the king inquired if his guest might next improvise another, this time with *six* voices.

"Imagine improvising such a fugue!" Josef nodded, fascinated by this tale of someone he knew quite well, along with someone he deeply admired from afar. "I am sure that such an undertaking was well within my master's powers," I continued, "but he declined due to the bizarre nature of the royal theme and in fear that under such circumstances he would fail to do justice to his art. Instead, he requested to improvise upon a subject of his choice, which he subsequently dispatched with the king's permission.

"Bach was not a pompous man. Yet his pride was stung. He said as much to me years later and remained determinedly fixated on Frederick's challenge. On the return trip, only a few days after the scene I have just described, he conceived of this entire collection," I said, taking ahold of the score. "Back at home in Leipzig, he worked on it unremittingly, until he was satisfied. He then had his *Musical Offering* engraved in copper, at his own expense, and sent what appears to be this very copy to His Majesty.

"My master received neither word of thanks nor acknowledgment that his precious cargo had even arrived. So, while he was proud of his accomplishment, his feelings about the entire enterprise were conflicted. By the time he related the saga to me, he admitted great sadness over it."

Josef coughed and looked sharply at me.

"Carl, I was there that night."

"But how?" I cried. "Where?"

"In Potsdam, at court. The Kapelle musicians knew that Frederick had invited Bach to play for him, and my father did not want his children to miss any opportunity to hear 'the master.' As I recall, he was not entirely certain Bach would call that evening but had us nearby, just in case."

I interrupted. "Bach said he was shown to the king almost immediately after his bone-jarring journey. Having no time to rest flustered him and from that point forward he felt manipulated—as if he was a pawn on a chessboard. He did recall, however, that families with children were present during the king's manipulations. They were seated off to one side, I believe he said. How marvelous that you were among them!"

Josef sighed. "I recollect that he held his own and was, at all times, most respectful. And what he demonstrated at court that evening was truly astounding. Though I was too young to perceive the extent of Bach's genius, I had heard enough stories about his mythical abilities to understand the rare nature of the event. Everyone at court revered Bach, my father and my uncle included, along with Carl Phillip, naturally. Accordingly, His Majesty heard about 'old Bach' so often that he began pressing the composer's son to bring him north, 'to see what all the fuss is about,' as he put it."

Josef crossed the room to his cot and sat before continuing.

"Well, you've heard the story from Bach himself, so there is little more for me to add. You should know, however, that in the weeks and months after Bach's visit, my father remained so overwhelmed that he evoked that night often, ensuring we would never forget it. As for the king, indeed he is a very proud man. He's also a sophisticated musician, albeit his taste tends toward a lighter style than that which flowed from Bach's pen. Nevertheless, as he dragged his guest from one fortepiano to another, the king appeared as astonished as everyone else by what he heard and saw.

"I suspect he may also have wanted to push Bach to his limits, either to understand what was humanly possible or as some vain display of his authority. Whether or not Frederick or one of his musicians dreamed up this 'royal theme,' as you call it, I cannot say, but whatever the case, I deeply regret learning that Bach found the experience so distressing. I repeat—it is to his credit that he disguised it well.

"As for the keyboard works in his *Offering*, they are brilliant, if also mentally and physically taxing. Admittedly, I have yet to decipher the final puzzle canons, but I'm itching to read the trio sonata, which appears to be the heart of the work. Carl, I have a colleague here at headquarters who's not a bad violinist. I'm sure I could persuade him to sit down with us some evening and play through the trio if that would appeal to you. Can you secure a flautist in town?"

I told him I was confident I could locate someone and that nothing would make me happier than to play through this score with him, particularly as my master had given it up for lost. I wondered aloud how Josef had discovered the music.

"I was in the royal library, selecting music to bring to Leipzig. I knew I would find all the Bach I wanted at St. Thomas, so I mostly borrowed music of other composers, although I did make off with a copy of the *Well-Tempered Clavier*. Carl Phillip occasionally turned to it for pedagogical purposes, and I hoped he would not go looking for it while I was away.

"Perusing the various shelves, I happened upon a bundle wrapped in brown cloth and tied with twine. It appeared to have never been opened, so I carefully unwrapped it. And, *voilà*—Bach's *Musical Offering*! Whether it had been misshelved, forgotten, or ignored, I felt certain it would never be missed.

"Of course, when I am recalled to Berlin, I shall return it, along with the rest of the music I borrowed. And now that I have the precious knowledge of the events that led to its creation, I'm doubly desirous to play the trio with you."

As my host accompanied me downstairs to the great front door, Josef told me again how honored he was that I had shared Bach's cello music with him.

"What a pity I'm here in Leipzig representing the enemy," he murmured. "Well, Carl, let's hope politics never disturbs our friendship or our shared love of Bach's music."

I told him I felt the same way. Regardless of his uniform, I had ceased to regard him in an adversarial light. "Truly, Josef, had it not been for our present circumstances, we certainly would have never met, much less have had the opportunity to make music together."

"Carl, that's a worthy sentiment, and when next we meet, we shall raise a glass to it!"

I remained on the front steps for a few minutes, taking in the bracing air. Somehow the temperature seemed warmer, the dark less foreboding. I looked toward the marketplace and reflected on the events that had brought me to this door. What a twist of fate that I had become friends—and was soon to make music—with someone connected to Frederick's court, the root of Bach's personal conflict with Prussia!

Moreover, how fortunate that my association with Josef was even possible! Life among the Prussians had relaxed, as initial tensions had calmed in Leipzig. And while the army still maintained authority that could not be challenged, they mingled more freely with us in the streets, churches, taverns, and coffeehouses. I felt that I could safely trust Josef's sincerity, and harbored no misgivings about inviting a fellow musician to return with me for an afternoon of chamber music.

A fortnight later, I was back at The Fireball, this time alongside Johann Tromlitz, a flautist and flute maker of considerable renown in town. Although he had never worked under Bach's direction, his curiosity was piqued by the opportunity to play this mysterious music and he embraced my invitation. Josef welcomed us both and introduced us to his comrade, a violinist and former pupil of Josef's father.

"It took only a few dozen lessons with Papa Graun," Haupner grinned, "to make it clear to us both that I was meant for another line of work! Still, I love to play, and will strive not to hold the rest of you back."

Josef now ushered us all into the great drawing room. "Given the aristocratic nature of the music, this seemed a far more fitting location. This morning several of us transported the keyboard from my chamber upstairs." Everyone agreed that the setting was ideal. And so we gathered around the keyboard and prepared to become the first to play the trio sonata from Bach's *Musical Offering*.

Bach never shared his intentions for the flute part with me, but from the start of the sorrowful *Largo*, it quickly became apparent that Frederick's favored instrument was *not* the center of attention. Indeed, the flute entered two bars *after* the violin, submissively, in strict imitation. And the flute's delayed entrance in the spirited *Allegro* that followed seemed even more conspicuous! I assumed these were subtle pokes at Frederick, particularly in that Bach handed the flute the *Thema Regium* only *after* everyone else had their turn; indeed, it came so late as to impress the experienced listener as an afterthought.

Secretly, I took great pleasure in each of these cunning jokes, conjuring an image of my bewigged master seated at his desk, puffing on his pipe and indulging in hearty laughter at the king's expense.

We had just begun discussing Bach's subtle integration of the royal theme in the finale, another playful *Allegro,* when we heard a commotion in the foyer. A moment later, a sentry appeared at the door in the company of two guests. One, the cherub-faced chessmaster Ephraim Lessing, I immediately recognized. His companion, larger and in uniform, projected the melancholy air of a man who longed for something he could not have. Josef introduced him as Ewald Christian von Kleist.

The new guests sat and became a polite audience as we restarted the last movement, which we had abandoned upon considering its finer points. Though this second *Allegro* began with the flute, the 'royal theme' was practically undetectable, so furtively had it been woven into the musical texture. A spirited, bounding accompaniment provided a further foil to the winding theme. Soon enough, Frederick's thorny musical subject had been subsumed by Bach's gleeful, inexhaustible inventiveness, until the trio's very last bars, when the bass, unfurling a ribbon of scales, swiftly brought the music to a close.

Lessing and Kleist stood as one, exclaiming "Bravo!" and clapping loudly. Stepping forward, Lessing inquired about the music, and Josef explained about Sebastian Bach, the former St. Thomas cantor. "What you just heard was but a small part of a larger musical composition, a gift from the composer to His Majesty, King Frederick the Great. We believe it had never been performed before this night."

Lessing acknowledged that he had become aware of Bach while attending Leipzig University but had never heard any of his music performed. "I was riveted," he admitted, "although I must confess to having no better ear for music than the fellow next to me." Teasingly, he draped his arm around Kleist's shoulder. "So, as regards any worthwhile account of what you have played, we must trust the musicians."

The three of us spoke over each other to assure him that this was music of unsurpassable skill. I added, as my companions nodded in agreement, that Bach never having heard the work performed made the experience doubly poignant for us all.

Tromlitz soon departed for a rehearsal and the rest adjourned to the dining room. The table was laid with an assortment of meats, cheeses, and dark bread, along with pewter tankards of Gose, appropriately a favorite of my master's. As promised, we stood to toast the serendipitous, complicated circumstances that had brought us together. But next, we sat, and clinked our tankards in memory of our venerated Johann Sebastian Bach: "Let his music and his genius soon be recognized universally!" Our tributes complete, we fell to the feast before us. I could not recall the last time I had eaten so well.

With scarce common ground to continue discussing music, the company veered toward politics, with Lessing and Kleist eagerly returning to the spirited debate they had paused upon entering the drawing room. These were obviously devoted friends despite being cut from very different cloth. Kleist, born into a military life, was the scion of an illustrious family that had long fought in the service of the House of Hohenzollern. He had been an officer in the Danish army until recalled by "The Old Fritz," as he boldly referred to His Majesty. Kleist's mission in Leipzig involved refashioning defeated Saxon troops into proud fighting Prussians. But administrative duties were both irksome and tedious for him, and he wished for nothing more than to return to the field of battle.

"Look how His Majesty has already transformed Prussia," Kleist remarked. "Under his father's rule, it was no more than a backwater state; under Frederick's enlightened reforms, it has become economically and politically sound *and* religiously tolerant. I daresay no other European monarch can make such a claim!

"I'm truly sorry for the plight of Leipzig," he added, turning to me. "Your fair city is a blameless casualty of the present conflict. Still, Frederick will never allow his august dynasty to yield to the House of Habsburg or Austria's allies."

Lessing's loyalties, I soon learned, were conflicted. Saxon born, he had spent much time in Berlin and longed to return. Yet he considered himself a *Weltbürger*, a citizen of the world, while holding European values in the highest regard. To complicate his position further, Lessing disparaged ruling dynasties and the warfare that ameliorated such empires.

"Kleist, I admire your passion and, to an extent, your willingness to die for such a cause," Lessing said, patiently and not, I suspected, for the first time. "But as you know well, I detest war. I find it undignified. And while I appreciate Prussia's dynastic claims and the belief that Austria has taken Silesia unrightfully, in no way can any war of expansion justify the significant loss of human life."

Kleist, who believed he was wasting away in Leipzig and was pressing hard to return to service, interjected that he was not only unafraid to die but could think of no greater honor than to do so for king and country.

"Regardless of our differences on this or any other subject, you, Lessing, will forever remain among my dearest friends. Still, I believe that the more land Prussia rules the better it will be in the long run for the health of the Germanic Nation. As for the present hardships, only time will tell if they may bring about a better future."

I listened intently to this debate, which was superior to similar arguments among my university classmates in both its tone and its participants' depth of experience. I could not help but identify more with Lessing's humanistic spirit, and though I shared little of Kleist's fervent nationalism, I admired the passion that buttressed his conviction.

It came to light that this unusual friendship—Kleist was also fourteen years Lessing's senior—found its greatest common ground in literature. Lessing was engaged with several projects, including various translations, as his English was impeccable. Additionally, he served as editor of a Berlin literary journal and had authored plays, one of which had been staged while he was still at university. Kleist, for his part, was a published poet of note. Years later, I would learn that both men were regarded as seminal figures in the German Enlightenment, a movement whose origins sprang from Leipzig's native son, Gottfried Wilhelm Leibniz, and that proliferated across the continent into a broad quest for scientific knowledge, spiritual fulfillment, and human happiness.

Lessing told us he had learned of Kleist, who had been affectionately dubbed the Poet of the Spring, long before they met. "I was introduced as a student to his expansive poem *Der Frühling* —'The Spring,' hence the nickname—which earned our friend much notice. The acclaim was probably as much a consequence of the work's sentiment as its construction, built as it was of hexameter, the rhythmic pattern common to classical Greek verse. That he sustained the ancient meter for pages was an astounding feat," Lessing declared, raising his tankard once more, "and I'm honored to call him my friend!"

Kleist shifted in his chair, implying unease at Lessing's praise.

"But, my dear man," Lessing continued, "while I marvel at the skillful framing of your words, I find my struggle increasing with your allegiance to the Prussian cause. For instance, your 'Ode on the Prussian Army'—how does it begin?"

Kleist laughed for the first time that evening. "As if you didn't know!" he chided. But all the same, he recited the opening verse:

> Unsurpassed army! with death and destruction
> Enemies penetrate legions,
> Around which the joyful victory swings golden wings,
> Fifty troops, ready to win or die.

"Yes ... *'Ready to win or die,'* Lessing repeated. "I suppose you faithfully capture the essence of warfare, but I'm no soldier and can hardly be expected to align with such sentiments. Admittedly, I possess no more knowledge of war than of music. Still, I would suggest that what music expresses is pure, whether in the abstract or visceral sense—such as the intensely moving musical performance we were treated to earlier. The same can hardly be said of poetry. And your words, Kleist, are a call to arms!

"Be that as it may," Lessing continued before Kleist could respond, "I do confess to an emotional surrender to the epic poem with which you are currently at work. If I may?" Kleist nodded.

Lessing went on. "The poem of which I am speaking tells the story of Cissides and Paches, Thessalian companions who died for their country fighting the Athenians." At this point, Kleist successfully interjected that the poem's essence was not merely about the companions' loyalty or sacrifice, but also warfare itself.

"As you say," Lessing concurred. "But for me, it's less about war's heroics and more about brotherhood, particularly brotherhood inspired by loyalty and sacrifice. Yes, your protagonists' fate is the tragedy of war, to which I believe all can fully relate. Yet the poem appeals to me on account of the friendship it depicts. I must also confess, however, that I'm drawn to its connection to the ancient world of Homer."

"Well, Lessing," Kleist retorted, "my prose can't be all ancient myth and love of the natural world, can it? I hoped that my Prussian ode would inspire my comrades, even if many of them do not share my devotion to our king or my commitment to army life. Certainly not the Saxon recruits, at any rate!"

Finally, Lessing broke off the banter. "Pardon us, gentlemen, for the diversion of our pedantic prattle. Herr Barth, tell us of your maestro. What else should we know about him? Is his music performed anywhere other than at Prussian headquarters?"

Josef turned to me. Smiling a bit tightly at Lessing's goodhearted jest, I acknowledged that Bach had traveled little despite his abundant genius. Consequently, while generations of Bach musicians were well known in and around Thuringia, the composer's sublime gifts had yet to be widely embraced.

"I'm sure it's only a matter of time," I added confidently. "Tragically, his death, which followed on the heels of a calamitous surgery, could have been avoided." I briefly recounted John Taylor's misdeeds—Lessing recalled seeing his distinctive carriage about town—and Bach's subsequent decline.

Lessing broke in to request more of his music, as he and Kleist had heard only the final portion of the Trio earlier that evening. "Carl," Josef asked, "why don't you play one of his cello suites?" After the others urged me on, as if in chorus, I responded that I'd be honored.

Well fed and in good spirits, we returned to the ballroom, where I tuned my cello as Josef spoke more about Bach's music.

"Gentlemen, Carl played one of the cello suites for me a few weeks ago, and I can attest that they are bona fide treasures of his repertoire. You may be unaware that my enthusiasm for Bach is why I requested a post here in Leipzig. It is my great good luck that the request also brought me into contact with Carl. My dear friends, you have your poetry. We have our Bach!"

I chose to play the First Suite, a work I had committed to memory, supposing its buoyant prelude with its uplifting dance movements would best captivate our neophytes. I was not mistaken. After I had concluded the spirited final bars, Lessing rose to his feet and exclaimed that this was spectacular music, even to the uninitiated.

As I packed up the cello, he continued. "Gentlemen, I thank all of you for one of the most enjoyable evenings I have had in a long while. As it happens, I arrived with fond memories of this house. Kleist is aware that I lived here with Herr Winkler, the owner, before the tenancy of tonight's hosts. To be honest, things between Winkler and myself had already begun to sour when he announced to me one fine evening that my Prussian friends were making him 'uncomfortable.'

"The next thing I knew, he kicked me out. But truthfully, I was only too willing to go. What a twist of fate! I was once an unhappy and unwanted lodger inside these walls, and tonight I have dined as a delighted and welcomed guest! Anyway, regarding lodgings, should any of you come across something affordable nearby, please let me know. My resources are less than abundant, but my needs are also few."

"Herr Lessing, you are most cordially invited to view my humble dwelling around the corner," I immediately replied. "It is hardly spacious, but in my opinion, its charming courtyard view compensates for the lack of elbow or even headroom. And

I would welcome the company. Should you find it suitable, perhaps you could tutor me in chess? That would be far more valuable to me than a few groschen per week to offset my rent."

Lessing replied that it sounded like a promising pact. We thanked our Prussian hosts for the delicious repast and bid them good night. Lessing accompanied me around the corner to my garret, where I quickly apologized for its lack of resemblance to The Fireball.

"Nonsense, it's perfect!" Lessing exclaimed, "as I shall be leaving soon for Berlin and require little more than a place to lay my head until then. I plan to return occasionally, however, so as long as you do not mind an itinerant guest, I would be most grateful. And if it's chess lessons you truly desire, chess it will be!"

"Along with some English tutoring?" I added.

"English too? My dear fellow, that'll cost you! How about you throw an occasional Bach cello suite into the bargain?"

And we shook on it.

Chapter 15

LIFE CONTINUED TO DEVELOP IN familiar patterns. My university studies were both challenging and inspiring, and I was teaching once more at St. Thomas and performing when the church needed an extra cellist or singer. Thus, I earned just enough to remain comfortable. My leisure hours were often spent at one of Leipzig's coffeehouses, near the newspaper racks, or at the chessboards. Josef and I made music as often as our schedules permitted.

English lessons were to be had whenever Lessing was in residence. Indeed, he demanded that we speak only English to each other, and he occasionally produced a British newspaper for me to read aloud. We moved on to my chess instruction only when he was satisfied with my progress. On the beautiful board he brought to my garret, he took me slowly through the nuances of controlling the center of play. Lessing's remarkable understanding of the game was matched by his seemingly infinite patience with his new pupil as I began to grasp previously unimagined concepts. And as we had agreed, I played Bach for him in return.

In short, I enjoyed a predictable, uncomplicated life, cheerfully filled with learning, friends, and music. But one evening in 1759, the tragedy of world events visited my doorstep.

Lessing entered the garret, entirely lacking his usual *joie de vivre*, dropped into a chair, and handed me a letter. His gloomy air was enough to alert me that the charmed existence I had led for so long was about to change.

The missive, Lessing informed me without a trace of his characteristic wit, came from Johann Ludwig Gleim, a Prussian soldier and close friend of Kleist. Gleim was also a poet whose writing Lessing encouraged, despite reservations over its intense militarism, similar to his misgivings about Kleist's work. Gleim related that their mutual friend had finally been granted his wish to return to the front but fell at the Battle of Kunersdorf. Kleist had died a hero's death, Gleim maintained: after being struck by several musket balls, he had stubbornly continued to lead his troops and had succumbed only after one leg was crushed by shrapnel. He had fallen from his horse, been thrown into a swamp by the enemy, and left for dead.

"Kleist was later discovered alive," I read, "and carried to Frankfurt for care. But blood loss had ultimately felled the Poet of the Spring."

"He perished for his fatherland and his king," Lessing muttered in a strangled voice. "I took issue with this devotion, yet how many would be willing to die for such a cause? It is said that Frederick the Great once assailed hesitant troops by railing, 'Dogs, do you wish to live forever?' Kleist, may his soul rest in peace, took the message to heart. I shall see that the words he left behind will not be forgotten. Yet, the pain of wondering what he might still have created will never forsake me."

"I did not know him nearly as well as you, nor for as long," I answered warmly, "but I deeply admired his spirit and courage. And I certainly understand your anguish over what might have been; similar feelings about my late master are never far from my heart. Ephraim, please accept my deepest condolences."

I was able to persuade him to leave the garret for a meal, and we stopped by The Fireball to give Josef the sad news. Then the three of us walked to the *Thüringer Hof* in the Brühl, which had been a favorite of Kleist and, centuries earlier, Martin Luther. As we dined within the storied walls, Lessing recalled the devotion between himself and Kleist: the time his friend had nursed him back to health, shortly after his first arrival in Leipzig; Lessing's concerns about Kleist's melancholic tendencies and frustrated hopes of marriage; the late soldier's rigorous self-discipline and disregard for physical pain; and, not least, his unfailing generosity.

"He even tried to secure a salaried position for me. He will truly be missed by all who knew him, and none more than his troops. Speaking of which," Lessing continued, "how much longer can this war drag on? It would seem all sides must have exhausted their resources and energies, yet no end appears in sight."

Looking at Josef, he struck a slightly more cheerful attitude. "Well, my friend, with any luck we shall soon find ourselves in Berlin. I shall return there shortly and would very much like to continue our camaraderie in that enlightened city ... if that is also your wish."

"Lessing, I too hope that our friendship will carry on. And Carl," Josef said, turning to me, "you must visit. I long to introduce you to my father, and of course, you must become acquainted with Bach's son Carl Phillip. The two of you should have much to discuss!"

I now spoke for the first time since we had entered the establishment.

"Nothing, aside from the conclusion of this war, would make me happier than to visit the two of you in Berlin. But once my studies have ended, I shall have to find employment with all haste. You must promise to keep me abreast of all the city's musical happenings."

We raised a glass to Kleist's memory and headed home in due course.

We parted ways with Josef when we reached the Fireball, and as Lessing and I continued to my garret, I noted how the weight of his loss was bearing down upon my friend. He departed for Berlin a week or so later.

Happily for me, he would return to Leipzig with some frequency in the years that followed, especially after the city's theater life was revived and his plays became all the rage. Josef remained in Leipzig for a few more years, a situation that contributed greatly to my happiness although his presence also signaled the continuance of war.

───✦───

John Taylor roared back into my life on a spring evening in 1761, as I neared the end of my time at university. I might never have seen the notice had I stuck to my usual German periodicals while waiting for an open seat at a chessboard in the Café Zimmermann. But on this occasion, as I enjoyed the intoxicating air of cigar smoke and Arabian coffee, I occupied myself with the *London Gazette*, thinking to enrich my English by studying the present British activities in India as well as their campaigns against the French in America. When I flipped to the journal's last page, this advertisement just below the fold immediately caught my eye:

The HISTORY of the
TRAVELS and ADVENTURES
OF THE
Chevalier JOHN TAYLOR,
OPHTHALMIATER;

Pontifical—Imperial and Royal——The Kings of Poland, Denmark, Sweden, The Electors of the holy Empire——The Princes of Saxegotha, Mecklenberg, Anfpach, Brunfwick, Parme, Modena, Zerbit, Loraine, Saxony, Heffe Caffel, Holftein, Salzbourg, Baviere, Leige, Barcith, Georgia, &c. Pr. in Opt. C. of Rom. M. D.—C. D.—Author of 45 Works in different Languages: the Produce for upwards of thirty Years, of the greateft Practice in the Cure of diftempered Eyes, of any in the Age we live—Who has been in every Court, Kingdom, Province, State, City, and Town of the leaft Confideration in all Europe, without exception.

Written by HIMSELF.

This Work contains all moft worthy the Attention of a Traveller—alfo a Differtation on the Art of pleafing, with the moft interefting Obfervations on the Force of Prejudice; numberlefs Adventures as well amongft Nuns and Friars, as with Perfons in high Life; with a Defcription of a great Variety of the moft admirable Relations, which, though told *in his well known peculiar Manner*, each one is ftrictly true, and within the Chevalier's own Obfervations and Knowledge. — Interfperfed with the Sentiments of crowned Heads, &c. in Favour of his Enterprizes; and an Addrefs to the public, fhewing, that his Profeffion is diftinct and independant of every other Part of Phyfic.

Introduced by an humble Appeal, of the Author, to the Sovereigns of Europe.

Addreffed to his only SON.

VOL. I.

Qui Vifum Vitam Dat.

LONDON:
Printed for J. WILLIAMS, on Ludgate-Hill. 1761.

The elegant Chevalier, it seemed, was still hard at work. Was he crafting the second volume of his memoir or preparing a *communiqué* for his next stopover at that very moment, possibly while waiting for laudanum to take effect on yet another hapless patient? How many more procedures had he undertaken since the ones that caused my dear master's blindness and fatal decline? And how many had similarly failed? Had Taylor ever reflected on his time in Leipzig, or did Bach's surgery blend in with so many others far and wide?

Josef's hand on my shoulder interrupted my reverie. "Carl? Are you all right? My friend, you look as if you've seen a ghost. I've repeatedly called your name—a table has opened up."

"Josef, never mind the game. Please, sit."

He pulled up a chair as I laid the folded page between us. "Here is my ghost," I said, pointing to the notice.

Josef read it under his breath and sighed. "This is the man who operated on Bach, isn't it?"

"The very one," I whispered, fearing to distract players at the nearby tables. "His memoirs appeared this very year," I said, pointing at the information at the bottom of the advertisement. "I suppose the manuscript could have been submitted posthumously, but Taylor might just as easily be alive and preparing a successive volume—or two.

"What would I give to confront this man, to ask him what he remembers, and learn what's become of him! He could be anywhere—in London, perhaps, but just as likely Paris or St. Petersburg. Despite the sheaves upon sheaves of papers I have read in this room, this is the first time I have come across Taylor's name since he departed Leipzig!"

"Carl," Josef began, "it seems this turmoil will not be fully quieted until you have faced him directly. When you first told me of this awful experience and your role in it, as you will recall I maintained that you were in no way responsible for what transpired, neither at the time nor afterward. But still the matter haunts you."

I closed my eyes and rested my head in my hands, overwhelmed by the weight of memories and feelings. After a moment, I looked back at Josef.

"Right or wrong, my friend, I have never been able to think about Bach, nor even play any of his music, without reimagining my role during the procedure. However twisted it may seem, the Chevalier—or perhaps his ghost, if he has passed from this earth since this book's publication—remains inextricably linked to my past. I can't help but imagine how it would be to stand before him, whether in this world or the next!"

After a pause, Josef stood, returned the *Gazette* to its place in the rack, and said, "Come, my friend. Let's play chess."

We claimed our table and played well into the night, yet I continually imagined the Chevalier, instead of Josef, sitting opposite me. As I pictured the aged Englishman moving his pieces about the board, I longed for both the opportunity to confront him and the strength to accept whatever responsibility was mine to bear.

Chapter 16

In February 1763, Frederick the Great entered a hunting lodge a day's ride from Leipzig and brokered peace with Austria. The long war's end had been slow in coming, particularly as Frederick's Prussians had seemed on the verge of collapse a full three years earlier. Drained of manpower, materials, and money, and with Russian and Austrian forces occupying Berlin, some thought Frederick had little hope of continuing the fight.

But the king's defensive genius continued to keep his armies alive, and the death of Russia's Empress Elizabeth, in January 1762, was the last miracle he needed. Elizabeth's successor, Peter III, dramatically shifted the balance of power by not only striking an unexpected alliance with Prussia but also by offering Frederick more than ten thousand troops. Less than a year later, Frederick brought Austria and Saxony to the peace table at Hubertusburg, thus concluding seven years of bloody strife.

A condition of the treaty reverted Silesia, the swath of land at the source of so much conflict, to Frederick's control. But so little had been gained, so many had died—and, in the end, for what? At long last, Frederick's maneuvers had gained Prussia a place among the European powers. Yet I could not help but wonder if even Kleist would have found the cost worthwhile.

The conclusion of hostilities naturally signaled the welcome end of our occupation, but it also meant that Josef would be recalled to Berlin. I remained only too aware of how dearly I would miss him. Beyond our friendship, I had never known anyone who shared my love of and appreciation for Bach's music. His departure would create a void impossible to fill.

With my theological studies now complete, I remained in Leipzig until such time as work might materialize elsewhere. Summer passed slowly, but the fall proved cheerful, and in early October, the Michaelmas Fair commenced in full regalia. One afternoon, after winding through the labyrinth of stalls teeming with merchants and unfamiliar languages, I rounded the corner by my garret to find Josef waiting on a bench.

His appearance was a marvel, wholly unanticipated, yet he sat there as naturally as if he had just come from The Fireball. His changed appearance, though, struck me at once. Dressed in riding gear from top to toe, boots splattered with mud, and officer's uniform noticeably absent, Josef looked to have been on the road for some time. A leather valise rested at his feet, and next to him sat a twine-wrapped paper package. He broke into a broad smile as I eagerly stepped toward him.

"All hail the conquering hero!" I exclaimed over the din at my back. "How marvelous to see you! How is it that you have returned so soon? Not another war, please God!"

"Thank heavens, no! I come in peace," Josef assured me as we embraced. "And I had not thought of Michaelmas until at least a dozen foreign dialects reminded me at the last changing station! Well, given the celebratory hubbub, I'm doubly thrilled to have found you. I have been in England and took a detour on the way home to Berlin, though sadly, I must depart first thing tomorrow." Stepping back, he said with mock sternness, "Carl, you look svelte and handsome as ever."

"You, conversely, look completely worn out. Thinner, too. I guess the English diet wasn't your cup of tea?" I quipped, winking at my old friend. "Well, nearby are the means to fatten you up with any delicacy you could possibly want—Russian pierogi, Greek lamb, Turkish delight, and the rest. But first, you must tell me what brings you to town," I said, seizing his arm and herding him toward the steps.

When we reached the hush of my garret, we sat while Josef explained. "Not long after my return to Berlin, I was sent to London with a team of delegates to help sort out Prussia's relationship with Britain. As you might imagine, it's a messy business. We spent several days in the company of high-ranking ministers, each of whom wanted to do everything possible to placate the Prussians, never mind that the British chose to withhold badly needed subsidies during the war.

"Anyway, I don't believe much was accomplished, at least as far as the British were concerned. Frederick has emerged from the war stronger than ever; if nothing else, our delegation established that Prussia requires no further assistance from King George!

"After many tedious meetings without much progress, our little band was set to return home. But I begged off for a few days. It seemed a pity to come all that way and not take advantage of London's theaters and her sights. Such a splendid town! Then one day, among the stalls and bookstores in St. James Street, I happened upon this!" And he handed me the paper package.

I tugged at the twine until it fell away. The title of the gift, a handsome book, was in English. I had to read it twice before fully grasping its significance.

The HISTORY of the
TRAVELS and ADVENTURES
of the
Chevalier JOHN TAYLOR,
OPHTHALMIATER

I looked at Josef with a mixture of surprise and incredulity.

"I took the liberty of perusing it and marked the page I believe you will find most interesting," Josef said. I turned to the place held with a silk ribbon and read the following paragraph aloud:

> But to proceed, I have seen a vast variety of singular animals, such as dromedaries, camels, &c and particularly in *Leipsick*, where a celebrated master of music, who had already arrived to his 88th year, received his sight by my hands; it is with this very man that the famous Handel was first educated, and with whom I once thought to have had the same success, having all circumstances in his favor, motions of the pupil, light, &c but upon drawing the curtain, we found the bottom defective, from a paralytic disorder.

I was dumbstruck. After so many years, how could Taylor continue to promote these lies?

"Josef, this description is both astounding and utter nonsense!" I exclaimed. "Where to begin? First, Bach never mentored Handel. Indeed, they never even met, though admittedly, it is an astonishing coincidence that the oculist tended to both men. And how could Taylor have mistaken my master's age for 88, when he must have remembered him being decades younger when he operated on him?

"Yet none of that truly matters. It is this ..." I stammered, tracing the words with my finger, "... received his sight by my hands ..."

I let off and breathed a deep sigh.

"Taylor either chose to suppress the truth and paint the surgery in a positive light," I continued, "believing no one would ever be the wiser, or his memory was playing tricks on him. The latter, though, seems unlikely."

I briefly related Taylor's false claim of surgical success destined for the *Berlinische Zeitung*. "That was hard enough to stomach. But continuing to suppress the truth for posterity is reprehensible. Was he delusional about his own prophecies?"

I closed the book and leaned back heavily in my chair.

I apologize, Carl," Josef interposed, "for it seems I've only brought you added distress with this gift."

"To the contrary, Josef. You have done me a great service and I am indebted to you. That you would ride to Leipzig on my behalf is the sign of our truest friendship. But what am I to do now?"

Josef walked to the window and studied the courtyard below. With his back to me, he replied with deliberation.

"Carl, when I saw Taylor's book, I only knew that you needed to see it. What you do with the information it contains is something only you can answer. Of course, there's no guarantee that Taylor is still alive—forgive me, but I lacked sufficient time to explore the matter. To put this history behind you at last, I'm afraid you will need to take action yourself.

He now turned toward me. "To be sure, Carl, getting to London is a formidable undertaking, even for a member of a diplomatic corps. I enjoyed the best and most secure of conditions; for you, I fear it will prove far more challenging. Still, my good friend, I'm certain an attempt will prove well worth the effort. Of course, you may or may not find your man. But if you don't try, your persistent doubts about your role in Bach's surgery, so many years ago, persuade me you are likely to spend the rest of your life wishing you had. And anyway, Carl, what is there to keep you from your wanderlust?"

"My English, for one thing," I responded.

"Oh, come now! Your English is easily good enough for what you want to accomplish. And if you find Taylor, language will be no barrier, from what you told me about his German."

"Time?" I ventured.

"Make the time!" Josef declared. "With your studies completed and no pressing responsibilities to employer or family, there will be no better time to undertake such a mission. Not only can you make it happen, I believe you *need* to. And in your place, I wouldn't wait too long. Taylor may be alive still, but his remaining days are unknown. Besides, it's high time you experienced what lies beyond Leipzig's city walls."

I promised Josef I would consider the matter. We then toasted our reunion.

"Come, Carl. I'm starving. Let's enjoy the fair while the night is young."

In fact, the fair would have been impossible to avoid. The central marketplace, neighboring streets, and alleys were overflowing. One saw Persians and Jews, Italians and Armenians. Indeed, merchants from every European land were present to buy, barter, and sell leather goods, earthenware and ironware, toys, books, porcelain, glass, spices, coffee, confectionery, furs, and garments of cotton, linen, wool, and silk. Buyers haggled over hens and horses and fortunes were told by itinerant wanderers. For the next three weeks, Leipzig would remain fully transformed into a *mélange* of brilliant costumes, exotic fragrances, and the clamor of foreign tongues.

The marketplace had become a second city of tents and carts. We pushed along rows of hides, fabrics, and carpets of myriad designs. The sun was already setting when we caught the scent of searing meat and were led by the wafting aromas to a square lined with food stalls, where we enjoyed pierogi and stuffed cabbage leaves.

Now ready to leave the throngs, we passed through a city gate beyond which lay expansive fields dotted with chestnut and elm. Tents of all shapes and sizes spread seemingly to the horizon. To this domain, merchants and their families would return for the night.

Drawn by the sounds of strings to a nearby campfire, we found two performers in festive white garb—Hungarian masters of violin and cimbalom. Around them, dancers similarly clad moved in well-practiced rings, bending low and kicking out their feet to the music's pulse. At the opposite end of the field, we could make out the energetic strumming of lutes and vihuelas; these were the Spanish and Portuguese traders. As we moved between the two displays, Josef dubbed the polyphony of folk song "Michaelmas goulash"—an international stew of sound.

Mindful that Josef must rise early, we started for the city gate. But at the edge of the field, we came upon a small tent in which a young woman sat before a low table that held a few candles and a deck of cards. With a bright silk scarf about her head, her dark curls spilling beyond its edges, and an embroidered blouse cut low to reveal an ample bosom, she was, without doubt, the most exotically entrancing woman I had ever beheld. In the candlelight, I could just see a small, dark mark above her lip and the sparkle of her dark eyes. I stood frozen before her.

At her gesture, I nervously moved inside and dropped onto a stool. In charmingly accented German, the fortuneteller gently asked to see my hand. I gladly placed it in hers, hoping my perspiration wouldn't betray my attraction. My heart pounded so loudly that I was certain she could hear it.

She began by telling me the lines in my hand were strong, and for a few pfennigs, she would reveal their significance. Josef looked on from the tent's entrance as I withdrew a few coppers from my pocket with my free hand and placed them gently on the table, opposite the cards.

"Yes, you have solid lines … and beautiful hands. Are you perhaps an artist?"

I nodded.

She smiled, then traced the shorter of several creases. "I see here that you have lost someone dear to you. This loss has affected you deeply, and though it happened many years ago, you carry it with you, both the loss and some sort of burden connected to it."

I glanced over my shoulder at Josef. The candlelight was enough for me to see his raised eyebrows, suggesting he was impressed with these powers of perception.

"And my future?" I shyly inquired. "Can you see what might lie before me?"

"Very much so, Herr …?"

"Barth," I stammered. Her slender forefinger traveled the length of the longest line on my palm, sending a pleasant tingling to the base of my neck. I could no longer tell which vexed me more: her keen intuition or her alluring beauty.

"Herr Barth, this line indicates that you are to undertake a very long journey. However, this journey is not—how do you say—symbolic?"

"A true journey, then? A physical journey?"

"Yes, an actual journey ... and it appears to be an important one," she added as she looked up from my hand. Overcome by the intimacy of her warm eyes fixed on mine, I looked away, again catching Josef's face in the flickering candlelight.

"Would you like to know more?" she asked.

"Only if it's fortuitous," I said, only half joking.

"Then, Herr Barth, I shall tell you something more. You will find your mate, though not soon and not here," she said as she motioned behind her, which I took to indicate the city. "Nor will you remain much longer in Leipzig. Your future lies elsewhere."

I glanced down at the lines of my hand and then back at her, wondering if all she said could possibly be true.

"And finally, this line," she continued, slowly tracing a more shallow crease, "suggests you will be content with your life. That is good, yes?"

I responded in the affirmative, not wanting to remove my hand from hers. She tenderly turned it to look at the back and ran her thumb across the veins before placing it gently on the table, palm down.

Then, softly, "That is all."

I sat for a moment, looking down at the table, and then raised my eyes again to meet her gaze. Her lips curved into an easy smile.

"And you, Fräuline?" I asked, unsure how to engage her in conversation. "May I ask your name ... if you don't consider my request too forward?"

"I am called Dafir. This name comes from Trandafir, which means 'rose' in Romani, my language."

"It is a fittingly lovely name. And, of course, I read neither palms nor cards, but where will *your* journey end?"

"Ah … the journey of my people never ends. We travel, we arrive, and we travel again. This is not my first time in Leipzig, and who knows when we shall return? I do not know where I shall be a week from today."

"It seems a sad existence, never having a place to call your own."

"What does it mean to 'own' a place?" she responded. "You cannot leave with it nor take it with you when you die. We roam between towns and villages, but we experience a full life and build memories all the while. Because of you, Herr Barth, this night will remain with me as a cherished memory of Leipzig. That is a beautiful thing, and all I can ask."

Her words stirred me deeply. As a creature of place and habit, I could not envision moving on, day after day, but I could certainly understand her sentiment. Not knowing what else to say, I thanked her.

"Fräulein…Dafir, I'm grateful for your time and counsel. I shall dwell greatly on both in the days and weeks ahead."

She bowed her head in farewell as I stood and exited the tent. But I could not stop myself from turning back to catch her eye once more. Beside me, Josef sensed that I was shaken. "She is as lovely as she is prescient," he said as we passed beneath a copse of birch.

"She is hardly the first woman I have noticed in my lifetime," I replied, "but she is easily the most captivating. I'm unsure if it was due to her striking features, the rhythms of her accent, the intimacy of the scene, or the accuracy of her impressions, but she moved me to the quick."

"Well, Carl, it's high time someone caught your eye. I was beginning to think it would never happen!" he teased, clapping my shoulder.

We passed again through the gate and retraced our steps through the marketplace, its streets and stalls now settling for the night. Soon, we reached the courtyard before my garret. As we ascended the staircase, Josef thanked me for a memorable afternoon and told me how glad he was that he had made the journey here.

"And now to bed, Carl. I must rise before dawn and ride double quick to Berlin, where my presence has undoubtedly been missed."

Josef took the space formerly occupied by Lessing, whom I had not seen for some months. His presence was represented by his chessboard, still at its place of honor.

As we lay in wait for sleep, I spoke softly. "Josef, I'm deeply humbled that you traveled all this way to deliver the book to me in person. Thank you."

"Trust me, Carl, it was my honor. Besides, I needed an excuse to avoid returning home with such stuffy diplomats. So it is I who should thank you! But between the book and the words of your lovely acquaintance, I believe you need to prioritize the journey we discussed. Next time we meet, I hope you will be able to regale me with your own stories of London. And now, good night, dear friend."

∽

Josef rose first, well before dawn, and awakened me from a dream. In it, I again sat in Dafir's tent and requested a reading, but this time from the cards.

"You must know it is unwise to tempt fate, Herr Barth."

"Perhaps," I answered. "Or, perhaps, my destiny includes an enchanting, dark-eyed companion?"

"This cannot be," she responded, but I saw her smile. Emboldened, I asked if she would meet me at the fountain of St. Nicholas Church, just on the other side of the city wall.

"At the risk of sounding forward," I pleaded, "it would be my honor to show you a little of my city. It is very charming, particularly under the moonlight. You have my word as a gentleman that you will come to no harm."

I waited at the fountain until well after sunset and had just about given up hope when Dafir appeared, seemingly from thin air. Together, we wandered through the market stalls toward St. Thomas school, and I told her about my life there.

Then we were strolling along the bank of the River Pleisse, her hand in mine, and she told me about her travels and country. Before long, we stood beneath a linden, wrapped in each other's arms. But she retreated when I attempted to kiss her.

"I cannot. We leave tomorrow. And as I have told you, your destiny lies with someone else."

I was gazing into the deep mystery of her eyes when the vision melted away.

"Josef, is it time? I was dreaming."

"You certainly were," he answered, smiling. "And I can well imagine what about! But yes, I must depart."

Dawn had not yet arrived as Josef and I walked the gaslit streets to the stable where he had boarded his handsome gelding. We embraced before he swung into the saddle.

"Carl, be well until next time. If last night's palmistry proves accurate, don't forget to let me know where you end up. Riding back to Leipzig and not finding you would be tragic!"

Josef nudged his mount into a canter and began to turn toward the Grimma Gate. Reining in, he paused long enough to call back over his shoulder. "You can always send notice to Berlin's Royal Palace. They will know where to find me!" He then swept his riding cap in a gallant arc of farewell.

Late that afternoon, I found myself again beyond the city wall and returning to the same tent as the night before. But the woman behind the table was a stranger.

"I hoped to find Fräuline Dafir. She … read my fortune last night. Might you know her whereabouts?"

"The Fräuline left early this morning, in a caravan of several families. Perhaps they were headed south. May I be of service?" she asked, motioning toward the table.

Disappointed, I thanked her and backed out of the tent. Across the field, where Josef and I had watched the dancers, a pair of musicians playing a zither and a shepherd's flute now accompanied a chorus of singers. I dropped onto the grass and listened as I reflected upon the events of the past day and night.

I felt the absence of Josef and Dafir in the pit of my stomach. I knew nothing about this woman or her alien ways, yet she had left a profound impression. Moreover, she had awakened feelings I had never truly experienced, and I could not help but desire more.

In time, the assemblage before me broke up and everyone returned to their tents. As I crossed the broad expanse and walked toward the city gate, I continued ruminating on Josef and Dafir, for both had materialized unexpectedly and vanished just as quickly.

Back inside my garret, I was struck by the coincidence of the two unanticipated meetings, one with an old and trusted friend and another with an unknown and beguiling charmer. Remarkably, both presaged the same inescapable journey. I climbed into bed, unable to quiet my mind. I knew I would go in search of the oculist.

PART III
JOURNEY

Chapter 17

The Michaelmas Fair concluded and the merchant army, tents struck and carts loaded, drove their horses back through Leipzig's gates. Some were destined for home across faraway lakes and mountains, others for fairs elsewhere. As the streets and markets returned to normal, I was left to ponder the dark-eyed woman, her prophecies, and John Taylor's book. Josef's gift beckoned me daily, and I became consumed with the certainty of my destiny.

I knew I could have no more excuses when an offer of a single term's employment arrived from Halle, inviting me to fill in for the ailing cantor. I was to teach Latin, give music lessons, and help prepare the Sunday performances, for which I would be more than adequately compensated. I accepted at once. The post would likely continue for the better part of the year, or at least until Gottfried Mittag, cantor of Halle's Market Church of Our Dear Lady, was well enough to return. Even better, my new position would supply me with ample funds for travel. I decided to head for England as soon as my time in Halle concluded.

Curiously, Bach's son Wilhelm Friedemann had served in Halle as the Market Church organist until conflicts with Mittag convinced him to resign. Friedemann and I had met when he came to Leipzig for his father's funeral and again to help settle the estate. I had not seen him since, nor were we to meet again. Later, it became known that Friedemann had left Halle before securing another position; subsequently, he unsuccessfully reapplied for his old job. I could not help but wonder if the younger Bach was carrying on the paternal tradition of scorning his employers.

I knew Halle had also been the home of Handel, whom the newspapers reported as having died in 1759. The city remained proud of its native son, and I recalled Bach's mentioning that the famous composer had returned there on occasion. By the time I arrived, however, no family remained. His niece, born Johanna Friderica Michaelsen, had married a law professor named Floercke and set up house in Gotha, a Thuringian town one hundred miles to the southwest. As far as I could ascertain, she was still alive. And as I was now aware that John Taylor had tended to both men, I determined that Gotha would be my first stop on my way to London.

My time in Halle was pleasant enough, but the longer I tarried, the greater my preoccupation grew with what awaited me westward. Upon Cantor Mittag's full recovery, I returned briefly to Leipzig, where I put my affairs in order before embarking on what I calculated could be an absence of several months. From Gotha, I would proceed to Calais, cross the English Channel on the Dover ferry, and take a coach to London. By departing in September, I hoped to be back on Saxon soil before winter could wreak havoc on my itinerary.

I purchased a leather trunk and at the last minute, having been warned of highwaymen—some of whom were known to be in league with the drivers—had most of my travel funds sewn into a false bottom. Along with a professional letter of introduction from the rector in Halle, I decided John Taylor's book would be among the few effects I would carry. As for communication on foreign soil, I would have to rely on whatever English fluency I had gathered from the London press and Lessing's magnanimous coaching, along with the French and Latin I learned in school. I trusted all of this would see me through.

The initial stretch to Gotha proved blissfully uneventful. The weather was hot and dry, the roads dusty, and the rigs, whether post-chaise or, more commonly, the commercial coach, made good time. So long as the weather held out, I preferred sitting alongside the driver or upon the imperial, where as many as five or six other passengers were likely to join me. We typically made seven or even eight miles in an hour and thus required just over two days to reach Gotha, which I was delighted to find had retained its medieval flavor.

I took a room before making inquiry about Frau Johanna Floercke, Handel's niece, now a widow but wealthy, thanks to the successes of both her uncle and husband. Locating her posed little challenge, for she occupied one of Gotha's most prominent residences, a conspicuous two-story house in the center of town. Her doorman solemnly accepted my letter of introduction from Halle and requested that I wait while he brought it to his employer. Given Johanna Floercke's family connection to Halle, I hoped my impression would be favorable. From a well-appointed sitting room, I was soon shown into a spacious parlor, where my hostess awaited.

Frau Floercke was a handsome woman, some 50 years old. To my relief, she was not merely gracious but genuinely curious to speak with me. I told her that before my employment in Halle, I was schooled in Leipzig, where I had been apprenticed to the composer Sebastian Bach at St. Thomas.

"Naturally, I am familiar with the name Friedemann Bach, organist of the Market Church in my birthplace of Halle," she said, in animated tones. "I understand his father was also a skilled organist, though I never heard him play. My uncle may have mentioned your Sebastian Bach once or twice."

I informed her that Friedemann was no longer the organist in Halle. "I have been given to understand that he and his employer did not see eye to eye, a trait that seemed to run in the family. In defense of my master, I can confidently state that he was far more than a 'skilled organist.' Indeed, my humble opinion is that his keyboard playing and improvisational abilities were second to none."

I quickly regretted the latter statement, as Frau Floercke might well have believed the same of her late uncle. "I see …," she ventured. "And did he also compose?"

Though disappointed that my hostess was unaware of Bach's music, I could not be surprised. Few musicians beyond his immediate orbit were familiar with him or even aware of his existence. That her uncle had achieved such international acclaim during his lifetime made these facts, of which I was acutely aware, especially poignant.

"He composed a great deal … both in Leipzig and earlier," I said. "Unfortunately, when I came to serve him, his eyesight had deteriorated so much that composition had become nearly impossible. He underwent eye surgery in his sixty-fifth year, but matters quickly went from bad to worse. He died, much to my grief, not long thereafter."

I continued, as she wanted to know why I had made the journey to Gotha. "During his examination, which I observed from the doorway along with Frau Bach, who has also since died, my master made a point of telling the surgeon that he had on more than one occasion attempted to *rendezvous* with your uncle in Halle.

"Bach was a supremely gifted composer himself," I continued, "and that he held Herr Handel in such high estimation inspired me to make the trip here. The first time Bach came to Halle, hoping to meet your uncle, he arrived too late, for Handel had just left the city. And when he learned of Handel's visit to Halle years later, he again hoped to meet him but was taken ill. He thus lamented that his endeavor failed not once, but twice."

Frau Floercke replied that she had loved her uncle dearly and regretted that he had moved so far away. "Unfortunately, shortly following his last visit, he suffered a terrible carriage accident in the Netherlands, and soon after that, one of *his* eyes began to fail. It seems highly possible that this event was the cause of his complete blindness in his later years. I understand that a famous eye surgeon examined him but concluded that his blindness was irreversible."

Here I interrupted, apologizing as I did so.

"Frau Floercke, fantastic as it seems, your uncle's oculist was the same man who operated on my master. His name is John Taylor, assuming he's still alive, and he wrote of having seen both men in his memoir, which is among my present effects. In the same paragraph wherein he declares to have cured Bach of blindness, which I assure you *was not the case*, he also claims to have examined your uncle and to have discovered in him a paralytic disorder that prohibited surgery. Whether Taylor's description of Handel's condition was entirely accurate, or even honest, I cannot say, but this is the very man I am traveling to London to find."

"I'm so sorry to hear about your master's misfortunes with the doctor," Frau Floercke said. "But what, may I ask, is your intent should you locate him?"

I acknowledged that I was not entirely sure. "I've spent far more time contemplating past events and far less predicting what might become of such a meeting. I was present for Bach's surgeries and witnessed disturbing events that reflected poorly on John Taylor, not only as a doctor of medicine but also as a man. I imagine what I shall say will largely depend on *who* I find.

"In other words, is the doctor the same man he was all those years ago? Taylor believes—or at least would have posterity believe—that he returned the precious gift of sight to Bach. Yet the tragic reality is that Bach never recovered and was dead within three months."

I stopped then and briefly closed my eyes. "Well, everything naturally depends on whether Taylor is alive, whether I find him, and whether he will be willing to see me," I resumed. "I suspect I shall have ample opportunity to ponder these possibilities over the next fortnight, as I make my way to London."

Frau Floercke listened patiently as I unburdened myself. "Given what you've told me," she observed, "It sounds as if my uncle was fortunate that Taylor declined to operate. I'm no musician, so I can only imagine the hardships he and Herr Bach must have endured, having been deprived of their sight."

At that moment a servant knocked and entered, bearing a small samovar of coffee, fine china cups and saucers, linen napkins, and a silver platter of little cakes. I gladly accepted these elegant refreshments before urging my hostess to continue.

"The lawyer who settled Handel's estate told me that despite spending his final nine years in total darkness, his celebrated status only increased. When he died, the entire city mourned—some three thousand Londoners turned up at the funeral. Imagine that!" she exclaimed, shaking her head. Recalling Bach's simple service further underscored how different these two composers' lives had been.

She next praised her uncle's generosity. "He had amassed a fine art collection, much of which was auctioned off, but in his will he remembered a great many people. For instance, his musical instruments went to his copyist and he passed on his house in Brook Street to his manservant. Those were loving acts indeed!

"I will say, however," she continued, "that he was also a very proud man, acutely aware of his importance in the music world. Thus, he requested interment in Westminster Abbey. In return for this honor, my uncle bequeathed the necessary funds for a grand monument!" She laughed at this extravagance but also admitted that while she harbored no great desire to see the tomb her uncle had commissioned, she did regret never visiting him in London.

When Frau Floercke placed her demitasse on the platter and rested her hands in her lap, I understood that our time together was nearing its end. But our conversation continued as she herself walked me to the front door.

"I'm only sorry that Herr Bach and my uncle never met, given what you have told me about your late master," she said. "Herr Barth, our meeting may not have been as grand as that between two maestros but I'm so glad you made the effort to find me! If you like, I would be most happy to provide you with a letter of introduction to my uncle's manservant, John Duburk, whom I believe still lives in Brook Street. I think it will be worthwhile for you to inquire if he knows of Taylor's whereabouts."

I assured her that such a letter would be most welcome, and promised to make Brook Street among my first calls in London.

"I shall have the letter in readiness for you first thing tomorrow morning," she declared. "And, if I may add, your love and admiration of your late master is deeply touching and evident in all you have imparted today. Surely, Herr Bach is smiling down upon you from heaven and will accompany you in spirit as you journey on in his memory. I wish you Godspeed, safe travels to London and back home to Leipzig."

I thanked her sincerely and told her how honored I was to have made her acquaintance. She then called for a servant to instruct the cook to prepare a lunch of bread and sausage for me to collect on the morrow, along with her introductory letter. We clasped hands warmly and wished each other a pleasant evening. It was the last I would see of her.

I rose early the next morning and retrieved the letter and lunch parcel on my way to the station. Soon I was aboard a coach passing through Gotha's western gate.

———

The next fortnight introduced me to a swath of Europe that I had only imagined. My westward path took me through Eisenach, which I knew to be Bach's birthplace, and then through the German states of Hesse and Westphalia. From Cologne, with its dizzying twin gothic spires, I passed through the tidy Netherlands and finally into the lushness of France and the sunswept docks of Calais, having lumbered through lowland bogs and dense forests, traversed Rhenish mountains and hills, and swept over the mighty Rhine.

The coaches were most often drawn by a team of four horses, though occasionally my fellow travelers and I found ourselves behind a *unicorn*, a team of three. At such times we moved at a grueling four miles per hour, even on flat terrain. In the steep hills and true mountains, we were often called upon to walk so as to lighten the carriage; during and after heavy rains, the male passengers were not infrequently needed to help the coachmen extricate our vehicle from muddy ruts.

The many thrilling experiences I relished quite compensated for these inconveniences, however, and none more so than approaching a town gate aboard a post-chaise! As the post maintained the right of free passage, the coachman would sound his horn, which alerted the guard to open the gate. Then the coach and its jostling occupants would charge through like cavalry, at full speed toward the next changing station.

One of the last coaches in which I had the pleasure of traveling to Calais was a French diligence pulled by hearty and handsome Norman horses. The conveyance, said to have ample room for twelve, was chock-full of passengers within the coach itself, seated high alongside the driver, and crowded into the rear cabriolet beneath its folding leather hood. Given the mountain of luggage, baskets, bandboxes, and other receptacles loaded on top, our pace was laggard. But the amicable, lively companionship more than compensated for this delay.

These weeks also afforded me welcome opportunities to contemplate how best to approach a reunion with John Taylor, should it come to pass. The contents of his book reinvigorated my ambivalence about the man, from his impressive accomplishments and fierce intelligence to his untrustworthy nature and pernicious vanity. The first few pages were enough to convince me anew of his mighty shortcomings, yet I left none unread.

The frontispiece featured an engraving of the bewigged Chevalier much as I had encountered him: distinguished, handsome, attired in splendid finery, haughty and proud. After claiming to be Ophthalmiater Pontifical, Imperial, and Royal, in the service of "the King of Poland, Denmark, Sweden, the Electors of the holy Empire, the Princes of Saxe-Gotha, Mecklenburg, Anspach, Brunswick, Parme, Modena, Zerbst, Lorraine, Saxony, Hesse, Cassel, Holstein, Salzburg, Baviere, Liege, Bareith and Georgia," Taylor boasted that for some thirty years, his practice had taken him to every "Court, Kingdom, Province, State, City and Town of the least Consideration in all Europe, without exception." Additionally, there were claims that he had authored forty-five works in an array of languages!

One pronouncement in particular stood out: Taylor's concern that his son, the work's dedicatee, would defend his father's honor:

> 'May I not *presume*, that you, my son, will defend your father's cause?—
> May I not *affirm*, that you, my son, will support your father's fame?

I found these lines most peculiar. They suggested that while others might rise to defame the doctor's work and reputation—or perhaps already had—he hoped his son would not be among them.

At the turn of each page, I was obliged to temper my grievances with Taylor's tedious prose, not to mention his tiresome flattery of, and bloated claims of friendship with, a neverending parade of crowned sovereigns, lesser royalty, venerated potentates, and even the pope. I was tempted to toss the volume out the carriage window when I came across his pious hope that the town of Norwich might one day include his birth among its most significant events. In their entirety, his unfailing overstatements about his accomplishments made their veracity seem ever less likely.

For the record, I include the following vainglorious excerpt concerning Taylor's choice to take his medical practice on the road:

> I well knew, that any miscarriage in a settled life would be so fatal to me, that my practice would soon be at an end, and with it, in consequence, all my hopes of improvement, and that I knew no way to avoid this great evil, but by traveling, a design that must expose me to a thousand dangers ... there was no other way but traveling, for me to acquire sufficient practice for improvement; and that, if I inclined to become this way great, by the services I might do mankind hereafter, I must hazard all, and my merit and reward, possibly might prove in proportion to the danger ... The advantages of traveling in a design like mine, considering my education and knowledge in general practice, must be very great; because if at home, I could only hope to imitate my masters, and nothing could I attempt that was new without the greatest risque; for should I miscarry, they would be the first to blame me, and join their voice with the public against me; whereas the scene is changed, by my continual movements from place to place, my hopes of success in my enterprises; I mean with regard to my being supplied with subjects, and consequently with

the power of improvement; would necessarily be kept alive.

With this view behold me, in my native country, flattering myself, that ... one and all will with one voice agree, that what I have done towards the perfection of this admirable and invaluable branch of physic, is well worthy of applause; not forgetting, that the first sovereigns of the world, as well as the most learned bodies now existing, have all in this agreed; that I was born in this age for this great and important undertaking, and that all mankind were convinced, before I left the world, that my labours had not been in vain.

The delights of reading notwithstanding, I was a happy man the day I reached the final page of Taylor's irksome epic.

The weather turned blustery once we crossed into northern France, and when we disembarked in Calais, the Channel appeared unnavigable. A Dover packet ship was scheduled to sail the next morning, but only if conditions were favorable. Thus I secured a room near the docks, not knowing how long the delay might last, and set out on a short excursion about town. In clear weather, I knew the chalky cliffs that beckoned beyond the Strait of Dover were visible to the naked eye, but for the moment I could do little but wonder when I would see them myself.

By the time I wandered back to the *Place d'Armes*, only a few fishmongers were hawking the last of the day's catch, the stalls of tinsmiths and lacemakers having already closed up for the evening. So I strolled about the sixteenth-century citadel before returning to the inn, taking dinner, and retiring.

I woke well before sunrise, surprised to see it had dawned calm. Even though whitecaps skimmed across the strait, I was informed that the ferry would soon set sail. After quickly gathering my belongings, I made haste for the wharf, following the sounds of screeching gulls competing for breakfast and the complaint of overburdened wagons hauling cargo destined for foreign shores.

We were blessed with favorable winds, and once aboard, learned that the crew expected to make landfall by early afternoon. With the lines cast off and the vessel oriented toward open water, I looked behind and watched the steeples of Calais recede beyond our gentle wake.

Chapter 18

When I arrived in Dover, I had been traveling for the better part of three weeks. I had endured sleepless nights, driving rain, biting insects, knee-deep mud, and inept coachmen. But the hours it took to cross the English Channel were the most fraught of all. In less than an hour after setting sail, I felt as if I'd been relieved of everything I had swallowed the previous two days, and it came as little comfort to know that I was not suffering alone. Sprawled on the ship's bow, I attempted to keep my eyes trained on the distant cliffs, but there was little to be done beyond feeling grateful that I was crossing the strait at its narrowest point.

Upon reaching shore, I was helped off the ship and taken to an inn, where I attempted to sleep off the unpleasant effects of seasickness. The night was short, however, for I boarded a basket coach before dawn the next day. My fellow passengers on the way to Charing Cross were smartly dressed Englishfolk returning home from Paris.

However rough I had found the channel, little changed on English soil. The coach system to London was exceptionally well run, but constant traffic along the Dover road left it deeply rutted and marred by potholes, making for bone-crushing travel. Not infrequently, I was hurtled into the passenger seated next to me, or he into me, whether we were seated aloft in the cabriolet or inside the carriage.

I found little relief at the changing stations and inns, where we paused for refreshment en route. The first was Canterbury's Red Lion, where I ate almost no breakfast, as my stomach remained unsettled from both the previous day's crossing and the morning's ride. Notwithstanding my discomfort, our driver remained confident we would make London by suppertime. Indeed, at dusk, we could detect the glow of foundry fires and the stench of tanneries on the outskirts and knew we were fast approaching something far more significant than a mere village or hamlet.

As promised, the Dover coach pulled into Charing Cross at nightfall. The team trotted past a bronze equestrian statue of the ill-fated Charles I, whose silhouette I could just make out in the darkness, before striding under an archway and into the courtyard of the Golden Cross Inn. I disembarked gingerly on wobbly legs, crossed the courtyard, and secured lodging. With my luggage brought up behind me, I made straight for my room, desiring nothing but a motionless bed in which to recover.

I immediately fell into a deep sleep. It was not until the following afternoon that I awoke, my appetite having suddenly returned, demanding to be sated. With some effort, I raised myself from bed and procured a meal at the inn, then returned directly to my room, where I slept undisturbed until the following morning. This time I awoke to the sounds of horse-drawn carts and the shouts of workers, some in languages I did not recognize. Upon gaining my senses and whereabouts, I dressed and inquired about directions to Brook Street, Handel's former residence.

The darkness shrouding my arrival in Charing Cross two nights earlier had afforded me little appreciation of London's vastness. But as I threaded my way northwest, through the

Haymarket and toward Hanover Square, I encountered an uninterrupted series of building projects that appeared to spread to the horizon. Upon reaching 25 Brook Street, I stood and rang, assuming that visitors to such a handsome house, three stories in height, would be greeted by a doorman. The heavy oak door soon swung open to reveal before me in the transom a jovial-looking fellow, well-dressed, about shoulder height to me, with fluffs of gray curls ringing an otherwise hairless head.

"Pardon me. I am here to see Mr. Duburk … if that is possible?" I asked haltingly, hoping my conspicuous German pronunciation wouldn't compromise my chances.

"If your accent is any indication," the man responded good-humoredly, "you've traveled a long way to find him, and found him you have! What might I do for you, my good man?"

I remained confused, having expected to be greeted by a servant.

"I beg your pardon," I responded. "Are you Mr. John Duburk?"

"Indeed I am! And you are …?"

I promptly reached into my breast pocket, withdrew my letter of introduction from Johanna Floercke, and passed it to him. After quickly reading over the document, he muttered the name of the signature several times, evidently trying to remember why it seemed familiar.

"Ah! My late master's niece. Has she sent you?"

"Not quite," I replied. "I have come to London for personal reasons, but I met Frau Floercke at the start of my journey. She was of the opinion that I should make your acquaintance. As my recent days of travel were rather punishing, I immediately took to bed in Charing Cross. At any rate, Frau Floercke would be glad to know that I have finally made it here in good time and health," I said, glancing down at my legs. Only now did

I realize how fatigued they were, as until this morning I had used them relatively little since my departure from Leipzig.

"Herr … excuse me … Mr. Duburk, I must beg pardon for my English."

"It is I who should apologize," Duburk responded, "for keeping you on the doorstep after traveling such a great distance! Please," he said, beckoning me inside and leading me to the anteroom.

"For years, I worked in the stewardship of my master, so after his passing, it did not seem right that I should be so served in return. Thus, I live alone. This was the cause of your confusion at the door and for that, I beg your pardon. Am I speaking too quickly?"

"Perhaps only a little," I answered. "I trust my English will improve in due time. But if you wouldn't mind speaking just a bit more slowly, I think it will benefit us both."

"Capital that you are here in London, Mr. Barth," Duburk said, now slowly *and* at noticeably greater volume, a reaction to my labored English that would prove typical during my stay. "But before you tell me why you are here, might I offer you some refreshment? I am familiar with the trip from Dover and am only too aware of how excruciating it can be. Even in the best of weather, most of my acquaintances would say they should prefer the instruments of torture in the Tower of London," he added with a hearty laugh.

When I acknowledged that some repast would be most welcome, my host eagerly showed me to the next room and bid me to be seated at the elaborately carved oak table. He spread out a linen pulled from the nearby sideboard, then quickly lay two place settings.

"I was just in the act of preparing a meal for myself when you rang. I am delighted to break bread with a guest from abroad. I'll only be a moment."

Duburk promptly excused himself. He returned a short time later with a tray of meat pies, two bowls of broth, and bread rolls, then drew two beautifully stemmed silver cups from a majestic corner cabinet. These he filled with pale, fragrant wine.

"The wine is an English specialty," he said with pride. "It was produced from birch tree sap this past March and is only now truly ready to drink. Some believe it prevents baldness but I am left to question its efficacy, given that I've drunk my share over the years!" he exclaimed, tapping his pate.

Raising his cup, Duburk continued, "To the health and long life of His Majesty, King George, and your arrival in our country, Mr. Barth! May it prove a prosperous visit. Now, what brings you to London?"

By now, I had taken several bites of the fare and a few generous sips of wine and felt more settled. As Duburk had proven most gracious and welcoming, I proceeded to impart my oft-told story.

"As a student in Leipzig, I served Sebastian Bach, a composer and contemporary of your master, Handel. As it so happened, Bach lived and worked not so far from Handel's birthplace in Halle. As my master had become nearly blind, he sought the services of an oculist who had recently arrived in our town. The surgeon, a man named John Taylor, would also tend to Handel at a later date, at least according to his memoir.

"Taylor also claimed, on more than one occasion, to have restored my master's eyesight. This was an absolute fabrication. The fact is, Bach died shortly thereafter, a consequence of the surgeon's ineptitude. To be clear, the matter is far more complicated and I have carried the weight of these events, which transpired over a decade ago, with me ever since. Thus, I have traveled to London hoping to confront the oculist and put my mind at ease. That is, assuming Taylor is still alive."

Duburk sat in silence, contemplating what I had told him. After an ample sip of wine, which he savored, he responded.

"That's quite an undertaking, Mr. Barth, and I admire your persistence on behalf of your late master. As you know, I too served a composer, and a great one at that. As for Taylor, yes, I am familiar with the man and his dubious reputation. Whether he still lives, I cannot say, but I can point you in the direction of someone who most likely can. His son and namesake is an oculist as well. He is known to be a compassionate soul with a professional reputation beyond reproach. And his place of business is not far from Brook Street."

We continued to speak at some length about our masters, men linked by music, country, and language, yet who led such disparate lives. I learned that Handel often held rehearsals in the very room where we were seated, and following our meal, Duburk led me on a tour of the house, showing me his master's study in the adjacent room and the bedrooms on the floor above.

"Toward the end of Handel's life, I occupied the garret," Duburk said, pointing overhead. "Formerly, the quarters belonged to my uncle, Peter le Blond, and it was to him that this house was initially willed, but with my uncle's death, Mr. Handel kindly altered his instructions. I should add that these walls were once hung with lovely artwork, including paintings by Poussin and Watteau, for my master was a discerning collector. Alas, the great pieces have been sold off, save for the few lesser works I could afford to keep."

We returned to the front of the house, where my host wanted to share something more.

"In light of your quest, Mr. Barth, I believe you will find this quite interesting." I followed Duburk to a handsome, waist-high walnut chest, where he withdrew a sizeable stack of papers from one of the deep drawers. These he placed on top.

"These are largely notices and reviews of Handel performances I collected over the years, but a few other curiosities concern your Dr. Taylor. To my knowledge, Taylor regarded Handel's eyes as untreatable, though that determination was made long before I came into his employ. What is certain is that Handel had lost his eyesight, or at least most of it, long before Taylor saw him south of London. Some said that it may have been a consequence of a stroke suffered years earlier, which for a period caused Mr. Handel some paralysis in his right arm. Others claimed that his eyesight was an indirect result of a horrible carriage accident he suffered on returning home from his birthplace in Halle.

"Whatever the case, I believe Doctor Bromfield was the first to operate on Mr. Handel. Years later, by which time Handel had become quite desperate, he sought out John Taylor, though what came of that visit I cannot say. What I *can* say, however, is that Taylor possessed a dubious reputation."

Duburk turned to a page containing what appeared to be lines of verse.

"As you must know," he said, passing the page to me, "Taylor's appearances were often preceded by fantastic proclamations. This anonymous poem was published in the *London Chronicle*, near the period when Taylor saw Handel, in Tunbridge Wells, some thirty miles south of here. Even for me, one whose native tongue is English, the prosaic language is difficult to understand. Still, the essence is of Euterpe—the muse who presides over music—urging Apollo and Aesculapius to help cure Handel of his blindness. However, Apollo says there is no need to intervene, for Taylor will be the one to cure him. Given that no less than the Greek gods are portending Taylor's talents, I wonder if Taylor himself was not the poem's author!"

Duburk thumbed through the pile and showed me various other cuttings.

"Here's another poem, entitled *An Epistle to a Young Student at Cambridge, with the Characters of the Three Great Quacks, M..p, T..1.r, and W..d*. This one was published in 1737, so it's comparatively old. Still, Taylor's reputation as a charlatan—obviously, he is the '*T..1.r*'—appears to have been well established by this point, along with that of a Mrs.

Mapp—'*M..p*'—another notorious fraud, known to some as 'Crazy Sally,' and a Mr. Ward, or '*W..d*.'"

As the poem went on for pages, Duburk drew my attention to the lines referencing Taylor's misdeeds:

> *Come up to Town, then, Harry, leave the School,*
> *Your gilded Coach shall be upheld by Fools.*
> *Pall-Mall be thy Abode, or Grov'nor-Square,*
> *An ample Crop of Fools you'll harvest there.*
> *But This, you say, 's against the plainest Sense,*
> *The more is due to glorious IMPUDENCE.*
> *T..l.r and M.pp too here her Reign exalt,*
> *And to her Foot-stool lead the Blind and Halt.*
> *T..l..r, with Learning, wise as any Grandam,*
> *Brushes away, and ventures all at Random.*
> *With Lady's Hand,' and Play-Things bright and keen,*
> *Can Cataracts remove, and Drop serene*
> *He to the Poor, most charitably kind*
> *Can, if they want a Trade, soon make them blind.*

"I don't know when Taylor was born," Duburk went on, "but given the year of this poetry, he must have acquired his suspicious reputation early on. The verses were likely inspired by this engraving of Hogarth from a year earlier," he explained, extracting yet another page and pointing to the three figures at the top of the illustration. "These are our three humbugs. Taylor is on the far left, winking mischievously and holding a walking stick with an eye on its grip."

Staring at this brazen depiction, I felt no small amount of vindication. In light of the poems and this scathing caricature, I also took great comfort in knowing that my long-held misgivings about the Chevalier were, in fact, widely held beliefs!

"And what about his son?" I inquired.

"Ah, yes." Duburk returned the documents to the chest. "From what little I understand, the junior John is far more modest, sympathetic, and charitable than his father ever was. He is known to care for the indigent, which sheds light on his character. He works in Hatton-Garden, east of here and northeast of Charing Cross. With a few inquiries, you will undoubtedly find him with little difficulty."

I stood and thanked my host warmly for feeding me and sharing his knowledge of Taylor. As we walked to the door, he stopped and asked if I might like to attend a concert of Handel's music.

"Tomorrow night, the Royal Opera is giving a semi-staged performance of *Samson,* one of Handel's greatest oratorios. By all accounts, it is a notably dramatic work, though regrettably, I have never had the pleasure of experiencing it myself. I had arranged to take a lady friend, but she is indisposed, so it would be my pleasure to offer you her seat."

I replied that, although it would be my honor to attend, I had traveled with limited attire and feared I had brought nothing suitable for such an occasion.

"Mr. Barth, my late uncle was a man more or less your size and some of his garments still hang upstairs, in the garret. Why don't we have a look?"

We ascended, once more coercing my aching legs, where we promptly found a reasonably well-fitting waistcoat, dress coat, and breeches.

"Capital!" Duburk exclaimed after I donned the ensemble. "That will do splendidly, especially with a silk cravat! Why, it may as well have been tailored for you! And I'm delighted at the prospect of sharing your company tomorrow evening! It will be my honor to introduce you to London's exhilarating cultural life."

Having established that I would return to Brook Street a few hours before the performance, my host bade me a successful visit with the younger Taylor and hoped I would encounter little trouble locating him. I thanked him yet again and departed in the direction whence I had come. Then, thinking better of it, and with ample time, I decided to take a series of detours.

With renewed vigor, I walked the length of the Pall Mall, browsing several shops and reflecting on the verses Duburk had shown me. Thence, I continued to Buckingham Palace and Westminster Chapel. At the Palace of Westminster, I could not help but imagine my friend Josef, seated at a long table surrounded by Frederick's representatives and English lords, the assembly seeking a way forward after the war.

Later, after walking north and enjoying a meal at a chophouse along the Strand, I returned to my bed in Charing Cross, exhausted. And in the minutes before sleep, I leafed through John Taylor's book once more, as I envisioned my possible encounter with the son on the morrow.

Chapter 19

As Duburk predicted, the Chevalier's son was easily enough found. An innkeeper in Charterhouse Street directed me to a modest residence nearby, where a shingle above the door advertised *John Taylor, Oculist*. The fine mist that had met me when I stepped out of the Golden Cross Inn late that morning accompanied me to Hatton-Garden, so the warmth and serenity of Taylor's practice and residence that afternoon were most welcome.

I was shown to the downstairs waiting room, where I was asked to remain until the doctor concluded his present appointment. Soon, Dr. Taylor entered and introduced himself. Apologizing for my English, I haltingly delivered my well-rehearsed lines about meeting his father years earlier, when he operated on the celebrated German organist and composer Sebastian Bach. At the mention of Bach's name, I sensed a hint of recognition in Taylor's expression.

"I hope to confer with your father, the Chevalier," I said pointedly. Grasping the nature of my visit, Taylor kindly asked if I wouldn't mind waiting another hour or so until his last patient of the day had departed, "so we shall be able to speak at leisure." I quickly agreed.

In due time, Taylor returned and invited me upstairs to his examination room. I immediately recognized a high-back chair similar to the one I had helped move into Bach's study almost two decades earlier. This model, however, was noticeably free of adornments. Nearby, various medical instruments lay on a table. Charts of the human eye's anatomy hung from the far wall, and beneath these, dozens of medical books and journals crowded the shelves of a substantial walnut bookcase. Taylor offered me a seat and took his place behind a handsome, yet simple, oak desk, upon which several medical books lay open. My attention was momentarily drawn to a diagram of eye muscles, partly illuminated by the gray mid-afternoon light, when my host politely inquired about my memories of his father.

Looking closely at this John Taylor for the first time, I noted how much he resembled the man I encountered years earlier. Father and son shared the same prominent nose and upturned lips, but the younger man's modest vestments and unaffected demeanor offered a stark contrast. Moreover, he immediately put me at ease by showing sincere interest in learning more about my experience with his father. And it soon became evident that this encounter would be very different from the one I had long imagined between myself and the Chevalier.

Although not fully disarmed by Taylor's genuine curiosity and gracious manner, I nonetheless decided to speak openly about my mission to confront his father about the botched surgery that led to my master's death. To my relief, the Chevalier's son sat quietly and patiently, encouraging me. For the next quarter hour, I recounted my memories of the eminent oculist and that fateful operation, shying away from none of the worrisome episodes that had haunted me since, such as his evident dependency on opiates, all the while trying not to come across as disrespectful.

Finally, I communicated my own desperate need to find peace of mind and my belief that confronting the oculist would bring about that end. "Despite my suspicions throughout the procedure that your father appeared unfit to operate, I failed to act. I continued to assist him and consented to all his instructions, to the detriment of my late master."

John Taylor, who had sat motionless thus far, now appeared visibly distressed. After a moment, he nodded faintly.

"Herr Barth, what you have related saddens me more than I can say, but unfortunately, it is not a surprise. I would like to help you in your search, for my father may still live. I have, at least, received no news to the contrary."

My stomach tightened as I realized my hope for a rendezvous with the Chevalier remained alive. Concealing my tension, I held my silence. "My father is a deeply complicated man," Taylor continued. "I am confident he was meant to be a great surgeon, and perhaps, when he was at his best, he was indeed that. But in all impartiality, he was destined to fail. My father was born with a silver spoon in his mouth, as they say in Scotland. His father was a surgeon and his mother an apothecary; thus, he came of age in a world of medicine.

"But my grandfather was something of a conjurer. Perhaps because of his education and dignified appearance, rare attributes in and around their town of Norwich, he developed something of a mythical reputation. The townsfolk thought he could do no wrong; thus he was sought not only for his medical expertise but also to comfort mourners and the downtrodden.

"I don't mean to suggest that my father inherited—or exploited—all of his own father's traits. But at the very least, I believe the seeds of my father's brazen confidence and sense of infallibility were sown in his youth. I might even venture that his predilection for extravagant dress is a legacy of my grandfather's penchant for showmanship.

"As for our relationship, he was not harsh; I received no beatings. But neither was he a good provider. Never did he send home funds from the fees he earned during his prolonged absences, so the responsibility of supporting my mother fell to me at a young age. I can also tell you that many press reports have defamed him over the years. His transgressions have been exposed, sometimes luridly, from here to Berlin—running from bail, a fugitive beyond the seas, abandoning his family in distress, and so forth. But most damning are foreign reports suggesting my father blinded many by way of his negligence."

Taylor's son maintained that his father had once been a man of great integrity and had the best intentions. Before his hubris got the better of him, he made significant contributions to his profession. Then, as the father's medical failures began outnumbering his successes, the son believed he chose an itinerant lifestyle to dodge the myriad conflicts arising in the town where he was living and attempting to practice. Whether the medical community was jealous, critical, or skeptical of his abilities, the younger man could not say, but in the end, his father thought better than to remain in one place.

The oculist soon found that a traveling practice was also far more lucrative than permanency, for it brought an endless parade of patients and a constant shower of compelling financial rewards, especially from the nobility. Eventually, his father's prosperity led him to crave a living beyond his means.

"He appreciated fine spirits, fashionable attire, and beautiful women, and undoubtedly, many other outlays, such as conveyance and entourage, also required significant and steady income. It all proved unsustainable. As to your suspicions,

Herr Barth, of my father's addiction to laudanum, of this I was unaware. But given his other tendencies, such an addiction seems a possibility."

I related that his father had no surgical assistant when he visited Leipzig. Hence, I had been recruited.

"I imagine that by the time he arrived in Leipzig, my father could no longer afford to keep such a man on his payroll," Taylor observed. "The fact is, he ran into debt early on and only managed to stay a step ahead of creditors by constant travel. Of course, moving about conferred another advantage. By fleeing each town, he never had to answer for bungled results, as you tragically experienced.

"I do not for one moment mean to imply that my father appeared at the gate of each town or city with the *intent* to defraud or injure. I'm certain that his medical aspirations were sound, even if his performance was not. His abilities may have become compromised, in other words, but I don't believe he was malicious. Because his debts were mounting, he must have started to put his interests before those of his patients. I suspect this was the reason he wrote his last book. He must have anticipated significant returns from the sales, although I could not say whether such hopes were realized."

I mentioned that his father's memoir had accompanied me from Leipzig and that I had found the dedication somewhat curious.

"Yes, that is indeed a curiosity," Taylor responded. "Beyond the need to right his finances, the book was also my father's last attempt to prove himself and his worth to the world.

If you read it, you have likely become equally enlightened about his love of medicine, vanity, and his need for approbation. And as you say, it was also a means of attempting to reconcile with me.

"Frankly, Herr Barth, I struggle with my father's legacy. Who can predict how one will be remembered? If nothing else, the story of his life is a warning bell for me," Taylor confessed, gesturing at his humble surroundings. "Thus have I chosen to remain in one place and avail myself to all, even those who lack the means to pay.

"Well," he continued, "I hope you have gained an understanding of the chasm between my father and me. I am grieved to hear of his failings regarding your master, Sebastian Bach. Nevertheless, such experiences are in keeping with what appears to have led my father to his present state of absolution."

"Absolution?" I repeated, unsure that I had heard correctly.

"An hour ago you and I were strangers," he replied. "But as we have each unburdened ourselves, I can tell you, in full confidence, that from what I understand, my father is living in a Bohemian monastery. I do not know more, for it has been nearly a decade since I have seen him. The last time was when he was in London to see his book through to publication, and we had a *contretemps* ...much on account of the issues you and I have discussed.

"I should also say that the years had taken a discernible toll on my father's health. The robust man I once knew appeared old and listless, and he complained of his eyes, among a host of other ills. He would now be well over 60 years of age, so assuming he's alive, I should think time—in your case—is of the essence.

"My father will need to learn the truth about your master's fate if he is to be truly absolved of his deeds. For this reason, I have shared with you what I know of his whereabouts, but finding my father, even among a finite number of monasteries, may be akin to searching for a needle in a bundle of hay. Should you be so fortunate as to locate him, I ask that you remember he is attempting to make peace with his past by taking vows. While your story would ideally add a certain urgency to this objective, it should not undermine it. Please, Herr Barth, I beg of you—tread cautiously!"

I acknowledged his concerns and expressed my gratitude for his candor. "Dr. Taylor, having studied theology at university, I fully understand and appreciate the solemnity of your father's vows. Should I find him, I promise to treat our encounter with the utmost dignity."

Taylor stood, and we shook hands. "Herr Barth, you have undertaken an ambitious, if not impassioned, quest in the memory of your late master, which speaks volumes about your character. I regret you had to travel so far only to come up empty-handed."

"To the contrary, Dr. Taylor," I responded, "I have no regrets. And if I fail to locate your father, my journey will nevertheless have been worth the effort."

I thanked the good doctor again as he held the door open to the street and wished me luck in my pursuit. Stepping outside, I was again met by a steady mist and London's frenetic pulse.

My arrival at Brook Street was expected this time, and after making ready for the evening, John Duburk and I started for Covent Garden. As we walked, I only briefly remarked on my meeting with John Taylor, as Duburk was eager to point out various sights and play the role of guide. We walked to Drury Lane and then along the Strand, where Duburk noted the hapless preponderance of vagrants and the endemic prostitution. He explained that the streetwalkers plied their trade according to their backgrounds and location. For instance, some appealed to the ignoble class around Moll King's Coffee House. At the same time, the more smartly dressed "spells," as he called them, milled about the theaters and the opera house to lure affluent clients during the pause or after the conclusion of performances.

By the time we arrived at Bedford Street and St. Paul's Cathedral, Duburk's narrative had shifted to the significance of the Covent Garden Opera House, including Handel's long association with this venerated institution. I might as well have crossed an entire ocean by the time we traded the mud and poverty of the marketplace for the brilliantly lit, three-tiered Royal Opera.

As I strode the spacious foyer, I was instantly absorbed in this new world of brilliant music, glorious costumes, and thrilling drama. Handel's *Samson* played to a full house of a thousand spectators who packed into all available spaces, from the horseshoe-shaped pit to the tiers of boxes along the length of the theater and the gallery far above where no seats were provided.

Duburk had secured a pair of seats in the third tier from which we had a splendid view of the entire place. I was startled to discover that the clamor filling the theater upon our arrival did not cease with the stately opening strains of the overture. In actuality, two sets of entertainments played out simultaneously under the Covent Garden roof: the drama unfolding upon the stage and that of the audience members, whose boisterous banter competed with Handel's hunting horns. Indeed, many in attendance caroused until the final curtain—playing cards, calling out to friends, or whistling for sweetmeats from beleaguered stewards.

Many in the audience hushed only at the start of an aria, but Handel's brilliant "Let the Bright Seraphim," sung just before the closing chorus, elicited a thunderous ovation. The most stirring singing of the evening, however, occurred with Samson's first act air, "Total Eclipse." The moment was particularly poignant, as I knew Handel himself was blind by the time he crafted the blighted Nazirite's lines. I was twice brought to tears, first during the lament,

> *O loss of sight, of thee I most complain!*
> *Oh, worse than beggary, old age, or chains!*
> *My very soul in real darkness dwells!*

and then again during the aria itself, as Samson pitiably bewails his loss:

> *Total eclipse! No sun, no moon!*
> *All dark amidst the blaze of noon!*
> *Oh, glorious light! No cheering ray*
> *To glad my eyes with welcome day!*
> *Why thus depriv'd Thy prime decree?*
> *Sun, moon, and stars are dark to me!*

My fragile emotions during the aria naturally reflected my memories of Bach and one instance in particular. As I accompanied my master home from a cantata performance one morning, he spoke about his inspirations, Handel among them. His death several months later was probably around the time of Handel's carriage accident. Both men shared a similar destiny, except that Handel lived with his blindness for years, with considerable time to bemoan his bleak circumstances. As I listened to the heartrending aria, I wondered which composer's fate had been the more tragic.

Duburk and I parted after enjoying a draught at a nearby pub. The good fortune of finding him was no less than a godsend, and I told him as much. I added that I would be only too honored to return the favor, should he ever find himself in my corner of the world.

Upon awakening the next morning, I lay in bed contemplating all that had transpired. The man I had traveled so far to meet was, alas, not in London but possibly much closer to home. This thought fueled my urgency to reverse course at the earliest opportunity.

As the next packet ship bound for Calais would not depart for two more days, I spent my remaining hours in this grand city browsing its stalls, tasting its ale, and marveling at its sites. When it was time to embark upon the first leg of my return, I dropped into my seat on the Dover coach, sensing that I was now in an urgent race against time. What were the chances, I wondered, of finding the oculist before my funds were depleted or he vanished forever?

Chapter 20

Leipzig struck me as smaller than I remembered. The immensity of London, coupled with my peregrinations over so much land and water, compelled me to reconsider the place I had long called home. But not long after my return, I realized the change had little to do with size; the city had simply come to hold less for me. Friends and family had moved on or died, and my memories of the streets and shops now seemed strangely detached. The weight of the gray skies and the sense that the medieval walls were pressing inward validated what Dafir had foretold during the Michaelmas fair: my future lay elsewhere.

The return trip had not been without incident. Several days out of Calais, our coach was suddenly driven off the post road by a pair of highwaymen. The other passengers and I were forced to disembark from the coach one by one as our assailants demanded jewelry and money, threatening whoever failed to cooperate. Our trunks were thrown down, and their contents plundered for anything remotely worthy. But as the brigands had only the horses they were riding and a few bags in which to stash their pillage, they soon retreated.

Fortunately, in their haste, the bandits had overlooked the false bottom of my trunk, which had been resewn before I departed London. Had they discovered my funds, my travels might have been imperiled beyond recovery. Once safely at home, I considered my finances and concluded that if I lived modestly, my assets could sustain me for another month.

For the next several days, I threw myself into Bach's suites, practicing for hours at a time. At night I would visit the city's coffeehouses, renewing my love of chess and reading the papers. While charting my next course, I soon learned that Emperor Joseph II of Austria, whose enlightened views didn't square with contemplative religious life, had suppressed his empire's unproductive monasteries and sold off much of their lands. The institutions that survived his edicts did so because they provided needed services.

For me, these reforms signaled one of two possibilities: either Taylor would be found with less difficulty, for I would have fewer cloisters to scour, or he had already been expelled from under whatever roof he had taken refuge, in which case he might be all but impossible to locate. I dearly hoped it would be the former.

I set out for Bohemia in November. Nearly two months earlier, I had scheduled my journey to England while taking care to avoid hazardous weather. Now I was anxious to continue my quest, however threatening the skies. I traveled lightly, with most of my money again sewn into the bottom of my trunk. At the last moment, I decided to include the autograph of Bach's cello suites among my effects. A musical symbol of my late master, and the only actual music of his that I possessed, it represented my enduring bond to Bach. Assuming I located Taylor, perhaps tangible evidence would help alter the oculist's understanding of the magnitude of my master's life and allow him to finally accept the truth about his untimely death.

A light snowfall began within a few hours of my departure from Leipzig. But the roads remained dry and hard, which made travel reasonably swift, if cold. The route took me to Dresden and then southeast, deep into the forests of Bohemia. At each changing station, I inquired about the local monasteries and was informed that all those in the north had been shuttered. It was suggested that I proceed to the Strahov Monastery of Prague, among the few such institutions still functioning.

After some three days of travel, the coach rumbled to a stop before Prague's northern gate. To the west rose the spires of the medieval castle. To the south, pedestrian traffic moved across the Charles Bridge, with the city's terracotta roofs visible just beyond. After examining the papers of each passenger, a guard waved us on. The horses clopped through a series of rutted, labyrinthine alleys before swinging into Hradčanské Square a few hours past noon. I disembarked, was directed to a modest guest house near St. Nikolaus Church, and comfortably settled in. Before taking a long-awaited rest, I sent a message to the Strahov abbot, stating my name and present location and asking for any information about the Chevalier John Taylor.

Not long thereafter, I was awakened from a deep sleep by repeated knocking. A postboy stood at the door with a small envelope, the reverse of which was sealed with a crimson wax stamp bearing the initials WM. I hastily broke open the seal and read the following:

> *The estimable Herr Barth-*
> *Concerning your inquiry, Brother John*
> *Taylor is indeed a resident of our abbey.*
> *Before informing him of your presence,*
> *however, I must first ascertain the grounds*
> *for your visit.*

Please announce yourself upon arrival, whereupon you will be directed to my study forthwith.
  Servus Christi,
  Wenceslaus Mayer
  Abbot, Cloister Strahovský

As I had anticipated an exhaustive search with a frustrating series of dead ends, I stared at the message in disbelief. Here was the oculist, but a short distance by foot from where I now stood!

Realizing that the postboy was still outside the door, waiting patiently, I apologized and tipped him generously. I then hastened to dress and set off for the monastery. My long-awaited *rendezvous* with the man who had haunted my thoughts for nearly two decades appeared imminent.

Just beyond the last of New Town's snow-dusted streets, a timeworn path led me beyond dormant fields toward the monastery, a complex of interlaced buildings whose twin spires rose toward the irritable Bohemian sky. On the Strahov grounds, cassocked monks swept silently by, some heading away from the monastery toward nearby gardens, others moving in my direction. I had not yet reached the inner courtyard before I was met by a prior, who easily recognized me as a stranger to this place. Upon showing him Abbot Meyer's message, I was promptly shepherded inside.

We traversed a series of dark, noiseless hallways until we came to a pair of ornate doors, one of which stood open to reveal a cloaked figure seated at a table, absorbed in study. The prior knocked lightly against the open door and gestured I was to enter. The man who rose from his chair and turned toward me was perhaps a head shorter than I, with striking blue eyes and white hair that encircled his head just below his tonsure. He appeared both friendly and serene as he beckoned me inside.

From the large window at his back, gray light filtered into the room, illuminating a large wooden cross on one wall. A mural of St. Augustine, gazing heavenward with a book in one hand and quill in the other, was displayed on an adjacent wall. Although engulfed in shadow, the rendering of the venerated saint within a patch of rich golden sunlight caught my attention. The room also contained a pair of solid bookcases whose shelves labored under the weight of liturgical tomes.

"Welcome. I am Wenceslaus Mayer, Abbot of Strahov. I presume you are Herr Barth, whose message indicated you were searching for Brother Taylor?" I nodded as the abbot moved to a row of unadorned wooden chairs and drew one to his desk. This I took as my invitation to be seated. From his own chair, the abbot then asked how far I had traveled and the nature of my relationship with Brother Taylor.

"I am from Leipzig and am no relation to the man you call Brother Taylor. But I recently traveled to London in search of him, and there I had the good fortune of sharing time with his son." I added that it had been many years since Brother Taylor and I had crossed paths and that it was entirely possible he would not remember me.

"Father Wenceslaus, I served in Leipzig as an apprentice to composer and cantor Sebastian Bach. He was a surgical patient of Brother Taylor, who in those days practiced medicine. It is my belief that Bach died as a consequence of that operation."

I then inquired how long Brother Taylor had called the monastery home.

"He came to us perhaps a year ago," the abbot answered, "from a small abbey to the north shut down by the emperor. Strahov is one of the few such institutions in the region that remains functional. We thrive because our farm feeds the local parishes, and members of our flock are educators. Nor does it hurt that we also have a brewery," he added with a raised eyebrow.

"And what of John Taylor?" I asked.

"We offer shelter to many souls who have no other place to call home. Brother Taylor's knowledge of languages initially proved highly beneficial to our pedagogical needs. But not long after his arrival, his health began to deteriorate such that he could no longer teach. He is in pain, and his eyesight is failing. From what I understand, he was once a formidable oculist, so his condition seems both sad and ironic. Please understand: however you might recall him, he will appear much changed. That is, should he be willing to meet you."

Abbot Mayer now rose to shut the door. "Herr Barth," he said, returning to his desk, "visitors to Strahov are rare, and in such circumstances, we are compelled to safeguard our brethren. Some have come here because of a spiritual calling or awakening. They spend their time praying, meditating, and doing good work. Others have led lives for which they seek atonement. Their path to redemption is arguably the more strenuous, and your John Taylor has trodden one of these."

I acknowledged the abbot's concerns and added that I had not come to interfere with the life Taylor had chosen. "I do not know how much the Chevalier—pardon me, Brother Taylor—has shared with you about his past, but I have reason to believe that my experience with him was not uncommon. To be candid, when I knew him, he was unfit to operate on anyone. I am certain there was a time when Dr. Taylor helped many people, but I have learned that he may have harmed many more.

In the case of my late master, whom I regard as one of the great musicians of his day, his health was sound before his encounter with Taylor, and I believe the surgeon's hand hastened his death. If I may, I believe that in his quest for atonement, Taylor must acknowledge what transpired in Leipzig—a truth he has long suppressed."

The abbot sat silently for a moment, his expression bearing both sympathy and deep concern. "Herr Barth, I have served this monastery long enough to become a seasoned judge of character. That you have carried these travails with you for so many years and traversed long distances seeking answers speaks to both your passion and compassion, and I believe your words have great merit. Therefore, for Brother Taylor's benefit and your own, I shall encourage him to see you. Ultimately, however, the decision rests entirely with him."

My host then stood and courteously ushered me toward the door. "Herr Barth, it will soon be time for vespers. I shall approach Brother Taylor later this evening and send word about his decision. In the meantime, should you desire, you may join us in prayer."

I told the abbot I would very much like to attend the service. As we left his office, he placed his arm on mine.

"You said you were apprenticed to a cantor. Do you play or sing?"

"I am a cellist by training, but I was also a choirboy for years in Leipzig, so I am naturally familiar with the liturgy. I must admit, however, that it has been far too long."

"No matter," the abbot replied, tapping my arm gently. "It will be an honor to have you with us. Perhaps you'd like to explore the loft before the service begins? It has been quite some time since instrumental music has resounded within the basilica walls, but a few instruments have remained there. They might be of interest."

I took the abbot's suggestion and headed down the long corridor, carrying the candle he handed me. The sanctuary had yet to be lit for vespers, so after passing rows of pews I carefully climbed the steps to the loft with only the flicker of my candle to light the way. Upon cresting the top step, my eyes spied the outlines of several instruments, which, startlingly, lay scattered like victims of a violent storm. A violin was perched to my left, with but a single string, and just beyond, a scroll-less viola lay on its belly. Peering further into the shadows, I caught sight of a cello. I lifted it and was relieved that it appeared to be in playable condition, unlike its wounded comrades.

I held the candle close to one of the cello's exquisitely carved f-holes and peered through the other, searching for a label. I could just barely make out the following inscription glued to the inside back of the instrument:

Johannes Udalricus Eberle
Praha
Anno 1749

I set the cello gently down and turned to its closest neighbor, a violin of similar attributes. Its inner label also read Eberle, Praha, though dated several years earlier. I then returned to the viola, its lonesome scroll separated from its body, as if beheaded. Again, Eberle.

Even in the dim light, I noted that each of these instruments bore similar features, suggesting the work of the same hand. Whether Eberle had built them alone or with apprentices, I concluded that all had been created here in Prague as an instrumental family, probably commissioned by the church in which

I now stood. Standing in their midst, I could not help but wonder how they might have sounded when played together.

I was about to continue my examination of the loft when my attention was drawn to a murmur of voices below and the movement of shadows on the basilica walls. Vespers would soon begin.

I had slept neither well nor enough for days, so upon returning to my room after prayers, I collapsed onto my bed and fell into a profound slumber. In the morning, I awoke refreshed, hoping to find a note concerning John Taylor. Seeing none, I decided to tour Prague's Old Town. I crossed the Moldau by way of the Charles Bridge, and at the edge of what I soon learned was the Jewish Quarter, unexpectedly encountered waves of Jews dressed in splendid black frock coats and hats. It occurred to me that this was Saturday, their Sabbath.

Other than during fair season, I had rarely seen Jews in Leipzig until recently, when a small band of merchants and their families had taken up residence. But here, Jewish sons, alongside their bearded fathers and grandfathers, were spilling out into the streets, striding toward the medieval *Altneuschul*, their house of worship.

I soon found myself at the Old Town Hall. After gazing at its remarkable astronomical clock, I wandered through a labyrinth of narrow, winding streets. At the far end of an alley, I happened upon a quaint storefront with the outline of a violin etched into the wooden door. I knocked, hoping to learn more about the maker of the instruments I had discovered the previous evening. Peering through the leadlight, I searched for movement, but seeing none I continued on.

I then wove my way back to the inn, where I found a note under the door of my room. John Taylor would meet me in the monastery library this day, following the noontime meal. I had no idea what he had been told or what, if anything, he expected. But at long last, we were to reunite.

That afternoon, I noticed the instrument for the first time.

Having arrived at the church during the abbey's noon repast, I returned to the sanctuary loft to continue my exploration. The natural light now penetrating the basilica's leaded windows allowed me to move about with greater ease. Soon enough, I happened upon a long-forgotten cello.

It lay solitary on its back and against the wall. I inched toward it, my eyes carefully scanning the instrument from bottom to top as I assessed its lamentable state. The cello possessed neither bridge nor fingerboard and when I lifted it from the floor, I spotted a crack from the bottom of the belly halfway up the front. My gaze moved farther up and came to rest on the peg box. And in that instant, I beheld its most conspicuous feature: the cello was fitted with not four but *five* pegs!

I had thought, at times, that such an instrument could not exist, yet here was one before my very eyes. Immediately, I was overcome by thoughts of Bach's Sixth Suite, the only one I had yet to undertake, though my enthusiasm was tempered by this instrument's disrepair. Upon further study, I realized it was smaller than the cello I had purchased from Anna Magdalena and possessed a neck wide enough to accommodate the fifth string. Peering through one of the f-holes, I saw that it, too, had been made in Prague by Eberle, though in 1750, the year of my master's death. Like the others, this instrument appeared remarkably well crafted, and I was certain that it could come back to life if restored with patient, loving hands.

I carefully set this cello aside and returned to the one I had found the evening before. A brief search turned up a nub of rosin and several cello bows, one of which remained serviceable. I sat and drew the bow caressingly across the strings. Once tuned, the instrument's warm resonance sent wave after wave of sound into the sanctuary's remotest corners.

The resounding tone of the instrument lightened my spirits and temporarily mitigated my anxieties about meeting with the Chevalier. I remained completely swept up in the moment until the monastery bells, tolling the thirteenth hour, brought me sharply back to the present.

I found him near the back of the library, a lone figure seated at a chessboard. The room was two stories high and ringed by a balcony containing shelves of books and maps running along each wall. I approached with apprehension.

Taylor looked up, clearly awaiting a challenger. Despite the abbot's warning, I stood openmouthed at the all-but-unrecognizable figure sitting before me. The stylish attire and jewels were, of course, no more, and as with Bach years earlier, I initially found myself staring at a closely cropped white coif where once sat the dashing, shoulder-length wig. Despite a full beard extending well beyond his chin, Taylor's formerly proud visage had been supplanted by a diminished appearance, the consequence of a considerable loss of weight. But most shocking were his eyes. Formerly piercing, they were now hollow, as if the light had gone out of them.

"Dr. Taylor?" I uttered, not entirely certain that the man seated before me was, indeed, the oculist.

He nodded slightly, then gestured toward the board. "Do you play?" he asked in English, his tone soft, and somewhat beseeching.

I replied in the affirmative and took the opposite seat, at the white pieces. With a nod, he intimated that I should commence. To this day, I am unsure what I awaited when I finally came face to face with the Chevalier, though I had once fantasized about entering into a game of chess with the man I had come to loathe.

Immediately, as instructed by Lessing, I sought control of the board's center. I played aggressively and with confidence, although admittedly, I was distracted. I was not as finely attuned to the unfolding game as I was to the adversary seated before me. Still, I could hardly have imagined my competitor to have been as stealthy as he was. Taylor assumed a conservative, defensive strategy while leaning into the board and pondering every move. I assumed that his posture was either a consequence of poor eyesight or an artful type of gamesmanship honed over many years and many matches.

Gradually, I began to appreciate his tactics, and after a dozen or more exchanges of captures, it became obvious we were destined for a draw. There would be no winner, only two opponents calculating one another's motives. Years later, I would reflect upon our match and see it for what it was: a metaphor for our present conundrum—the accuser and the accused.

Taylor was the first to speak.

"Thank you for the fine game, " he uttered in German, taking me somewhat aback. "It has been so long since anyone was willing to play me, much less play so well."

I spoke briefly of having studied with a master before acknowledging his own estimable skill.

"It has indeed been many years, but I once played with frequency, and I learned from every competitor," Taylor confessed. "The continent is awash with vast and distinct languages, cultures, foods, and philosophies. Yet they all have one thing in common," he said, pointing at the squares in front of us, where a few pieces still stood resolutely. "You have a confident hand, if at times aggressive, bolstered by more than adequate skill, so I thought it best to cajole you into believing you were in control while I charted a more guarded course. In the end, neither of our methods prevailed."

Suddenly, Taylor turned the tables of discourse.

"But chess is not why you have come, Herr Barth, so please help me understand why you are here. I have had not a single visitor since entering the service of God. Despite my former standing in the world, I now live in total obscurity, so it's a wonder anyone found me. I understand that I operated on someone—a musician, the abbot said—in whose service you once labored. Admittedly, I have known many people over many years and across vast distances, so I beg your pardon for not remembering you. Alas, both my eyes and memory appear to be failing me, though they only follow suit with my other debilities. To be quite frank, I am counting my days."

"I recently traveled to London," I said, "hoping to find you there. With help, I managed to locate your son. He knew little of your whereabouts other than that you were likely living in a monastery somewhere in Bohemia. I then returned home to Leipzig—where your path, Dr. Taylor, crossed with mine some twenty years ago. I soon set out for Bohemia, intending to search for you until my resources were exhausted. It is my good fortune to have found you so quickly in Prague, in the first abbey I happened upon.

"It is much more complicated to explain why I have gone to such great lengths to find you. Years ago, you came to Leipzig, where you operated on my master, the great composer Sebastian Bach. I assisted: you no longer had an aide in your employ, and Bach deemed me the most trustworthy to serve in that capacity. Almost from the start, I harbored concerns about your acuity. During the procedure, your arm slipped from its position on the arm of your chair and the blade with which you were preparing to operate struck my master in the eye."

Calculating that now was the moment, I asked him directly. "Do you recall this incident?"

Taylor sat silently, his lips pursed, and appeared to be searching his memory. "Herr Barth, as best as I recall, your Bach underwent a couching procedure in his study. I also have a vague recollection of returning days later to re-examine him. And now that I think about it, I wrote—albeit briefly—about the success of that treatment in my memoir. Perhaps you should have a look if you can locate a copy."

"Dr. Taylor, I own a copy of your book and have also read other descriptions of the events, written by you, many times. I cannot speak to the accuracy concerning any of your other surgeries, but the procedure you undertook—with my assistance, I must repeat—was in no way a success. You left for Berlin shortly thereafter, and I remained with my master's family to care for him. Bach's health began to deteriorate immediately. You operated at the start of April and he died that July. He never recovered."

I watched Taylor most closely as I spoke. What I told him appeared to come as a shock. I continued.

"No doubt you had much success during your travels, and by your own accounts at least, your work was lauded by a great many people. But for reasons I do not understand, you grossly misrepresented the facts of your attending to my master. And while you claim not to remember much of what occurred, I remember every detail, for I have relived that day many times.

"Bach was a man arguably at the height of his creative powers," I continued. "Beyond the pain his eyes caused him and his deteriorating eyesight, a condition that troubled him long before you arrived in Leipzig, he was in excellent health, especially given his age. He was but 65, by the way, not 88, as you stated in your memoir."

My words began spilling out faster than I could organize my thoughts, despite all the times I had imagined this conversation. "Bach's age is but a trivial matter, however. Several things occurred during the procedure that startled me, and though I was young, I was certain about what I witnessed. That said, I was entirely unaware of what, if anything, I should have done—or could have done. So, I failed to act. And with that failing, I felt complicit.

My voice, hesitant at first, now grew stronger. "One needn't have been a trained professional to comprehend that my master's eyes and the rest of his body began to fail in the days after your departure. And nothing I witnessed that day sheds a positive light on *you*. I can detail many more of your transgressions as I vividly remember them, but for now, Dr. Taylor, this is why I have long sought to find you: to make you fully aware of what happened in Leipzig and, perchance, clear my guilty conscience."

Taylor, with some effort, pushed his chair from the table and slowly rose. "I am an old man and very tired. It is time I rest. I shall reflect on what you have told me. Despite little recollection of these events, your claims deeply unsettle me. If you are coming to me for money, I assure you it is all gone, along with the rest. If you are looking for answers, I'm not sure I have those either. Tomorrow, you will be notified if we are to meet again."

Taylor looked toward the library entrance and nodded, which I took as an invitation to help him in that direction. Without further discussion, I came to his side of the table, whereupon he took my arm. As I led him from the library, I knew not what he was thinking or whether he was confused or angered by our conversation, for he spoke not another word. After what seemed like an endless walk down numerous corridors, we reached his chamber, at which point he promptly let go of my arm and disappeared inside. Under the weight of much uncertainty, I turned from the heavy oak door, retraced my steps, and walked out into the night.

Chapter 21

THE WEATHER HAD STARTED TO turn since sitting down to chess with John Taylor. Thick banks of cloud were rolling in, the air was warmer, and the Bohemian sky looked to be ready to unleash a tempest. Departing the monastery grounds, I quickened my pace toward the Moldau's west bank, noted Old Town's flickering lights, and drew closer to the inn. All the while, I reflected on my conversation with the oculist. Could he truly have remembered so little about the operation? I found this unimaginable, given that every detail was so deeply etched in my memory.

The events surrounding the Chevalier's turbulent days in Leipzig unspooled before me for the hundredth or thousandth time. Every nuance, from Taylor's initial visit to Bach's apartment to his abrupt departure for Berlin, remained as if it had transpired yesterday. Yet he claimed to remember only the most basic details. I also wondered what was to come. Would he see me tomorrow, or would I return to Leipzig with nothing but a chess stalemate for all my troubles?

I awoke early Sunday morning and retraced my steps to Strahov, having decided to attend Mass. This time I took Bach's manuscript of the suites; if Taylor chose to see me again, my late master's music might make an impression. The rain had begun in earnest, so I did my best to protect the music and avoid the expanding puddles of mud and melting snow by keeping to the side of the path.

The holy place was crowded with white habits, the color of the Premonstratensian order. Taylor could have been any of them, or perhaps he was absent. I prayed along with those in my midst, reciting the Latin Rite from memory. Following the closing *Ite, missa est*, I rose to leave with the rest of the congregants. But just before the sanctuary door, I felt a hand on my shoulder and turned to see Abbot Mayer.

"Herr Barth, I am delighted you joined us for Mass. Might I have a moment of your time?" He motioned behind us as we departed, toward the loft. "Did you find anything of note up there?"

The question caught me off guard. "Father Wenceslaus … in truth, I have been up there twice and must confess …" He stopped walking and looked at me. "I beg your pardon. It's not a formal confession," I assured him, smiling. "I mean that I found instruments strewn about. And most are—how best to put it—in an unenviable state."

"Ah, yes," he sadly replied. "Nobody has been up there for quite some time. We remain fortunate that our life here at Strahov goes on more or less as intended, which is all we can ask for. But it has been years since anybody cared for those instruments, much less played them."

I nodded and then asked with some trepidation if he had spoken with Brother Taylor. "Indeed I have, and this is why I approached you just now. He has requested that you visit his cell, where he plans to remain for the day. He didn't reveal anything about your meeting yesterday, other than to say he had prayed on whether or not to speak with you again. This morning, he sought me out to ask if I would relay the message to you, so it was fortuitous that you returned for the service.

"I shall add only that he appeared to be struggling mightily. Therefore I again urge you, Herr Barth, to proceed with caution. As you must have noticed, he has become quite frail."

"I have not come to accuse Taylor so much as find answers," I replied. "My hope is to leave with a better understanding of what happened so many years ago." He said no more as we navigated the maze of hallways that led to Taylor's cell.

"Whatever answers you find, may they be a source of healing for you both," the abbot said as he left me there.

Taylor's cell was tiny, no more than twelve feet square. It barely held a straw mattress covered by a coarse woolen blanket, a small chest, and a wooden stand with a single candle stump perched on top. A walnut kneeler occupied a nook in one wall, a stark wooden cross above it. A small leaded window in the center wall barely relieved the gloom. The only sound was of rain slapping against the glass.

Directly beneath the window sat the Chevalier, moribund in a hard wooden chair. He appeared weary, and even more frail in this austere space. I assumed the equally comfortless chair next to him had been installed for my visit. Wasting no time with pleasantries, the former surgeon admitted he had slept little since our visit the day before, and had thought of nothing else. At once, he implored me to tell him everything I remembered about our encounter twenty years ago.

I sat down, clutching the manuscript of the six suites in my lap. Without hesitation, I began with my earliest memories of my time with the Bach family, thinking it necessary for Taylor to grasp my reverence for and loyalty to my master. Next, I precisely chronicled his visits, the surgery itself, its aftermath, my master's rapid demise, the race against time to assist him with his final works, and his death.

I don't believe I saw Taylor so much as shift in his seat during the entire time I spoke. Finally, I recalled the ring the oculist had thrust into my hand after the initial procedure. "Dr. Taylor, I accepted that duplicitous gesture with remorse but it later occurred to me that its monetary value could be put to use. Once I realized that Bach's widow was forced to part with almost all of the marital property and sell off her late husband's effects, including some of his manuscripts, I sold the ring. And with the money, I offered to purchase one of Bach's cellos. She insisted I also take this," I said, lifting the manuscript from my lap and placing it into his fragile hands. "The money from the ring did help ease her burden, if only for a short while. It was the most I could do at the time."

Taylor, as I knew, could not read music even before his eyesight began to diminish. He nevertheless opened the delicate pages one at a time, peering closely. As he did, I told him about my accidental discovery of the cello suites in the St. Thomas library and how I had dedicated myself to learning the music. He looked puzzled, as if despite my narration he still failed to understand the significance of these pages.

Taylor passed the manuscript back to me. After a prolonged silence, I uttered, "That is all," and lowered my gaze to the manuscript in my lap. We sat for what seemed like an eternity, listening to the rain.

Finally, he spoke. "Herr Barth, I have attended to everything you said, and, in return, I shall attempt to unburden myself about my past, including the days before I came to Leipzig. Doing so may help explain my actions which you have graphically recalled, and which I assure you bring me no pride. I had forgotten much about that time—or chose not to remember. What's certain is that, as you have vividly reminded me, I was not in good stead when I arrived, nor had I been for quite some time. I began ..."

At this point, Taylor broke off, no doubt gathering his thoughts. How would he commence to explain himself or his actions when such a vast gulf separated the unabashedly insolent professional he had been and the broken penitent he had become? He bowed his head, and I followed what appeared to be his gaze. Perhaps he was looking at the hands that once wielded the instruments of his trade. We had that in common. When he looked up, his expression was one of surrender."

"I found trouble nearly from the start." he resumed. "As I wrote in my memoir, life in a small town had its challenges. I sensed early in my career that others in my profession were jealous of my knowledge and skills. So, I departed Norwich and took my practice on the road. At first, I traveled as an itinerant by postal and commercial coach, although I was soon able to keep a private conveyance and driver.

But in the Netherlands, a terrible accident occurred when a storm felled a tree directly onto the road in front of us. When the horses veered into a ditch, I was thrown against the coach door and greatly injured my back and neck. My poor driver was launched from his perch into our very path. So, while I lay crumpled on the coach floor, he was trapped beneath a wheel with his legs shattered. As neither of us could move, we were forced to wait for aid but were not discovered for quite some time.

"The disaster left my driver crippled. I recovered, albeit very slowly. I quelled the pain with laudanum, which assuaged my suffering but which I soon could not do without. This was the initial phase of my decline.

"Once I was back on my feet and traveling again, my practice flourished. I had inherited my father's love of fine things—a trait I have come to regret, along with so many others. I could afford most anything I desired—wine, women, even the white chaise that brought me to Leipzig. I also traveled with an assistant, who aided me in my work.

But I was soon living beyond my means. As my debts mounted, I sought to travel and work more. To be sure, I had many successes, with patients from royalty to peasantry. I also made sure to copy every notice I posted in each town I visited and to preserve the copies carefully. Years later, I drew upon this record when I chronicled my history and travels. When I composed the notice to Berlin that you referred to, I did so under the assumption that Bach would regain his eyesight, as so many did under my carp's tongue needle."

The shock of hearing Taylor's mention of that tool, which I had all but forgotten, struck me as a painful reminder of our shared past.

"When you called at the inn," Taylor went on, "I understood that matters had taken a turn for the worse. You would not have found me but for an unexpected dalliance in the company of an *inamorata*, which delayed my departure. When I returned to the patient, it was clear, just as you witnessed, that I had damaged one of his eyes. But other than draining the wound, applying a laxative, and bleeding him, there was little I could do.

"While the technique of couching is often routine, there is no guarantee of success. And my profession, like many others, will occasionally endure accidents. In most trades, such as yours, Herr Barth, mishaps are not life-threatening, but in the arena of medicine, treatment sometimes goes amiss. While I have successfully restored sight to many patients, others have suffered more regrettable fates. Lamentably, your Bach was among the latter."

My breath caught in my chest when I heard Taylor's admission of culpability for the first time.

"We will never know for sure what killed your master, but it seems likely, from what you have told me, that the accident he suffered at my unsteady hand was the genesis of his decline. I regret this deeply. Yet I must remark on something you said yesterday which indicates to me now, and probably did also at the time, that there may have been other maladies at work.

"You spoke of the pain Bach's eyes were causing him," he continued, "and this was, in part, why he sought my help. He may even have said as much to me during my examination. I do not recall. But there is no connection, Herr Barth, between pain and cataracts. I knew I could help with the latter; as for the former, I surmise it was indicative of something far more complicated and nefarious.

"Had I performed a more thorough examination, I might have detected further medical issues. Admittedly, I was hasty, and my experience, if not my arrogance, suggested that I could remedy your master's cataracts swiftly and with minimal invasion. Yes, I chose the less complicated route, in the immediate attempt to restore your master's sight. Had I pursued a more vigorous course, he would have suffered terribly, perhaps to no avail. Treating diseases of the eye presents profound dilemmas to the practitioner, for such surgery is still in its infancy. Success is less than certain and it is always staggeringly painful, both during the procedure and afterward. And doing nothing would, in time, have been equally debilitating. Either way, he would have suffered years of increasing and ultimately unbearable agony. I have encountered such torment during my travels, and I can assure you, no matter how great a composer Bach might have been or how much he had yet to express by way of his music, he was destined to become wholly incapacitated.

"As to your role in what happened, I concede that I chastised you unfairly. In truth, you could not have anticipated such a violent thrust of your master's head, for which I am entirely to blame. Thus, you could not have continued to hold his head securely."

"I appreciate your admission of fault, Dr. Taylor," I said and paused to steady my voice through a flood of emotion. "But neither did I attempt to stop you," I added. "What I observed was wrong, and I knew it was wrong. Yet I did nothing."

"I daresay you had little recourse to intervene," he replied. "I was a man buoyed by fame, and I conducted myself like some kind of demigod. My reputation was buttressed by some of the world's most powerful regents, and you were but a child. A brave child, to be sure, but a child nonetheless."

I asked him why he had fabricated the accounts of success in his memoir. "That is a fair but complicated question," he began. "I never learned of your master's fate but felt obliged to assume he would fully recover—for the sake of my reputation. Because one of his eyes did show positive signs of a successful procedure, I chose to believe the other would heal as well. I could have excluded Bach from my memoir as one of my patients, but over time I had become aware he was a figure of some repute. I therefore mentioned him, albeit briefly.

"Herr Barth, while I never could have dreamt that I would one day be sitting before Bach's student and trusted attendant and held accountable for my actions, you have done the right thing. For all you have told me and the tenacity you have demonstrated in pursuing this course of action, you have earned my utmost respect. No doubt your master must have felt the same when he trusted you to be his attendant during the surgery. You have done him a tremendous honor."

Now the wave of emotion, so long in forming, broke in me, and I wept. For all that my thoughts, apprehensions, and aspirations had been fixed on this moment, I had never paused to consider how much of my life had been consumed by them. Along with my tears, though, came a curious release: the unburdening I had hoped to experience for so long. John Taylor reached out and touched my shoulder.

"It is I who should be in tears," he said, "but from the repentance I have undertaken within these walls, it would seem I have no more to shed. Still, I have learned that one's past should inform his future deeds. And certainly, your rich experiences have rendered you a man of worth. I have no doubt your compassion and perseverance will one day be put to other excellent uses.

He sat silent for a moment, then continued. "I am so grateful you bore the courage to confront me with such forthrightness. I shall carry the remorse of my past with me until the end of my days. Your visit has been a precious gift. And for this reason, I am under an obligation. What may I now do for you?"

I wiped my face and caught my breath. "Before I reply, Brother Taylor, please allow me to escort you to the sanctuary."

As we walked, the former oculist spoke about his son and namesake. "I know he is disappointed in me, if not altogether ashamed. One of the reasons I undertook to publish my memoir was to reconcile our estrangement and regain his good graces. It's also why I dedicated the work to him. I hoped that by reading it, he would see beyond my transgressions and come to take pride in my achievements."

I assured Taylor that he had a profound impact on his son, as was evident in the younger man's charitable work. "Write to him," I urged. "I know he will want to hear from you. Tell him where you are and that I found you. I believe he will want to know that as well."

Taylor assured me he would. But whether he ever did, I cannot say.

We arrived at the basilica, empty and tranquil at this hour. Candles emitted a golden glow against the walls, while the fading luminescence of day found its way through the chancel's narrow windows. Taylor seated himself in a pew near the front of the sanctuary as I carefully made my way to the loft and returned with the cello I had played the day before.

I set a chair upon the altar and, after tuning the instrument per Bach's instructions, played the entirety of the Fifth Suite. Never had I been so intent on bringing forth every shade of meaning from each movement. As I became absorbed in the fugal Prelude, a stunning demonstration of counterpoint, and the poignant and solemn Sarabande at the work's center, my master's image arose almost preternaturally in my mind.

When the final tone of the concluding Gigue had evaporated into the shadows, I opened my eyes for the first time since commencing to play. Taylor and I were no longer alone. To my astonishment, many of his brothers had quietly joined us in the sacred space. I laid the cello down and stepped off the altar, into the embrace of several monks, Abbot Mayer among them. "Please return to my chambers when you are finished here," he whispered. Taylor remained seated, his face flush with tears despite his earlier protestation of having cried himself dry. The music had gripped his emotions, exactly as I had hoped.

"I fear my words will fail me, but that was the most stirring music I have ever heard," he said.

"*That* was Bach," I answered promptly.

At these words, he closed his eyes and bowed his head. I suspected that, at last, he fully appreciated the gravity of everything that had occurred, and allowed him a moment to do so before sitting down next to him.

"Brother Taylor, I am ready to tell you what you might do, as you have asked. Someday I hope to write about all my experiences with Bach, including our encounter here today. Few presently know of Bach's genius, but word will spread; there will come a day when people will want to know as much as possible about his life *and* death. But they will not learn the truth from the tale you have told.

"So, I ask for your admission that publication of a full account is the right thing to do, and your permission to contradict what you yourself have written. I believe that your agreement would lighten your burden of regret, and also imagine your son would be heartened to know that you gave me your blessing."

After wiping his tears, Taylor turned to me.

"Herr Barth, until now, I knew Bach only as one patient among thousands. But having heard you play his music, I understand much more about him—and even about you, though you had already revealed so much.

"Yes. Share your story as you see fit. The world will want to know. It *needs* to know. I regret I shall not live long enough to learn what you record, but this is also as it should be. And rest assured that, if your visit was indeed a precious gift, as I expressed in my cell, your performance was a divine blessing, for which I shall remain eternally grateful."

Silently, I placed my hand on the white sleeve of his arm. He bowed his head again and closed his eyes, signaling his wish to remain in the sanctuary, alone and in prayer. As I walked away, I wondered if I would ever see John Taylor again.

Chapter 22

I FOUND THE ABBOT IN HIS study. "Herr Barth, I had nearly forgotten what such music sounded like in our sanctuary and the uplifting effect it can have on one's soul. In return for what you have given all of us, I hope you will accept a token of appreciation. Nobody here will play the cello you used, or even miss it, and hearing it today made me aware that it deserves better. It is yours if you would like it."

The generosity of his offer stunned me so much that I hesitated, to gather my thoughts. "Abbot Mayer, your thoughtfulness touches my heart. What you suggest is a most tempting prospect, but if I may be so bold—might you be willing to part with another that is unplayable in its current state?"

He looked at me quizzically.

"If I may …," I continued. "I own and play a four-string cello not unlike the one you so kindly offer. It belonged to my late master, and I have developed a deep fondness for it. However, among the other instruments in the loft is a *five-string* cello, the first I have ever encountered. Bach wrote specifically for just such an instrument, but that music has remained inaccessible. The cello I speak of requires great care, but yesterday, in Old Town, I came across a luthier's shop.

"If you agree, I could call for this cello tomorrow and deliver it to the luthier, to be repaired at my expense. Once the restoration is complete, I shall return to Prague to fetch it, and when I do, I shall come to Strahov and pay my respects."

"Consider the instrument yours, Herr Barth," the abbot said, smiling. "It heartens me yet more to know that my token … *our* token of appreciation will be of such value to you. I scarcely thought, when you first wrote to me, that my brethren would be so honored by your presence and your music. I shall await your next visit, and until then, Godspeed."

I timed my return to Strahov the next morning to fall between Terce and Sext, so as not to interfere with morning prayers. As I had hoped, the sanctuary was empty when I arrived. Pausing to take in the silence, I recalled the bittersweet moments of the afternoon before. In the loft, I found a cloth wedged into a corner, large enough to wrap the cello. I then stopped at the abbot's study. As he was not to be found, I departed with my prize.

Under threatening skies but little rain, I went immediately to the luthier's shop. This time, my knock was answered. Before me stood an aproned man, with the broad shoulders of a saddler or smith, who introduced himself as Tomáš Hulinsky. When he saw the cello scroll protruding from the cloth in my arms, he pulled me from the soggy street into his dry workshop. The rich smells of wood and varnish worked on me as a tonic, and I felt immediately at ease. After introducing myself, I briefly explained my business in Prague.

Hulinsky was perhaps 50, with a head of fine red curls. I sensed a genuine, sincere nature from his cheerful, intelligent expression. He eased the cello from my arms and gently laid it on a nearby table atop a strip of thick cloth.

"Ah, this one has seen better days," the luthier sighed, then thoroughly inspected the instrument. As he peered inside it, using a candle with a reflecting hood, I stole a better look around the shop. Several instruments were suspended from their scrolls on a nearby wall. Chisels, clamps, templates, and other tools hung organized above a work table dotted with bottles of glue and candle stubs. And at the far end of the room, slabs of wood—maple, spruce, willow, and rosewood—were stacked, patiently waiting to be brought to life again.

"Even before I read the label, the design of the scroll and hue of the varnish suggested the work of Eberle," Hulinsky proclaimed, blowing out the candle.

"You know of the maker?" I was pleased to hear it.

"Indeed, yes. I apprenticed under him, in this very place. Master Eberle died not long ago and quite suddenly. All of this," he said, gesturing about, "has fallen to me. And this violoncello piccolo…I recognize it! It was the only five-string cello to leave the shop during my time here. Eberle and I built a series of instruments for Strahov, though it has been years since any have been brought in for repair. I suspect there is no longer use for music in the monastery. Dare I ask about the other instruments? Have you seen them as well?"

I shared with Hulinsky that everything I had seen appeared neglected, though this cello was arguably in the worst condition.

Hulinsky winced. He then asked how I had come to possess the cello.

"It was a generous gift from Abbot Mayer, who was happy to put it in the hands of someone who appreciates its rarity and will put it to good use. If you are willing to do the work, I shall entrust it to you. I plan to depart for Leipzig as soon as possible, but when you notify me that the work is complete, I shall return posthaste."

Hulinsky assured me that restoring his master's cello would bring him great satisfaction, though it would be months before he could turn his attention to the project. "Currently, I am working alone. As you might imagine, finding knowledgeable help is difficult, at best. Bohemia isn't Italy, after all," he added with a wink. "And as you can see, I have more than a few projects ahead of yours." I had already noticed numerous instruments in various states of disrepair.

"To address the crack, the cello's top must be removed. Once complete, however, that repair, along with the others, will be nearly imperceptible. Of course, the instrument requires much more work in addition, so I beg your patience, Herr Barth. You should not expect to hear from me in less than a half year."

I assured him everything was in order, and that I was sincerely grateful for his help. Having written out my Leipzig address, I bid Hulinsky adieu and returned to the inn to fetch my belongings.

Late that afternoon, I took a seat aboard a post coach alongside another gentleman, across from his wife and two adult daughters. Rain began again, this time in earnest, just as we were about to leave. Our driver shut the coach door, dropped the leather curtains over the windows, mounted his box, and urged his team toward Prague's northern gate. I took care to tuck Bach's manuscript securely between myself and my fellow passenger as I settled in.

By the time the coach was well north of Prague, night had fallen. To the rhythmic sound of hoofbeats, I passed into a fitful sleep of uneasy dreams that passed before my mind's eye in vague fragments. Hopelessly lost amidst Old Town's cramped, winding streets, I was accosted in turn by white-robed Monks and black-clad Jews. They attempted to engage me, but their words were lost among pounding hoofbeats and creaking wheels. My panic mounted until it became nearly unbearable, but at that juncture, I was shaken awake. Delivered from one nightmare, I quickly found myself living another.

We were traveling along a chain of small hills that ran alongside the Moldau and had been caught in a violent storm. The rush of water, caused by recent snows and the present deluge, was overflowing the riverbank and submerging our path; even the hoofbeats could no longer be heard over the water battering the coach's roof and the sound of the wheels sloshing through mud. Mercilessly, the driver urged his team ever onward, hoping to clear the raging water.

We had no sooner crested one hill before the driver drove the horses relentlessly down the other side. And then, the carriage slammed to a stop. The driver, nearly blind to what lay ahead, had plunged us into a water-filled channel.

I was thrown helplessly against the door to my right, my weight forcing it open a hand's breadth. I thought I had not sustained serious injury, albeit I was stunned by the blow. For a moment, I hearkened back to the devastating coach accidents endured by Taylor and Handel. Such thoughts were quickly banished, however, by the threat of our present situation.

The wheel beneath me was stuck fast, and the carriage itself listed precariously. Floodwaters began seeping through the splintered floorboards and streaming in through the door, which I could neither pull shut nor force open. The next sounds we heard were those of the driver. He had been thrown from his high seat and, though injured, was wading to our aid.

He screamed that we should crawl out the window at the front of the coach before the vehicle overturned completely and became lost to the flood. I now perceived that my shoulder was throbbing, but nonetheless began to assist the other passengers through the aperture before following them and dropping off into the swirling waters.

By the grace of God, all made their way to slightly higher ground. The other male passenger and I then pushed our way back toward the coach, intending to assist the driver. He stood at the head of the terrified horses, still hitched, whipping and berating them as they strove to pull the carriage forward and right it. But despite desperate efforts of man and animal, the top-heavy wagon was now perilously close to foundering.

I had frightful thoughts of the savage torrent sweeping all downstream. Thus I compelled myself to climb onto the rooftop, untie the trunks, and push them over the side. The other male passenger and I managed to pull them to where his wife and daughters waited before returning to the compromised coach. With the gentleman now at the reins, the driver and I moved to the rear and, with our backs against the wagon, augmented the horses' efforts by pushing off against the trench with all our might, slipping and sliding all the while.

With a groan, the wagon lurched up and forward; as it did so, the door jerked free of its hinges and fell away. Water rushed out of the cabin and carried the splintered door toward the river.

The driver now scrambled around to the front of the coach, where he took hold of the reins and led the team to higher ground. The damaged wheel shimmied throughout, yet somehow remained on the axle. The other passengers and I then worked together, dropping the trunks into the carriage's footwell, which forced the excess water out the doorless opening. With the others aboard in what little space could be had, I walked alongside the compromised wheel just far enough to be sure it would remain attached, then climbed onto the box next to the driver.

Only at that moment did I remember Bach's manuscript, which I had placed at my side when we set out from Prague. I gasped, then howled at the driver to stop. Startled, he brought the team to a halt as I jumped back off, returned whence we had come, and stared out at the raging Moldau. And I cried out into the blackness, overcome by the realization that the river had devoured Bach's precious music.

Aboard the coach once more, I tried to take comfort in the knowledge that Anna Magdalena's copy of the suites, along with my own, resided safely within the St. Thomas library. Though the disappearance of Bach's original was heartrending, we had blessedly averted disaster. Neither human nor animal life had been lost, and we had salvaged nearly all the cargo. A final glance behind us, toward the river, revealed nothing but the rush of water streaming over its bank.

Safety and warmth were now all we sought, and the damaged wheel held well enough to get us to the next station without further incident. In Leipzig at last—muddy, grieved, and exhausted—I collapsed onto my bed in my old garret.

I awoke with a start at first light, my only thought to ascertain that the copies of the Bach suites were where I had left them. Heart pounding, I dressed and sprinted to the library, where I scanned the familiar shelves until my eyes beheld Anna Magdalena's faithful copy, along with my own.

My shoulder still ached, but I felt as if I could breathe again. The tempest had lamentably claimed the original, but the cello suites would endure. And, without further cataclysm, I would have the means to play the very last one before the year was out.

My return to Leipzig only confirmed what I already suspected: my emotional ties to the city were now gone. Where there had once been friends and family, only strangers remained. I had too little employment, and my paltry savings would soon be depleted. The rector of St. Thomas offered me some light teaching duties, but I politely declined, as they would not provide even a subsistence wage. Mulling over my prospects, I thought about Tomáš Hulinsky in Prague. He had expressed a need for assistance in his shop, so I wrote to tell him that, while I continued to hold out hope of securing employment as a cantor, I hoped he might accept my services until such might present itself. I admitted to having no experience as a luthier but assured him that I was a quick study, good with my hands, and well understood the nature of stringed instruments.

His reply came a week later. Hulinsky would pay me a modest wage and offered me board in the small room at the rear of the shop until more suitable accommodations could be obtained. He would not consider this arrangement a proper apprenticeship, as these typically lasted several years. Still, if I could dedicate a minimum of one year to his service, he would engage me immediately.

I replied, stating my intent to arrive forthwith. Then, with mixed feelings of trepidation and exhilaration, I put my modest affairs in order. I quickly sold off my belongings, save for things of particular value, such as Bach's cello, the lap desk, and the chessboard Lessing had graciously told me was my own to keep.

I terminated the lease on my garret and left a forwarding address with the rector at St. Thomas. Only one final task remained: to make a new copy of Bach's Sixth and final cello Suite. As I hoped to be in Prague for less than a year and had long ago memorized several of the other suites, it would be enough to return to Bohemia with only this one in tow.

―

I arrived at Hulinsky's door a week later, after a mercifully uneventful journey. The violin maker warmly greeted me and showed me to the small room I would temporarily call home. No sooner had I lifted one latch of my trunk than he seized my arm and insisted on feeding me with a loaf of dark bread, a hunk of cheese, and a leg of lamb. We drank to my arrival with a flask of pilsner, and I again thanked the luthier for his generosity and willingness to trust me. As soon as I had finished my meal, we began.

After a close look around the shop, Hulinsky informed me that my initial duties would be limited to tidying up and running errands. As I gradually learned more about the intricate workings of his craft, I began to assist him with minor repairs; soon I was carving blocks of wood for bridges and mixing varnish. Occasionally, I traveled for wood and other supplies, trips that more than once took me to the farthest reaches of Bohemia. My skills and instincts continued to sharpen, and before long Hulinsky entrusted me with choosing the most promising maple and spruce planks based on their inherent resonance and patterns of healthy grain.

After several months, with the shop cleared of dozens of projects, we turned our attention to the cello piccolo. I watched as Hulinsky expertly removed the instrument's top and again appraised the interior damage. He first noted wormholes, then meticulously differentiated between hairline cracks that wanted only glue and larger ones that required expert patching.

The work had proceeded for several days, during which I gratefully observed the painstaking, unhurried process of Hulinsky's method, when I was awakened at dawn by an ominous dream. John Taylor and I were to meet over a chess game, but I had been left alone in the shop. With each completed task, more work piled up. As a fading sun cast longer shadows across the wooden tables, it became apparent that I would neither attend to all the repairs nor make my appointment with Taylor.

I woke in a sweat, with the anxious feeling that time was running short. Perhaps I was also feeling some guilt, as I had yet to cross the Moldau to visit the monastery, even though I had been in Prague for months. I had repeatedly reasoned that I was too weary from long days and hard work. But in truth, I harbored great trepidation about returning to Strahov. I was unsure how to form a relationship with Taylor or if such was possible.

This time, compelled by the dream, I determined to visit that very evening. I closed the shop at dusk, pulled on a wool coat and hat, and made my way through Old Town, across the Charles Bridge, and down the old footpath. Fighting a sudden chill, I crossed the monastery courtyard and headed to Abbot Mayer's study. He was surprised to see me but also professed delight and greeted me with his customary warmth. After some pleasantries, however, he regretfully informed me that Brother Taylor had taken a turn for the worse not long after my previous visit. He was now completely blind and hovering close to death. A few days before, he had received the last rites.

"If I visit his cell, will he remember me or even know I am near?" I asked.

"Brother Taylor is unconscious. As to what he may be aware of, I cannot say. In the days following your visit, he spoke to me on more than one occasion about Bach's music and how deeply your playing had moved him. If you were to play for him now, I could only hope he might sense your presence. Let us go now and retrieve an instrument for you."

I nodded, and as we walked toward the sanctuary, I told the abbot of my return to Prague and present position, adding that I expected to remain in Prague for a time but still aspired to a position as a cantor, the pursuit of which might take me elsewhere. In the loft, I found the cello and bow as I had left them. We then proceeded in silence to Taylor's cell. At the door, the abbot placed a small, wrapped object in my hand.

"Brother Taylor entrusted me with this. We had no idea when you might return and he feared he might not live long enough to meet you again. He said it was his last remaining possession from earlier days."

Thanking him, I tucked the package safely into my coat.

The odor of decay blew over me through the open door. Taylor lay motionless, his head tilted back into the straw of his mattress. His eyes were open but stared vacantly heavenward. His shallow breaths did not quicken when I knelt, nor did he react when I spoke. I slid his timeworn chair closer to the bedside, then steadied my cello and tightened the bow.

For two quarters of an hour, I played, uninterrupted, the music of my master. After each movement, I looked down at Taylor but perceived no motion. My mood remained tempered, far from the passionate abandon of my performance in the sanctuary. I had arrived hoping that something of the music's spirit would penetrate Taylor's drift into final sleep but now had the peculiar sensation of both walls and time pressing in on me. I whispered in his ear that I would return on the morrow, yet wondered if he had the strength to survive another night.

It was not until I lay in my own bed, hours later, that I recalled the cloth-wrapped object in my coat pocket. I rose, lit the candle, and found it to be a silver tool about the length of my index finger. This was a carp's tongue needle such as the one Taylor had used to operate on Bach's cataracts. It brought to mind his silver case, engraved with fleur de lis and lined with red velvet, that had held several such instruments. Had he sold it to help settle his debts? I stared at the slender yet sturdy instrument until the candle flame caught a draft and flickered out.

A banging on the shop door roused me from my slumber the following morning. A messenger stood there, stomping his feet and breathing hard into his ungloved hands. The envelope he gave me bore the crimson seal and initials of the abbot, and the missive within informed me that Brother Taylor had passed from this world only a few hours before.

That afternoon, I stood on a patch of frozen ground west of the monastery, surrounded by dozens of white robes. Gazing through the twin cupolas of Strahov and off toward the bleak, gray horizon, I recalled the only other sepulchral ceremony I had attended: the burial of my master nearly two decades ago. But that hot July day stood in sharp contrast to the biting wind and tiny snowflakes of this occasion. Otherwise, Taylor's funeral was a similarly brief, modest affair.

While the abbot spoke of the man laid out in cloth at our feet, I held the needle and pressed its sharp point against my palm. Numb from the cold, I sensed only a dull pain from its tip against my skin as I imagined Taylor working Bach's cataract away from the center of his eye. When the abbot began intoning the prayers for the dead, I wondered if John Taylor had fully reconciled his past at last or, despite absolution, if his transgressions followed him to his grave. When Bach understood his end was near, he found peace in music. What had the former oculist contemplated in his final hours? Had he continued to wrestle with his misdeeds or longed for the son he would never again meet in this world?

When the brothers lowered Taylor's enshrouded body into the earth, I resolved that one day I would return to Leipzig to visit the grounds where my master lay buried, and on that day I would not go empty-handed.

Chapter 23

Prague's steely gray skies had given way to sunshine and an eagerly awaited thaw when, several weeks after Taylor's death, Hulinsky stretched five strings across the bridge of the newly restored cello. When he tightened the E string, the gut groaned in complaint. Unlike its thicker, more durable neighbors, this highest, thinnest string was so brittle that it was likely to snap if not crafted to withstand maximum tension. So it had been wound according to Hulinsky's exact specifications. To be safe, he had ordered a half dozen spares.

I had watched each painstaking step of the repairs, as the luthier replaced the cello's top, reset the neck, attached a new fingerboard, and cut the bridge. He then asked me to touch up the superficial scratches the instrument had suffered over its many years. And now, at long last, I would have my formal introduction to Bach's Sixth Suite.

Naturally, I had long familiarized myself with the score, yet eyeing the notes on a page felt akin to reading a description of a painting I'd never viewed in person; hearing the majestic music under my ear was to behold the canvas with my own eyes. I had spoken to Hulinsky often about my late master, and he had listened raptly as I played movements from the other suites. But when I brought the Sixth to life on this instrument, discarded in a monastery loft and revived by the great luthier, the effect was wondrous.

Moments before I began to play, Hulinsky had propped open the shop door to welcome in a breath of warm, fresh air. From a workshop bench, arms crossed, he stared intently as I began to work my bow against the strings. Hulinsky could not have shared my unbridled thrill at crossing into the unknown terrain of the fifth string, but he was nodding and tapping his foot with evident satisfaction. I continued as he moved about the shop, studying the instrument's rich colors and warm tone from every corner.

At first, I struggled mightily, for the instrument felt very awkward in my hands. As Hulinsky had explained during the restoration, the cello piccolo was a compromise design that could accommodate both a deep C string and the significantly higher E string. I was also unaccustomed to the wider fingerboard required for the additional string that had so intrigued Bach. These factors, coupled with the demanding nature of my master's music—its rapid passagework, myriad string crossings, lavish embellishments, and challenging chords—proved daunting in a way I had not been able to anticipate. Yet none of these obstacles diminished my exuberance at playing the suite for the first time. I felt a door open within me, revealing a glorious, undiscovered vista too long denied.

The cello had been transformed into an undeniable beauty. The E string was resilient, penetrating, and sweet, reminding me of the crystalized ginger I once tasted at a Leipzig fair. Its middle range was resonant and warm, its lower end rich and chocolatey. Glancing up, I saw that Hulinsky was proud of his work. And when I finally laid down the bow, the good-natured luthier rushed forward, lifted the instrument by the neck, and turned it in his hands, admiringly.

"She looks and sounds like a dream: rich, ample, and remarkably even across all the strings. And that music is radiant! It seems you'll need to grow an extra finger to go along with that extra string," he said with a playfully raised eyebrow. "Well, I'll leave its eventual mastery to you, Barth, but I delight in what we have accomplished together! It's once more a hearty instrument worthy of Eberle, *my* master."

"Come," he said, placing the cello on a nearby worktable. "We've earned a drink or two." And giving my shoulder a gentle squeeze, the luthier ushered me out of the shop.

I was happy to continue under Hulinsky's tutelage until word came from Borna, a village south of Leipzig. The cantor at the Church of St. Mary had taken a position elsewhere without warning, so the school needed a replacement as soon as one could be found. I had come highly recommended by the St. Thomas rector, and it was sincerely hoped I could begin at once. The letter also indicated that should my work prove satisfactory as well as to my liking, I could expect a permanent contract.

Given the size of the school at St. Mary, it stood to reason that the post would offer fewer resources than Bach had at St. Thomas. But it would also entail far fewer demands. I could easily imagine a quaint school with a few talented boys, and some less so, whose welfare and education would be my responsibility in part. I assumed that the church also possessed a choir and orchestra, most likely of mediocre ability, but I would be free to program the music of my choice. I was being offered the steady employment and idyllic existence I had been waiting for.

As I perused the letter, standing in the doorway of Hulinsky's shop, the violin maker asked if everything was all right. "It's from the rector at Borna. The cantor has departed from St. Mary and I have been invited to step in immediately."

He laid down the neck of a violin whose scroll he had been carving and stood to face me. "It's what you've been so patiently waiting for, is it not?" he asked.

"It is—indeed," I admitted.

"That's marvelous news for you, Barth," he said sincerely. "It must make you feel very satisfied."

"Honestly, I'm a bit shocked," I replied. "I'm honored by the invitation, to be sure. It's just so sudden. I know little about the school or the village. And yet, such an opportunity may not come again for a long time, if ever. Pardon me, but … but …" I stammered, unable to complete my regrets.

"Barth!" Hulinsky exclaimed. "I will be sorry to see you go, but go you must. We agreed that you'd work for me until another opportunity appeared. Now that the cello is finished, what is left to keep you? If the school is not to your liking, there will be a workbench here, as long as I'm answering the door."

I thanked him for his generosity and laid the note on a bench before picking up a broom. Hulinsky gently took it from my hands. "The floor can wait. You must reply directly and accept the position. When you take your response to the post, inquire about the express schedule to Germany."

Two days later, Hulinsky walked me to the station, where we were met by a cart carrying both cellos and the rest of my belongings.

"Your weather looks promising, Barth. I predict a smoother trip than the last time you headed in that direction! My good man, it was an honor to have you under my wing, and I'm certain your new rector will feel the same. I wish you much happiness and success. And Godspeed to you!"

We embraced warmly and I thanked him again, choking back my tears. I took my seat and peered out the coach window as Hulinsky ambled back in the direction of his shop. He turned, caught my glance, and waved. The driver snapped the reins, and soon we were beyond the city gate. Moments later, the coach swung westward, just long enough for me to glimpse the Strahov Monastery and the city of Prague for the last time.

Borna's Church of St. Mary rested proudly atop a rise near the edge of town. The steeple appeared no larger than my thumbnail as we approached, set against a background of verdant farmland and ribbons of rolling hills. I disembarked at the town's Imperial Gate to the sound of the bells of St. Mary, after setting out from Leipig only that morning. I had hired a rig, as no public coach was scheduled for Borna until the following day. The brief journey south was nothing short of idyllic, its progress marked by elegant stone mileposts, green pastures, and roads shaded by chestnuts and elms. Along the way, we passed pilgrims traveling north in the footsteps of Martin Luther.

The rector expressed relief that I had turned up so soon. Following his greeting, he showed me to my modest but adequate quarters. Early the next morning, he escorted me to my first class, introduced me to my students, and bid me a good day. And with that, work was underway.

I soon felt a sense of familiarity in the small Saxon town, as the Church of St. Mary and St. Thomas bore certain similarities.

Both parishes traced their histories back over centuries, and each had welcomed Martin Luther within their walls. Even my accommodations and duties were comparable. As Bach had done, I occupied an apartment in the church's schoolhouse, taught music and Latin, and led the Sunday performances from the church loft. In short, I felt as if I was walking in my master's footsteps. Additionally, I was granted full support for travel to Leipzig whenever necessary to consult materials at the St. Thomas library. I felt no urge to stay in my former town but always enjoyed a coffee, and a game or two of chess, at the Café Zimmermann.

My dedication to my students and enthusiasm for my new post seemed to make a most favorable impression, for within weeks of my arrival, I was summoned to the rector's office to discuss a long-term contract. Admittedly, I initially felt some conflict upon settling into my new position. Borna was a fraction of Leipzig's size, with fewer than 2,500 inhabitants, and I wondered if I might outgrow it. But by the time I was asked to remain, I had come to appreciate the tranquility of this remote hamlet.

For close to a decade I remained a bachelor. I courted several women from respectable families, yet none of those relationships blossomed. Then, in my tenth year, a merchant and ropemaker by the name of Johann Gottlieb Hofmann moved to town, and with him, a daughter. I was told that Johanna Friedericka took after her late mother, a strong, beautiful woman who was said to have striking blue eyes. We were married in 1783, and our first night together was one of nervous fumbling, laughter, and joy. When my new wife fell asleep in my arms, I was certain we were a well-suited pair.

My instincts proved correct. Over the next seven years, Johanna gave birth to five children, and while three died far too young, our son Johann and daughter Henriette are with us still.

I remained active as the cantor of Borna for many more years, during which I proudly led performances of Bach's music and often performed his cello suites for my congregation. These efforts were always warmly embraced. Nonetheless, it was well to the north where I encountered the most meaningful appreciation and acclaim for my late master's music.

Chapter 24

MY OLD FRIEND JOSEF GRAUN and I kept up a frequent exchange of letters in the years that followed. Of course, I communicated about locating Taylor, though I merely outlined the tale in hopes of sharing the finer details in person. In later correspondence, I conveyed news of my work in the luthier's shop and my subsequent appointment in Borna.

Josef, in turn, wrote blissfully of marriage, then tragically of his wife's death in his arms during childbirth. And in early 1781, he informed me that Ephraim Lessing had died in Braunschweig, another sorrowful missive that I attempted to buoy with uplifting news of my own. Josef had humorously inquired, more than once, whether I had managed to catch up with the lovely Dafir. So I was overjoyed to announce at last that I was engaged, though not to a fortune teller!

Now, at the turn of the new century, I was 65 and Josef was all but demanding a visit from me.

> *Carl,*
>
> *I know you are resigned to that quaint little town of yours but you owe it to yourself, and me, to visit Berlin at the earliest opportunity.*

There is a woman here, Sara Levy, née Itzig, who was once a student of Sebastian Bach's eldest child, Wilhelm Friedemann. She is a marvelous pianist, wholly dedicated to the music of your former master, and runs a salon out of her stately home. As this year marks the fiftieth anniversary of Bach's death, she is devoting several of her brilliant salons entirely to his music. I have told her about you and she has expressed a keen interest in meeting you and hearing you perform. The cello suites are entirely unknown here.

Please consider escaping that domestic life of yours for a few days. Better yet, bring your family with you. Know that a fine instrument awaits you and that you will be my guest for as long as you can endure city life!

I remain your faithful friend and servant—

J. Graun, Berlin

    Learning that others were devoted to Bach's music delighted and heartened me beyond all expectation. For as long as I could remember, I had wondered when my master's music would find an audience both discerning and appreciative. Though his cantatas could occasionally be heard in Leipzig, performances elsewhere remained rare. I had planned to attend a concert of his music at St. Thomas in late July, on the anniversary of his death, but this proposed event in Berlin was something else entirely.

    Admittedly, the story of my master's brief sojourn to the court of Frederick the Great still struck a nerve. Though

"Old Fritz " had died in 1786, I had forgotten neither Bach's anguished recollection of that visit nor Josef's firsthand account. Granted, the monarchy had passed twice, first to Frederick's nephew, Frederick William II, and then to his son, Frederick William III. And, from what I could determine from Josef's invitation, a new generation appeared to be embracing my late master's music. Might the long overdue Bach revival happen after all? After considering the matter for several days, I decided to learn for certain.

I traveled to Berlin with my wife and children in the second week of July. I wanted them to share in the experience and hoped they could gain from it a better understanding of my lifelong dedication to Bach's memory and music. Furthermore, if Josef's enthusiasm for Frau Levy was any indication, I knew an introduction to her would be especially meaningful for my wife and daughter.

The nearer we drew to our destination, the more I thought of Bach's arrival at the monarch's palace. Exhausted and denied the opportunity to recover from his arduous travel, he had been at once dragooned to perform for king and court. But I smiled widely when we disembarked at Josef's residence near the Royal Palace, where good food, rest, and my dear friend's congeniality awaited. Josef, after rushing out to our coach to begin our reunion, commenced at once to shower us with hospitality.

Soon after our arrival, Josef began peppering our 17-year-old son Johann Friedrich and our 10-year-old daughter Henrietta with myriad questions. They both played keyboard and sang and were eager to tell him how much they enjoyed making music at home. I observed, quite immodestly, that both my wife and daughter "sang a fine soprano," a phrase Bach had once lovingly applied to Anna Magdalena. Johann expressed no wish to pursue a musical career but was soon interested in learning more about my good friend's work in a government post.

"I would most welcome your return to Berlin once you've begun at university," Josef offered. "That is, assuming your parents would ever let you leave Borna! Let's see how you like Berlin first, young man, for it's a far cry from the little town where you grew up." Johann, having taken an obvious liking to my old friend, graciously thanked Herr Graun for his kind offer, and added that he hoped to see as much of the city as time might allow.

Later that evening Josef and I excused ourselves and made our way across the nearby palace grounds. As we strolled over the grandiose estate, he recalled the recent king's love of music.

"Carl, you will be most interested to know that the late sire of our present monarch was quite an accomplished cellist and loved music as much as his uncle, Frederick the Great. Indeed, when Frederick the Second traveled, he often brought along his musicians, even in times of war! Several of the cellos from his collection remain in storage, so I took the liberty of speaking with the Royal Treasurer about borrowing one during your stay. I daresay you won't be disappointed."

We arrived at a gate to the palace courtyard, where a guard courteously greeted Josef before lighting two large candles for us. We proceeded through a grand portal and continued down several corridors, the flickering candlelight dancing off the richly appointed tapestries, until we entered a cavernous room that appeared to be used for storage. A pair of keyboards occupied its center, and against the far wall, I could make out a collection of large, gilt-framed paintings stacked several deep, their ornate gold leaf frames shimmering in the candlelight. All around were articles beyond count—mantel clocks, religious icons, *objets d'art*—tributes and gifts, I surmised, from foreign dignitaries and monarchs. Farther on, I glimpsed the reason we had come.

Several cellos and perhaps a half-dozen bows were spread across a table draped in rich cloth. I made out the label of a cello by Jacobus Stainer, a renowned Tyrolean maker whose work I had become familiar with during my time in Prague. But my attention was quickly captured by an instrument whose characteristics were unmistakable even in the shadows. Crafted of fine Venetian spruce, the deep red varnish, broad arches, bold f-holes, and the forward thrust of this cello's scroll suggested the work of Matteo Goffriller, a maker Hulinsky greatly admired. The label confirmed my suspicions:

Matteo Goffriller
Fece in Venezia
Anno 1731

I promptly slid into the nearest chair and reached for one of the bows. With the magnificent specimen braced between my legs, I drew the bow across the strings. The instrument responded as if it had been waiting to be set free, and the room resonated with a rich, complex, powerful sound. It was truly a marvel! I only wished Hulinsky had been there to share in my exultation.

"Exceptional, no?" Josef uttered from the shadows.

"It's astounding—unlike anything I've ever known. This was not built for the workaday cellist but for the player looking to project *above* an ensemble. This, my friend, was crafted for a virtuoso."

Josef urged me to bring the cello with us. I reeled in anticipation of performing my master's music on it at the salon. Yes, the music would speak for itself, but the Groffiller would allow me to mine the riches of my master's creation and give me the hope of creating an indelible impression on our audience.

Following a good night's rest and a sumptuous breakfast, Josef took us on a tour of the Royal Palace, in all its size and opulence, and then led us through the city. Though smaller than London, in the wake of a similar renaissance it had become an enterprising metropolis. After a brief stroll along the River Spree, we traversed several grand avenues. Our host drew attention to the Royal Opera and the spectacular library just opposite, the bustling *Gendarmenmarkt*, and St. Hedwig's Cathedral.

"We can thank Frederick the Great for this one, too," Josef announced as we stood before the structure, which he said had been inspired by the Pantheon itself. "Regardless of what one thinks of Old Fritz, it's difficult for Berliners not to appreciate such gifts!"

After a walk through the lush grounds of the Pleasure Garden, where we savored the sunset, we headed back along the Spree. As we drew near to his home, our host pointed southwest toward Potsdam, and then due west. "If we were to follow the river," Josef told us, "we would come upon Sara Levy's ornate grounds. But you will see all that soon enough. Tomorrow we shall visit Sanssouci, Frederick's royal playground in Potsdam. There, Carl, you will retrace your master's footsteps, and I am certain you will *all* find the place nothing short of breathtaking."

The next morning, we were met by a handsome black carriage, which Josef introduced as a *berline*, named for the city. "It's the very latest in travel comfort," he grinned and insisted we look underneath to admire the thick leather straps suspending the wagon. As promised, the journey was remarkably smooth, and as the wheels struck the uneven cobblestones, we all laughed in recollection of other, inhospitable rides.

Our path took us out through the city gate and hugged the river until the driver picked up the same road upon which Frederick the Great trundled to and from his palace in Potsdam. En route, Josef explained how he had come to know Frau Levy.

It seemed that our old friend Ephraim Lessing had been introduced to Moses Mendelssohn, a Jew but nonetheless one of Berlin's great men of letters. Mendelssohn himself sprang from a strictly religious home in Dessau, and his father, a Biblical scribe, assumed his son would take up the trade. But at only 14 years of age, Moses had made his way to Berlin, alone. He entered the city through the *Rosenthaler Tor*, the gate through which only Jews—and cattle—were permitted. Yet he attained prominence in the Prussian capital as an enlightened philosopher and theologian.

"It was Mendelssohn's brilliant intellect that drew Lessing to him," Josef exclaimed, "but when they first met, it wasn't philosophy or theology they discussed—you'll appreciate this, Carl—they played chess! And in time, the two men became great friends."

Josef recounted that the most visible of Mendelssohn's Jewish contemporaries was Daniel Itzig, a banker and court Jew to Frederick the Great who also served as mintmaster. Itzig had been among the few of his brethren to receive full Prussian citizenship—on account of his usefulness to the crown—and he used his stature to courageously speak out for the emancipation of his fellow Jews.

Mendelssohn and Itzig were linked in various ways. Both, Josef understood, were direct descendants of Moses Isserles, a sixteenth-century Old Testament scholar in Krakow. Itzig's son had helped found a private school for poor Jewish children that incorporated some of Mendelssohn's educational theories.

As we crossed a small bridge, Josef tidied up his story.

"Among Itzig's many children is Sara, a most remarkable woman. She married Solomon Levy, a banker, and they are the patrons and hosts of the salon at which you will perform. Like her father, Frau Levy is dedicated to causes of benefit to her people, but her true gift is making music. As you'll soon learn, she is a most accomplished keyboardist. She is a former student of Wilhelm Friedemann Bach—as I have written to you, Carl—and that is how she found her way to the music of your late master. It has become her passion."

Sensing my incredulity, Josef raised his eyebrows.

"It's a small world, no? And Lessing was the linchpin of it all! Knowing my interest in Bach's music, he introduced me to Frau Levy. And I have since attended many of her salons, which have become a cultural fixture of life in Berlin."

Shortly after Josef brought his byzantine story to a close, the *berline* pulled up before the magnificent façade of Sanssouci, Frederick the Great's summer palace, which proved every bit as impressive as Bach had recalled and Josef had described.

Again, my friend's royal appanage gained us access to rooms presently unoccupied. Naturally, my emotions were stirred as I entered the ballroom where Bach first encountered the king, and as I wandered through the successive chambers where he had performed on the royal keyboards. I savored my reverie before finding the others in the terraced gardens, in which Josef told us Frederick had hoped to be buried.

"This entire hill was once a forest of oak," Josef indicated. "It was all felled to accommodate Old Fritz's grand conception. Admittedly, the results are elegant, though I might have preferred nature as it was intended. He died in his study, up there," pointing again. "He was found in his armchair, having worked until the very end. Frederick wished to be here, buried alongside his beloved greyhounds, but his nephew ordered that he be entombed next to his father at the Garrison Church in the center of Potsdam."

Halting at the top of the steps leading back to the palace, Josef turned and urged us to take in the grand, sweeping view. "Frederick was quite an enigma, but undeniably brilliant!"

Hearing my friend's words, I recalled Bach harboring similar ambivalence toward the Prussian monarch.

On the day of the salon, we again boarded the comfortable *berline,* this time with the Goffriller. The Levy estate, a three-story mansion crowned with a red-roofed garet, was situated in one of Berlin's most stylish neighborhoods, on a swath of land west of the palace that abutted the River Spree. In front, a canopy of linden trees offered abundant protection from the warm July sun, while behind, rows of oaks stood like sentinels along the riverbank.

At the massive front door, Frau Levy herself welcomed my family with a mix of excitement and tenderness, expressing how honored she was that we had made such a trip. Her petite stature appeared particularly pronounced next to her husband, Solomon, who stood about my height, albeit of a slimmer build. Frau Levy had dark, intelligent eyes and waves of thick gray hair bound with a satin ribbon. She exuded confidence as well as grace.

Solomon kindly offered to carry my cello, while Sara linked arms with my wife and daughter before leading us all through the generous foyer and down a long hallway toward the rear of the house. In the elegant salon, the other guests were already seated and engaged in lively conversation. The listeners faced two keyboards at one end of the generously proportioned chamber, beyond which several handsome French doors had been thrown open, affording a magnificent view of the river in the distance. Josef, along with my wife and children, seated themselves in a back row while Sara and I made our way forward, followed by Solomon, still toting the Goffriller.

When Sara stepped before her guests, all conversation ceased. Without addressing them, she sat at one of the harpsichords and played a Bach toccata. Her touch was masterful, and I was certain the composer himself would have been swayed. She brought the stirring music to a close with a deft flourish, then rose.

"My dear friends, that was *Toccata* in D Major by Sebastian Bach—a work that my esteemed guest, Josef Graun, brought back from Leipzig many years ago and so generously introduced to me." Josef now stood and bowed modestly, to polite applause. "But Herr Graun has done us a greater service still, for he has brought with him today his dear friend, whose acquaintance he made in Leipzig many years ago.

"Herr Barth has traveled with his family from Borna, where he serves as cantor, and he has graciously accepted my invitation to perform music for cello alone by Sebastian Bach, whom he knew intimately. I must tell you that I am most anxious to hear it, for despite having long embraced Bach's music, I was entirely unaware—until quite recently—that he had written for unaccompanied cello. Herr Barth, if you would do us the great honor?"

I had seated myself next to the harpsichord while Sara spoke. Solomon Levy now handed me the cello and bow. After tuning the instrument, I announced that I would present the Fourth Cello Suite, and with a deep breath, I commenced.

The Goffriller's C string thundered out, filling the expansive space with a round, robust sound. The following phrases gave way to a velvety resonance, highlighting the cello's richest timbres. Throughout each movement I plumbed the instrument's potential, from *pianissimo* to *fortissimo*, perceiving no limit to its expressive range. The cello responded with all the colors, nuance, and power it had revealed in the palace several days earlier. By the time I reached the bounding Gigue, I felt I had spun a story of great merit—a most intimate view through the lens of my master, Sebastian Bach.

The guests rose as one, applauding furiously. Overwhelmed, I stood to acknowledge their appreciation, as Frau Levy came to embrace me before turning back to her guests.

"My friends, I believe I may speak for us all when I say, Herr Barth, you have given us much more than any of us were prepared for this afternoon. What glorious, exalted music! We are truly in your debt," this last remark sparking another round of applause. "You numbered this as the Fourth Suite—please, how many did your esteemed master compose?"

"Herr Bach wrote six, although the last was for an instrument of five strings." Glancing at the Goffriller, I continued. "This magnificent instrument, impressive though it is, possesses but four strings. I selected the Fourth because it is a particular favorite of mine."

"Herr Barth, let us hope these suites find more champions before much longer," Frau Levy responded. "In the meantime, we shall take a short interval before continuing our program."

I was at once surrounded by guests offering praise and inquiring about the music, but Frau Levy whisked me away to ensure I could partake of a light repast. When I returned to join my family in the salon, the room had been reset for a performance of Bach's *Concerto for Three Keyboards*. Our hostess announced that she would be joined in this performance by both Josef and Prince Louis Ferdinand of Prussia, a nephew of Frederick the Great. A frequent guest at the salon, the prince was not only a military man of the first rank but also a skilled composer and keyboardist, as his playing would soon show. The work, Frau Levy informed us, had been passed on to her by Wilhelm Friedemann, who had often played it with his younger brother Carl Phillip Emmanuel, and their father.

The performance was splendid; however, Frau Levy had one more surprise in store. She announced that we would all join for a set of glorious Bach chorales, to be led by another of her esteemed guests, Carl Zelter, the newly appointed director of Berlin's renowned *Singakademie*. It proved a fabulous tribute to my late master, and as we all sang to our hearts' delight, I could not help but tenderly recall the music-making in the Bach household that had brought me so much joy in my youth.

After the program concluded, I had the privilege of making the formal acquaintance of the prince, a delightful man, and Zelter, who confessed a like-minded passion for Bach's music. Frau Levy then urged me to share some of my memories of Bach. Everyone took great interest as I reflected on my time living with the family, then became rapt with attention as I chronicled the John Taylor odyssey.

Next, Frau Levy recalled Carl Phillip's obituary of his father, which alluded to the surgery, and the prince vividly recollected when his uncle had run the Chevalier out of Berlin. I then proceeded to divulge the dramatic carriage accident and subsequent loss of the original manuscript to Bach's cello suites, which I had never ceased to lament.

"Whether or not I did wrong," I told the group, "I hoped that God—and history—would look beyond it." Last, I expressed my eternal gratitude for the enthusiastic reception they had all given me.

Everyone left the Levy estate in high spirits, and as we climbed back into the *berline,* we bid a sincerely appreciative farewell to our hosts. Looking around the carriage, I noted my family's faces, so cheerful and content, and that of Josef, whom I had never seen more exultant.

───

Our departure early the next morning was one of both affection and sadness. These days with Josef had been sheer joy, but he and I understood they might be the last. Of course, our correspondence would continue, and we all looked forward to the possibility of Johann Friedrich one day benefitting from Josef's experienced and skillful guidance.

As my dear friend stood at the foot of the coach, I thanked him once more for his invitation and splendid hospitality. Then, according to our habit, I joked that I wasn't sure which I would miss most: his august company, the splendid Goffriller, or the convenient comforts of the *berline.*

For once, Josef did not respond in kind. "Carl, you and the Goffriller did yourselves proud, and the memories of your visit will remain fresh for the remainder of my days. Please promise me that you will commit to paper your experiences with Bach and his music. Some of the stories you told at the salon you had not even shared with me! Posterity deserves to have a record of everything you did on behalf of your master. The world will want to know. It *needs* to know."

I was eerily reminded that John Taylor had once spoken the exact words to me. "Carl," Josef continued, his hand on my arm, "I'm so grateful I stumbled upon John Taylor's memoir that day so long ago. It has all made for quite an adventure!"

After wishing us a safe and uneventful journey, my dear old friend stepped back from the coach and cried to the driver, "Godspeed!" As we pulled away, I turned to see Josef's hand raised in farewell against the backdrop of the Royal Palace, his white hair blowing in the warm July breeze.

Epilogue

JOSEF GRAUN AND I WOULD not meet again. True to his word, however, he did welcome Johann Friedrich to Berlin and mentored my son until the young man left to fight in the Napoleonic Wars. Thankfully, he returned unscathed to his mother and me. But Prince Louis Ferdinand, who played so beautifully alongside Josef and Frau Levy at her Berlin salon, was not so fortunate. In 1806, Josef informed me the prince had died heroically fighting the French.

Last year, the following letter arrived from Berlin:

> *Dearest Herr Barth,*
>
> *It is with deepest regret that I write to inform you that our dear friend Josef Graun has passed from this world. Several days ago he attended what was to be his last visit to our salon, and yesterday I was notified that he died peacefully in his sleep that night. I need not express to you how deeply he will be missed. May his memory serve as a blessing.*

We often think of you and your family's visit and how deeply your music-making affected all present that wonderful July afternoon.

With warmth and enduring friendship,

Sara Levy, Berlin

Shaken, I set the letter down and reflected on my first meeting with Josef inside Leipzig's St. Nicholas Church. What devoted comradeship had evolved from that chance encounter, and how greatly had it affected the course of my life! Through my grief, I soon began to honor his memory by transcribing my recollections of Bach, John Taylor and, of course, my dear departed friend.

That week of our final meeting, the performances of Bach's music at the Levy salon were not the only ones to celebrate my master's work. On 28 July 1800, the coach bearing my family passed through Leipzig's northern gate and we disembarked near the Brühl, where the familiar fragrance of lime trees welcomed us. Still, Johanna and the children were fatigued and anxious to complete the last leg of the journey, so I put them on a coach for Borna and remained behind.

That day marked the fiftieth anniversary of Bach's death and, in anticipation of the concert in his honor at the St. Thomas Church, I had timed the trip accordingly. After waving farewell to my wife and children, knowing I would rejoin them the following day, I walked the length of the city, through the central market and the Grimma Gate, until I reached the *Johannisfriedhof*, the city's common burial ground.

Because I had not traversed this plot of land since my master's death, I was no longer certain where he was interred. Alas, no stone or marker had ever been placed there. But my gait naturally slowed, and after a few more steps, I sensed I was standing above him. After noting several patches of freshly dug earth a short distance away, I turned to look at the ground below my feet. I tried to recall every detail of that day, including the small procession that had accompanied my master's body from the church to this sacred spot.

I also thought of John Taylor and pulled the carp's tongue needle from my pocket as I did so. I had lost track of it after leaving Prague for Borna, but recently my daughter had come to me with it in her hand, asking what it was for. She had discovered it wedged into a joint in the lap desk the Bachs gave to me that long-ago Christmas, a precious keepsake I had passed to her.

Now I beheld the needle for the last time, admiring its silver handiwork and pressing its fine point softly against my palm, as I had done at Taylor's interment. Bending down, I pushed it deep into the earth. To time and nature, it would surrender—dust to dust.

I left the gravesite and turned toward the apartment into which Bach and his family welcomed me, a penniless student and a stranger as well. As I neared St. Thomas, I could hear strains of his glorious music floating out of the open church doors. The sanctuary must have been filled to capacity, for listeners were crowded into the courtyard. Nearby, children ran and played in the cool shade of the linden trees, while a flock of swifts circled the spire, their full-throated song blending with the chorus of singers. The sun dipped behind the church as I reached the steps of the apartment, where I remained motionless for some moments. And when the sounds of festive trumpets and drums interrupted my meditation, I turned and strode lovingly toward the music.

AFTERWORD

This story came about as the confluence of two ideas. The first was to craft an account of the pair of eye surgeries that the English oculist John Taylor performed on Johann Sebastian Bach and the composer's ensuing death. We know little about the circumstances of either, save that these surgeries occurred around the first week of April 1750 and Bach died three months later. The *Nekrolog*, Bach's obituary as penned at least in part by his son C.P.E. Bach and published in 1754, maintains that the composer died as a direct consequence of these procedures. However, there may well have been extenuating or undetected factors that contributed to Bach's demise. In addition, because the importance of surgical asepsis would not be recognized for over a century, fatal infection in such cases was not uncommon.

Whether or not Taylor was as gifted an oculist as he claimed, he was undoubtedly a pioneer of self-promotion, which may have helped him gain the favor of European aristocracy and Pope Benedict XIV. Taylor published his first treatise about the eye around the age of 25 and went on to write much about himself, including *The History of the Travels and Adventures of the Chevalier Taylor*, from which I quote.

Whatever his authentic achievements might have been, Taylor also acquired a reputation as a charlatan that seems to have been deserved, though there is no indication that he was addicted to laudanum as I have portrayed. My depiction of Taylor living out his days in a Prague monastery is based on the following account by the surgeon's grandson:

> After many years of absence from this country, my grandfather's death was noticed in the following manner in a continental paper: Having given sight to many thousands, the celebrated Chevalier Taylor lately died blind, at a very advanced age, in a convent at Prague (*Records of My Life*, 1832).

This book's second, broader idea was to bestow Bach with a distinctive and characteristic voice. For all our knowledge about his music and manifest genius, he left very little to posterity by way of expressed personal thoughts. Extant documents and letters occasionally capture his frustrations about employment and humility about his abilities, but they rarely reveal a more profound sense of the man. Carl Friedrich Barth, then, became the means by which to elicit that voice, as the relationship between the young student and aging composer evolved during their relatively brief acquaintance.

I have taken some liberties with his history for the sake of this work, but Carl Barth (1734–1813) was a real person. He began his studies at St. Thomas in 1746 and was among Bach's last copyists. In the scholarly literature, he is sometimes referred to as Anon. N 5. Barth later worked as a cantor in nearby Borna, where, in 1781, he married Johanna Friedericka Hofmann (1760-1816), the daughter of a ropemaker and tradesman. Together, they had five children, two of whom—Johann Friedrich (b. 1783) and Henriette Friederike (b. 1790)—survived into adulthood.

Barth certainly would not have assisted Taylor during Bach's surgery. Most likely, the doctor traveled with an assistant (whose name is lost to history) or engaged help as needed. Given the excruciating pain associated with surgery in the 18th century, an aide by necessity would have been someone strong enough—and dispassionate enough—to render Taylor's patients immobile. However, as I needed my protagonist to be present, I assigned that role to Barth. And though we have no evidence that Carl Barth ever played the cello himself, or traveled to Berlin, I also required a protagonist who not only did both but also lived long enough to witness Bach's Berlin revival.

Whether or not Barth truly questioned his own spiritual beliefs—as was common during this epoch—I chose to portray him as a product of the Enlightenment, challenging the religious fervor of the older generation. Indeed, the actual Carl Barth studied theology and philosophy at Leipzig University, a hotbed of curiosity and intellectual thought. Still, it was important that my protagonist both characterize and recognize Bach's improvisations and compositions as divinely inspired and that he accept Bach's religious devotion, acknowledging it as a manifestation of the composer's musical-spiritual essence.

While the character of Josef Graun is fictitious, the man named as his father, Johann Gottlieb Graun (1703–1771), was concertmaster of Frederick the Great's Berlin Kapelle and among the most important violinists of his day. It is a testament to the senior Graun's reputation that Bach enlisted him to teach his son Wilhelm Friedemann (1710–1784). Graun sired three children, but I could not find any trace of the family's lineage.

Enlightenment figures Gotthold Ephraim Lessing (1729–1781) and Ewald Christian von Kleist (1715–1759) were not only friends who lived in Leipzig during the Prussian occupation, but they also occasionally lodged in the Great Fireball. Prince Louis Ferdinand of Prussia (1772–1806), a talented keyboardist and composer, and frequenter of Berlin's salon life, died fighting the French at the Battle of Saalfeld.

The remarkable Sara Levy, née Itzig (1761–1854), salonnière, patron, keyboardist, and music collector, was among those Berliners dedicated to studying and performing Bach's music. A pupil of Friedemann Bach, she passed on her love of J.S. Bach to her grandnephew, the composer and conductor Felix Mendelssohn Bartholdy (1809–1847), who is credited with Bach's overarching revival.

My depiction of European Jews and peregrine Roma families was written with awareness of the trappings of cliches and stereotypes. Fortune telling (*drabarimos*) was a specialized and well-documented practice of Roma women known as *drabardi*. Given the multicultural attendance at Leipzig's famous seasonal fairs, it is likely that nomadic peoples would have been present. Likewise, Jewish merchants and traders were active at Leipzig's fairs. Though only allowed to remain for short periods, they nevertheless played a significant role in the city's development as an international trade center.

Finally, like most cellists, I have often contemplated—and lamented—the fate of Bach's original manuscript to the cello suites. No autograph of this music survives, but the suites are believed to have been composed in or around 1720, while Bach was in the employ of Prince Leopold of Anhalt-Köthen. Modern editions of this music rely on copies made during or after the composer's lifetime. The earliest of these sources, by Peter Kellner, dates from around 1726. The date ascribed to Anna Magdalena's copy, 1730, is based on her handwriting and watermarks on the paper. A third source, from the second half of the eighteenth century, is the product of two anonymous copyists. And a fourth, from later in the eighteenth century, is similarly the product of an unknown hand.

The instrument for which Bach composed his Sixth Suite remains a source of great debate. Various five-string instruments existed during the composer's day, including the violoncello piccolo and the cello da spalla, the latter of which was braced against the chest. The Sixth Suite was a natural fit for either, although we have no words from Bach that indicate what he had in mind. Nor does the nomenclature surrounding these instruments clarify the matter, for just as the instruments themselves were then undergoing great experimentation, so were their names.

Although few such original instruments have stood the test of time, a cello piccolo built by Girolamo Amati, around 1610, is among the holdings of New York's Metropolitan Museum of Art. For those interested in seeing and hearing this splendid instrument, a performance of the Prelude to Bach's Sixth Suite can be found here: https://www.ludwig-van.com/main/2023/07/17/new-yorks-metropolitan-museum-acquires-of-one-of-worlds-only-17th-century-five-string-cellos/

ACKNOWLEDGMENTS

Books are not written in a vacuum and I am deeply indebted to a handful of individuals who helped me along the way. Eugene Downs read an early draft of my manuscript and made numerous insightful suggestions, which I heartily embraced. Ophthalmologist Dr. Stuart McCracken helped me understand the details surrounding and possible complications of Bach's surgery. He also shared a reprint of *De Oculis*, by Benvenutus Grassus of Jerusalem, and it is from this manual that Taylor quotes before Bach's surgery. Mirko Herzog, of Vienna's Technisches Museum, once again cheerfully found answers to my arcane questions, including those concerning eighteenth-century European travel. In Borna, Germany, Annemarie Englemann provided invaluable information about Carl Barth and his family. I dearly hope I have done her city's cantor justice. Brandeis University's Rachel Greenblatt answered my questions about Jewish life in Prague. And at the eleventh hour, my generous North Carolina Symphony colleague Craig Brown read the final manuscript and offered valuable suggestions.

Finally, it is impossible to put into words the depth of gratitude I owe to my dear friend Ron Samuels. With unflagging dedication, Ron repeatedly pored over every page and helped me create a far better book than it would otherwise have ever been. Ron, our decades-long friendship remains one of the great treasures of my life. Here's to our first Gose together in Leipzig!

CREDITS

Taylor, John. *The History and Adventures of the Chevalier John Taylor, Ophthalmiater* (London, 1761–62).

"An Epistle to a Young Student at Cambridge, with the Characters of the Three Great Quacks" is reproduced by Wood, S. "A Rare Manuscript of Chevalier Taylor, the Royal Oculist, With Notes On His Life." *The British Journal of Ophthalmology* (May 1930), p. 202.

Hogarth's *The Company of Undertakers*. Source: Wellcome Collection.

John Taylor's dispatches to the *Berlinische Privilegirte Zeitung* are reprinted from *The New Bach Reader*, ed. Hans T. David and Arthur Mendel, rev. Christoph Wolff (Norton, 1998), pp. 243–4.

www.ingramcontent.com/pod-product-compliance
Lightning Source LLC
LaVergne TN
LVHW090854120125
801048LV00001B/7